By David Morgan, the creator of the cult series of 2019 books.

He reputedly stores the contents of his brain every night on a memory stick but can never remember where he left it.

The 2019 Series

2019: The Beginning

The murder of a Countess starts an incredible series of events from Hong Kong and Paraguay to rural England. Why does billionaire Jessica Crowne want old documents? Who is the unseen Jerome Jones? What is the Octagon? Why do some people never age? Answers start on page one

ISBN 978-1846856495

2019: The Second Coming

Magick. Is the world changing? A mysterious man with two glamorous assistants launches an organisation promising peace and prosperity. Why do they seek an ancient golden cat? The Omasor Agency investigates, with help from Brick and Blonde, celebrity adventurers. Created from mostly natural English with no added squirrels but may contain nut residues and textual nudity.

ISBN 978-1846858932

2019: Athens 1 Atlantis 0

Atlantis fought Athens, 11,000 years ago for global domination. Their descendants intend to control the planet again using the Treasures of Poseidon and helped by the Temple Virgins, who are different to other women in interesting ways. Corruption, lust, kidnap, murder follow. Also some bad things. The Omasor Agency gets involved with help from Brick and Blonde, celebrity adventurers

ISBN 978-0-9559767-0-4

www.2019books.co.uk

Godsplay

DAVID MORGAN

Published by

Living Designs Publishing

Campion House, Campion Terrace, Leamington Spa, CV32 4SU

www.livingdesignspublishing.co.uk

First published by Living Designs Publishing 2008

ISBN-13: 978-0-9559767-1-1

This book is for Mike and Annie

1 Prolog

Jerome Jones knew it was unfair. He had solved the clues, found the key and was entering the Portal of the Gods.

He realised Selena was desperate to be the first to go through but she was away in northern Canada and he simply didn't want to wait. Maybe it was something else. He knew why she wanted to visit the gods and perhaps harboured a feeling that she wouldn't return. He reassured himself that this first visit would be brief, just long enough to discover what was on the other side of the entrance. Then he would return and accompany Selena on the next visit.

Jerome smiled as he entered the Portal. He was ready for the unexpected, although that was impossible to prepare for. Looking around at a new level of unexpectation, he found himself in a total, encompassing whiteness that positively discouraged any attempt to penetrate.

"We've been waiting for you," a woman's voice didn't say. The words simply came to him without need to vibrate the air.

"Sorry if I'm late," he replied and found the words bypassing his vocal chords.

She smiled deliciously. From her face, her age could have been about 45 but her torso was indistinct. He looked again and the body clarified into a well-proportioned figure wearing just delicate pink lace underwear.

"Nice job. Could you make the hips a little narrower and the chest slightly larger?" she asked.

He carefully amended his visualisation and her body changed in accord. She laughed and then leant forward, kissing him on the lips.

"You'll have to hope your people are as smart as you," she said cryptically but smiled deliciously.

Taking his hand, she led him into the whiteness.

2

Selena Bowman looked in good humour as she entered her underground office, concealed beneath an old building in Warwick, near the centre of England. She had just returned from two weeks in Canada, resolving the problem of a totemic bear cult that included eating people alive in their curriculum.

Her mood changed when she saw the note on her desk from Jerome Jones.

Selena managed Omasor, an extraordinary detective agency. It could not be contracted in the usual way. Assignments were selected, irrespective of any financial incentive and it was not uncommon for celebrities, millionaires or even royalty to be refused. The agency frequently offered their services to people who had not thought of using them. This was not an organisation you would contact for routine divorce or criminal investigations. It specialised in unusual and often paranormal cases. The only common factor was the success rate. Omasor had reputedly never failed.

Jerome Jones owned Omasor. He was one of the wealthiest men in England and certainly the richest unknown man. No photograph of him appeared to exist. He was never seen at meetings, deputising his various business dealings to a team of trusted associates whom he had carefully appointed within an impenetrable array of companies. His primary interest was property and it was rumoured that he owned a significant slice of central London plus other lands, hotels, offices and houses throughout Britain.

Assumed to be a recluse, he was actually rarely in his office. He spent a great deal of his time out on assignments that only he had knowledge of. He invariably wore a disguise, although this was unnecessary as only Selena knew his true appearance. He also employed several other men to impersonate him. They used his name but each was totally different in appearance.

A couple of months ago Selena had been involved in the Atlantis situation. Although that had been resolved, something had happened to her during the venture. She had encountered a powerful, unique woman who called herself Helen. She well remembered the touch of Helen's hand on her cheek that he had induced the most pleasurable experience of her life. She had also met a strange but extremely handsome man who had unsuccessfully tried to seduce her. Before leaving, the man had given Selena a small square of metal and told her it was an invitation to somewhere where she would meet him and Helen again. However, the invitation would need to be solved.

She had examined the metal square without success. It appeared to be a completely blank, polished piece of aluminium but much heavier. For no particular reason, she had given it a name. She called it the Squark. Eventually, she had asked Jerome Jones to try to discover its secrets. Now she had returned to find his note.

'Clue in the Squark. Portal of the Gods. Gone to confirm. Back soon. JJ.'

Selena cursed vehemently. Why hadn't he waited for her? She clicked the intercom. The caretaker would know when Jerome had left.

"Jeremy?"

"Yes, Ms Bowman?"

"When did Mr Jones depart?"

"Eight days ago."

A numbness ran through her.

"Eight days? Are you sure?"

"I'm sure. Is there a problem?"

"No. Thank you Jeremy."

She ended the call. Her annoyance had been replaced by a nagging concern. Selena rarely worried about Jerome Jones but this was a rare situation. 'Back soon' always meant within two or three days maximum. Eight was much too long. A problem and it had three edges.

First, Jerome was in trouble. Second, he had the metal square with him. Third, even if she had the square, she hadn't been able to solve the clue as Jerome obviously had.

A thought hit her. It was possible that Jerome hadn't taken the Squark with him. Perhaps he had even left the solution behind. She sprinted to his office and jabbed a combination into the keypad lock. Apart from him, she was the only one who knew the code.

The door swung open and she rushed to his desk. Everything neat and tidy. No notes, no metal square. Selena spent 30 minutes searching, including his computer records but she knew it was futile. She cursed again and slowly returned to her desk, deep in thought. Then she gasped.

In the 250 plus years of her life, Selena had rarely gasped. So rare, you could probably count the occasions on one hand, unless you were an alien when it could take up to five hands. A duck would find this counting process impossible and be forced to rely upon some external objects such as reeds. As it is well known that waterfowl are unable to count beyond two, the process would anyway be pointless. Hopefully, it has been established that Selena was a minimal gasper but now she gasped.

The Squark was lying on her desk, right in the centre. Someone had placed it there while she had been searching Jerome's office. She opened the video surveillance screen on her computer and replayed the previous 35 minutes. Initially, the corridor was empty and she fast forwarded. Then the display showed her running to Jerome's office and Selena reverted to normal speed, staring intently at the screen. 31 minutes later she saw herself walking back. No one had been in the corridor during her absence and there was no other access to her office.

She shrugged and picked up the Squark. This time she had to solve its mysteries.

It was 29 hours before Selena slumped in her chair, burning with frustration. She wasn't tired. The Blessing gave so much vitality that anyone taking it needed just three or four hours sleep and she frequently worked through the night.

She wasn't tired but she could not find a solution to the Squark. It remained just a plain square of polished metal. Selena cursed again and struck the desk in annoyance. She wasn't used to failure and certainly didn't like it. This was the first time she had needed help and Jerome Jones wasn't there to provide it.

Only one of her prime operators wasn't tied up on assignment. Chris Darmant had just returned from North Africa. After initial reservations, Selena had grown to like her and now knew Chris to be very reliable and astute.

3

Chris Darmant was sitting in the garden of her house just north of London. She was 26 and a millionaire. After attaining her degree at Cambridge University, she had joined the British Intelligence service but soon after was recruited by Omasor and she now worked directly for the attractive and intelligent Selena Bowman. She had also met Jerome Jones but only in one of his disguises. The Omasor offer was irresistible. Chris received an annual salary of two million pounds with a million pound signing on gift. One of the men that Jerome Jones employed as an impersonator had become her lover. She had christened him Jerome Two, a name he seemed happy to retain.

One other unique aspect of Omasor was that Jerome Jones possessed the Blessing. A liquid that guaranteed eternal youth if taken annually and also immunised against all illnesses. Within a few days, it brought the recipient to their physical peak, somewhere between the ages of 18 and 25 and they maintained that age whilst taking the Blessing. Death was possible, but only through anything immediately fatal such as a bullet in the heart or head. The mixture comprised nine everyday foodstuffs with a tenth constituent, the liquid that revived Lazarus. Only ten living people, five women and five men could be taking the Blessing at any time and if consumed by an 11th person, it acted for them like a poison. Chris knew Jerome Jones had agreed to allow an annual dose to four others. Herself and Jerome Two, Selena and Wincey Trellis, the probable future partner of Jerome Jones. Just five more to be chosen.

A spirit speaking through a man Edward Kelly in the 16th century had apparently provided the recipe for the Blessing and the location of the tenth constituent. Jerome Jones had told Chris that the spirit also warned of a terrible event to come. All human life would end on March 20, 2019 except for those taking the Blessing. Chris hadn't been told how this Armageddon would occur and also wasn't certain that it would happen, as he had been somewhat evasive on the subject. Chris still couldn't accept that the end of humanity was so close as she had heard so many other spurious doomsday predictions. However, none of the others had come with an eternal youth package that clearly worked.

The spirit had advised one other restriction. Although the Blessing enhanced sexual desires, no one taking it could procreate until after the event in 2019. Women could not conceive and men could not impregnate until then.

The phone rang.

"How fast can you get here?" Selena's voice.

"No more than two hours."

"See you then."

Chris smiled. Selena never wasted words. It took 27 minutes less than predicted when she arrived in Warwick and Selena's expression indicated a problem.

"What can I do?" she asked.

Selena didn't reply but simply handed her a small metal square.

"What is it?"

"I call it the Squark. You tell me."

"Looks like a wall tile from a doll's house."

"It contains a clue or message."

"Have you tried it under the microscope?"

"Yes. Both sides and edges. Nothing."

"Maybe chemicals?"

"I can't risk anything too powerful, it could destroy the message. But I've tried almost everything else."

"Does it fit into something?"

"I'm sure not. This was all I was given."

"Now you need to tell me the background."

Selena sighed. Then she recounted her meeting with Helen and the man, how she had been given the Squark and Jerome's disappearance.

Chris considered for a few seconds.

"Tell me what this man said when he gave it to you."

"His exact words were, 'In time, I think you might prefer me. She won't sleep with you, you know. But you can visit both of us if you solve the invitation.' That was all he said."

"He was saying that Helen wouldn't sleep with you?"

"Yes."

"You know who this man was?" Chris asked carefully.

"I believe I do now. Who do you think?"

"I'm sure it was Poseidon."

For the first time in the conversation, Selena gave a slight smile.

"Yes. It's the first time I've ever been propositioned by a god."

"I did a little bit on the Greek gods at university. I assume you also have an idea about the identity of Helen?"

"I think it was Athena."

"I think you're right."

"That doesn't help us to solve the Squark."

"Selena, it's not like you to be negative. Did you try immersing it in water?"

"Yes, I see. Poseidon. But I tried water and nothing."

"Sea water?"

A silence.

"No. Not sea water."

Selena grabbed Chris and kissed her hard on the lips.

"Hey, I've got a steady partner. And I could be wrong."

"I just know you're right. I tried a salt solution but it didn't work. It must be pure, fresh sea water. How fast can we get to the coast?"

Chris parked on the seafront in a little town on the east coast of England. Selena was out of the car and running for the beach before they stopped. Fortunately, it was high tide and the sea was just 30 metres away. Chris followed her and saw her scooping seawater with a bowl. She arrived as Selena was placing the Squark in the bowl.

Nothing. No change. Selena turned it over. It remained the same blank square.

Chris saw the look of bitter disappointment in her eyes.

"I was certain," Selena said. She sat down on the stony beach with the bowl in front of her and stared at the waves.

"Sorry, I was wrong. Maybe the man wasn't Poseidon," Chris said softly.

Selena looked back into the bowl and then her expression changed.

"This is sea water. It's not the sea," she said, jumping up and sprinting towards the breaking waves. Chris followed and knelt beside her as she carefully held the Squark under the water.

It began to glow.

First, a deep crimson and then a sudden rainbow of colours flashed across the square. After dazzling the eyes for a few seconds the Squark turned solid white and six words appeared.

"Take me out of the water."

Selena pulled it from the waves and then they heard a voice, crystal clear.

"You have now activated me. It took you so much longer than Jerome Jones."

"Where is he?" asked Selena.

"He is fit and well at the moment."

"At the moment?"

"He is scheduled to be killed in 23 days, 14 hours and 18 minutes of your time."

"What or who are you? asked Chris.

"I am a guide to the Portal. The Portal of the Gods, the fifth gift of Poseidon to his people in Atlantis."

"You're a portal? A gateway?"

"No. Your first task is to find it. I'm just here to guide you."

Selena had regained her composure.

"Please be exact. You say that there is a Portal to the gods here on earth?"

"Yes. Can't be more exact than that can I?"

"We have to find it and then you act as a key or invitation to go through?"

"No. I'm just here to provide a clue. You need to find the key."

"What's on the other side?"

"You must find out for yourself."

"What gods are we talking about?"

"You must discover that."

"And Jerome is there?"

"Yes."

"But you say he will die. Why?"

"That is the game."

"Game?"

"A test for you, a game for the gods. Do you want to see him?"

"Yes I do."

The Squark seemed to enlarge and become a video screen, depicting the head of a shaggy haired man. He was eating contentedly. Around his head was a shimmering, metallic looking circle. Like a halo but this ring hovered just above the level of his eyes.

"Is that Jerome Jones?" Chris enquired.

Selena nodded. "I'd recognise him in any disguise."

"What's that around his head?"

The image disappeared and then the Squark responded.

"The cause of his probable death. Did you see the inside of the ring? There are tiny little spikes in it. Every second they grow a little and in 23 days 14 hours and 15 minutes they will burrow into his eyes, his ears and his brain. Then he will die."

"How do we perform the rescue?"

"You just have to find him and take off the ring. It can only be removed by you or Selena."

"You know my name?"

"Yes you are Chris."

"So I'm invited as well?"

"Your names were selected some time ago."

Chris looked at Selena who shrugged and then spoke decisively.

"We will go. But this Gate could be anywhere on the planet."

"I can provide a clue. The same one I gave to Jerome Jones."

"I'm ready."

The Squark solemnly dictated lines of prose.

"The great Olympian came

From the North

Cloaked within another name

Isle of an isle

Across the circle.

With mighty fire

The lower path reveals

With treads of light

The upper path conceals.

Here lies the key

Past stone of wife

Infant mortals

42 North and 33 East."

The words displayed on the screen as they were spoken and Chris wrote them on a small pad while Selena simply memorised.

"Is that all you can tell us?"

"Yes. My job is done for the present."

The Squark disappeared. It simply vanished from Selena's hand.

"Well, we have a starting point," said Chris.

"This is not easy. Greek mythology, I think," she remarked.

"The words are too common to check on the internet. Maybe we should ask Brick and Blonde?"

Brick and Blonde were American archaeologists and adventurers that both Selena and Chris knew well.

"They're unobtainable for two weeks. Somewhere in South America and they've deliberately left their phones behind. Didn't want any contact and we don't have time to wait."

"Who else?"

"I've heard them mention someone. He's a professor at one of the top universities in England. Supposed to be an expert in mythology, particularly Greek."

"Then let's go. The game is afoot."

"Could be longer than that," responded Selena without humour.

Franco Goodfit had been Professor of Ancient Mythology at Camyford University for two years. His predecessor had held the post for so long that the envelopes had to be prised from his fingers after they realised he had expired.

A chunky man of below average height who looked about 35, Franco had earned the respect of his peers for an encyclopaedic knowledge of Greek mythology.

His university office was unexpectedly tidy. Not the usual book laden shelves and mass of papers scattered over the desk. Just a handful of volumes covering his subject and a large neat notepad in front of him.

"Ms Bowman and Ms Darmant, I believe." He rose and clasped their hands briefly. A firm, dry handshake. Chris noticed his smart suit was as tidy as his office and that his deep, dark eyes were fired with intellect.

"We need advice," Selena passed without preamble.

"Of course. You are friends of Brick and Blonde and I offer my services willingly."

"I have a text that I need to decipher."

"In ancient Greek? That's no problem."

"No, it's in English but I believe it refers to Greek deities. It's a sort of game we are playing with someone."

"Very well, a puzzle then. Please ask me."

Chris passed him a printed copy of the words she had transcribed.

Franco's expression changed.

"Where did the message come from?"

"As I said, it's just a game between friends. We like to set conundrums to solve."

Chris saw disbelief in his eyes but the smile returned.

"Yes, of course. I must say that I'm really intrigued by this. Is there any chance I could join the game? On your side, naturally."

Selena shook her head.

"Sorry, it's a private thing. What do you make of the text?"

"Not a lot at first glance. It mentions a great Olympian but that could be any of the primary Greek deities. The rest of it makes no sense at all. Let me think about it. If I come up with anything, I'll give you a call."

"It's very urgent. I was hoping to solve it today."

"I'm sorry. I'll try my best."

He shook them warmly by the hand with an increasingly infectious smile.

"You drive. I need to telephone," said Selena as they reached the car.

"That was disappointing," Chris remarked.

"No."

"But we didn't learn anything."

"Yes, we did," Selena responded and then began to talk on the phone.

Chris started the engine and pulled away from the university car park. As she reached the first crossroads, Selena spoke again.

"Go left, towards Tidnurgh. Reverse into the first side road and stop."

Chris didn't ask. A kilometre down the road, she reversed into a rough driveway that probably led to a country house hidden by the trees.

"What are we doing, Selena?"

"Waiting for Franco."

"Why?"

"He knew the solution. I could smell it."

"Why didn't he tell us?"

"It can only be because he wants to get there first."

"What makes you think he'll come this way?"

"His house is in Tidnurgh. I checked that before we visited."

She handed Chris a long dark wig from the glove compartment.

"I guess that's my disguise, what about you?" Chris asked.

"He won't see my face. I'll be kissing you."

They heard the sound of a car moving at speed. Selena turned to face Chris, ensuring she didn't mask her right eye.

"Make sure it's him," she whispered.

Chris saw a Caballini pass on the main road. Selena was right. It was Franco.

"Follow him but we mustn't be seen. We'll put a tracker on his car when he stops at his house."

Chris followed Selena's guidance and pulled up on the outskirts of the small village.

"Let's go," called Selena and they walked smartly past a clump of cottages.

"I see it," Chris said. The car was parked on the gravelled frontage of a larger house across the road.

"You've got the wig. I'll go back and wait."

Selena handed her the tracker. It was magnetic, no larger than a bottle cap and formed of black plastic. Chris crossed the road and walked slowly along the narrow pavement. She was conscious that the only other person in sight was an old man pruning bushes further down the road. As she neared the car she began to limp slightly and looked down at her feet. Then she leant briefly against the car, took off her shoe and pretended to tip out the offending stone. A second later, she continued her walk, crossed the road and returned back to the car, careful not to look across at the house as she passed.

Selena was in the driver's seat when she returned.

"It's under the rear bumper away from the exhaust," Chris reported.

Selena slid open a panel in the facia to reveal a map screen. A green dot shone brightly in the centre.

"Now we wait," she said.

The words 'now we wait' each contain a W, a letter with an interesting origin. It was originally inverted, rather like an M and represented the twin peaks of Everest and Kilimanjaro that were well known to the Romans who invented the letter. It then passed into other cultures, to people who hadn't heard of these mountains, like the Anglo-Saxons. As a gesture of disbelief aimed at the Romans, they turned it upside down to represent two letter V's. This stood for the words

'Viva Victorum', which translates as ' Long Live Victor The Uncertain'. This man Victor was probably one of their leaders but wasn't sure about it.

It was not a long wait. Six minutes and 14 seconds later the green dot began to move and Selena drove off to follow without urgency. Then she clicked on her headset and made a telephone call.

"Paul. Are you at the airport yet?"

A pause.

"Okay. Subject is Franco Goodfit. I confirm tracker number 932-844. I think she'll be coming there. Essential I know his destination."

She clicked off.

"You think he'll be flying somewhere?" asked Chris.

"The location could be anywhere in the world and the odds must be very much against it being within driving range."

Driving ranges are now very popular among golfers who cannot afford the escalating membership fees of Golf Clubs. Golf was invented by Sahara Desert nomads in 2819.5 BC to relieve the tedium of long camel journeys over monotonous sand. They used the leg bones of deceased camels as clubs and a dried pomegranate as a ball. Early games were played over two holes, each 129 miles long. The first hole was from one oasis to another and the second covered the return journey. The hole was simply the pool of water. After each stroke, the player remounted his camel to travel to the ball. The course record stands at 3,427. It would have been much lower but for the 693 putts.

"You're right, he's heading for the airport," said Chris, looking at the screen.

Selena turned off the road and sped along another route.

"This should be quicker. We may even get there before him."

A horse box thwarted that prospect. The route followed narrow country roads and oncoming traffic made it impossible to pass. Selena contentedly drove carefully, smiling as the horse's head appeared over the rear door.

"Beautiful animal. I'm not rushing past and risk upsetting it," she said calmly.

"I like horses too," Chris remarked. She had ridden occasionally around the age of 12 and had always treasured an equine affinity.

"More honest than most humans. I'd live with one if they didn't tear the bedclothes so much."

Selena's phone rang and she conversed for a minute.

"That was Paul. Franco has arrived at the airport. Paul is tailing him to the flight desk and we'll know soon."

They continued behind the horse for another 3 kilometres and then the phone rang again. Chris saw Selena smile as she disconnected.

"Now we have a destination," she said and turned off to the right while making another call.

"Annette, I'm heading for Undertoss airport. I need clearance to fly to Reykjavik within 20 minutes. Use Olaf if you have any difficulty."

"Iceland?" enquired Chris, after the call.

"Yes. I wish I knew how he solved the clue."

4

Chris invariably carried her passport, it was an Omasor rule. She was excited by the prospect of the journey to Iceland, one of the countries she had never visited. She knew that all the Omasor private aircraft carried an extensive wardrobe to suit almost any climate and didn't need to return home. They reached Undertoss in under 15 minutes and the compact passenger jet was waiting for them on the runway. Selena took the controls and they were in the air within 10 minutes. She was an expert pilot, experienced in all but the largest airliners.

"Who is Olaf?" asked Chris as she bought coffee from the mini kitchen.

"A travel writer with many friends and contacts, who lives near Reykjavik. He's actually Swedish and moved to Iceland 14 years ago. We don't employ him, he just receives an annual retainer for his services."

"Will Franco arrive before us?"

"Yes, by about 15 minutes. We are landing at a small airfield 25 kilometres from Reykjavik. I've contacted Olaf to fix a tracker if Franco takes a taxi or another vehicle. He'll also arrange to have a car waiting for us when we land."

"Have you been before?"

"Yes, many times. I used to visit Olaf regularly. You might say we slept together."

Chris was silent for a full six seconds.

"Together as in adjacent sleeping bags in the snow among the husky dogs?"

"Or as in naked bodies entwined in all-night sex in a centrally heated house? Is it important to know?"

Chris wished she hadn't asked.

"Not at all," she replied, hoping her blush was only inside.

The word blush is one of those that were changed in the Victorian era. In those times of strict morality, the upper classes abhorred the use of the letter 'F', which they considered a forerunner of indecent words. They usually replaced it with the letter 'B' and many of their amended words survive to this day. Thus, the word blush was originally flush and the change gives us a whole new meaning to current phrases such as barking dogs and musical beat. One can visualise the lounge of a manor house at that time where buxom Victorian ladies partook of bread, buns and butter whilst discussing recent blemish paintings and good books.

The journey and landing were uneventful. As they exited the craft, a young, dark hair girl approached.

"Ms Bowman?" she asked.

"Yes."

"I'm Hana. An urgent message from Olaf. He couldn't get through to you while you were flying."

"What's happened?"

"Your man didn't leave the airport. He's flying on to Akureyri."

"We need to catch him."

"There's no great rush. I know where he's going."

Selena looked at her sharply.

"How?"

Hana smiled.

"It didn't take great detective ability. He's booked another flight to travel on from Akureyri."

"Where?"

"To Grimsey," Hana said with an expression of self-satisfaction.

Selena looked surprised, not a normal emotion for her.

"Grimsey. There's almost nothing there. Why no rush?"

"The flights don't leave every day. He won't travel until tomorrow. You can catch him in Akureyri."

"Yes, I should have remembered."

Chris held up a hand.

"Okay guys. You need to let me in on the details."

Hana gave her a dazzling smile.

"Grimsey is an island off the north coast of our country, about 40 kilometres or 25 miles from the mainland. It's very small, only just over five square kilometres, a bit over two square miles. The Arctic Circle actually passes through the island."

"I guess it's covered with ice and penguins?"

"Not at all. The average temperature is only a fraction below zero in the winter and rises to about 8 degrees in the summer. The island is completely covered with grasses and mosses in a rich peat soil. The population is just over a hundred, mostly living along the southern coast. Sorry if I sound like a geography teacher."

"And what do you do?"

"I'm a geography teacher. That's probably why I sound like one."

Selena interrupted brusquely.

"Has Olaf cleared me to fly to Akureyri?"

"Yes, you can go immediately," Hana replied, immune to Selena's impoliteness that should have been called impoliticity.

Impoliti City was in Italy, north of the Riviera. Those of us who know a little ancient Italian had been told by him that it derives from a combination of three words. 'Impo' meaning 'we', 'lit' meaning 'are' and 'i' meaning 'the peoples who originally inhabited places further north and traded in gold, diamonds and other precious stones that were then made into jewellery and worn by many of the monarchs of Europe who invariably purchased from us when our caravans arrived bringing these wondrous articles'.

Selena and Chris returned to the aircraft.

"Fuel okay?" asked Chris.

"Plenty. We could fly to California and back."

They reached Akureyri after a smooth flight over the wonderful rugged purity of nature's scenery. Angular, yet always in harmony with the eye. Olaf had arranged another woman waiting with another car. This one (the woman) was fortyish with deep blonde hair and a lean face. The car was younger but hairless. The blonde didn't waste words.

"Your man arrived 20 minutes ago. He took a taxi to the International Imperial Emerald Hotel. The flight to Grimsey is 11.40 tomorrow morning. I'm Tana, by the way, Chris."

No smile but the information was complete.

"Is Olaf here?" asked Selena.

"No. He's in Hofn on the east coast. He has a new mistress there."

Chris was surprised at the extra information but noted Selena's lack of interest.

Tana drove them to the hotel and handed over the car keys.

"I must go now. A pleasure to meet you, Chris and you're looking quite well, Selena."

She left them standing by the car.

"You also look quite reasonable to me," said Chris, fishing.

Selena shrugged.

"We have met before. She has a strange idea that I took Olaf away from her."

"And did you?"

"Yes, in a way. But he's always had several women around Iceland."

"It would be interesting to meet him."

"I doubt if we will. Anyway, I wouldn't want you to be led astray."

"No chance of that. I only want Jerome Two. What is our next move?"

"We will pay a call on Franco."

"Really? I thought we were tailing him."

"That would be impossible on Grimsey. We need to know exactly where he's going. The island is so small, he can reach anywhere within minutes. I'm planning to offer him a lift."

The reception of the International Imperial Emerald Hotel was modern and impeccable. Akureyri is an ideal centre for touring Iceland and the hotel catered for the discerning traveller. Selena directed an irresistible smile to the small woman seated behind the desk.

"We'd like a room for tonight please."

The woman couldn't help returning the smile.

"Yes, of course. Have you booked?"

"We left it all to Franco Goodfit. He should have made the booking. I think he's arriving later today."

"Mr Goodfit is already here but I can't find a booking for you ladies."

Selena looked upwards.

"That's typical. He's very forgetful, isn't he Chris?"

Chris nodded dutifully as Selena continued.

"We want rooms next to Franco if possible."

"I have one vacant room with a double bed directly opposite but nothing else on the second floor."

"We'll take that one."

Formalities completed, they entered the elevator.

"We'll drop our bags and visit him now. I will require some answers," Selena said.

"He'll be surprised to see us here," Chris remarked.

They dropped off the bags and approached the opposite door. Chris held up a hand.

"I can hear the shower running," she said. She had a natural ability to direct her hearing.

"Can you open the door?"

Chris pulled out the set of skeleton keys she usually carried. A few seconds later, the door was open. A large, elegant room with original all paintings on the walls and ornate, hand carved wooden furniture. The bathroom was directly to their right and the door slightly ajar. From within came the sound of running water with a man's voice humming a melody.

Chris hesitated but Selena didn't. She kicked open the door. Franco was facing them, soaping his back in the shower. A look of incredulous shock appeared on his face, leaving no room for embarrassment. He completely forgot to cover himself. Chris saw his eyes travel to the pistol in Selena's hand.

"Hello again, Franco. I want you on the bed," she said icily.

He moved to grab a towel but she shook her head and herded him to the room.

"Lie down with your hands touching the headboard. You will note this is a silenced gun and no one will come if I have to use it."

He complied nervously. Selena moved to the foot of the bed and aimed the pistol directly between his legs.

Chris saw something in his eyes and felt sure it was fear.

"I'll tell you everything. Please don't shoot."

Selena didn't look amused. "That's good because I want to know everything. First, why are you here?"

"The message you showed me. This is the location."

"That is a bad start. This is not the location. I think I should shoot now."

She pushed the gun forward until it was almost touching a very sensitive area.

"No. Not here. Grimsey."

"Tell me exactly what the message means."

"It refers to Odin, the Norse equivalent of Zeus. The cloak refers to his usual garment when on earth. There is a legend, known only to a handful, that Odin or Zeus came from the North to Grimsey and there constructed access to both the heavens and the underworld. Zeus, Hades and Poseidon, the three brothers, combined to build an invisible stairway to the heavenly residence. In the same place, they also created some sort of tunnel or means of descending to the underworld."

"Then why has no one looked at Grimsey before?"

Franco was regaining some composure although it was continually undermined by his lack of clothing.

"As I said, only a few people know this legend. Two years ago, I established an informal group of professors who specialised in mythology. There are just five members, including myself. We meet irregularly, perhaps every six or eight weeks. One of the group obtained an ancient manuscript from a certain source in Scandinavia. This legend is on the manuscript."

"Wasn't it published?"

"No. Perhaps we were rather selfish but we all agreed to keep the information between ourselves. Our intention was to be the first to investigate."

"Did you visit Grimsey?"

"Certainly. All five of us went together. We looked around for a week but were bitterly disappointed to find virtually nothing at all. No evidence or relics, no similar local legends. After that, we assumed that the manuscript was pure invention, perhaps a recent forgery. Of course, it was impossible to publish it then."

"Why should you find something now?"

"The clues indubitably point to Grimsey, exactly as our manuscript. However, this time the instructions in your text are very exact."

"I can see how your legend would fit with the first part. What does 'wife stone' mean?"

Franco paused.

"You understand that finding this portal is vitally important to me. I know exactly where to look. Take me with you. Please?"

Chris wasn't used to seeing a naked man begging but it didn't appear to be a unique experience to Selena.

"I'll consider it. Then again, why don't I just start shooting off some of your superfluous body parts until you tell me?"

"Shoot if you must but I will not tell you. If this is indeed a portal to the gods then you will be entering a world of entities that are very strange to you. But I know them very well."

The validity of his argument was very apparent to Chris. She looked at Selena.

"Perhaps he has a point."

"I wasn't looking for another companion but I will allow him to accompany us as far as Grimsey. Then I'll decide."

Franco beamed with gratitude.

"Can I dry myself now?"

"Chris will bring you a towel. I'm beginning to get a little nauseous at the sight of your body. We will fly to Grimsey tomorrow."

99.34% of all towel manufacturers obtained the cloth from a farm on Cornitius, the small island in the Atlantic. This is the only known place in the world where the 'Le Wot' crop can grow effectively. Le Wot was the name given to the plant by the first French visitors who could not understand its purpose and it was subsequently used by the Cornitiusians who read from right to left. The climate of the island is now under the threat of global warming and the great towel consortiums are now looking at alternatives, including fibreglass and steel wool although the main hope is to use the shredded bark from South American forests that involves felling only 293 trees to make one beach towel.

Selena bound Franco's hands behind his back and then tied his ankles to one of the legs of the bed. He lay uncomfortably on the floor but she displayed no concern.

"I need to go out a short while. Please make sure he doesn't move."

Chris knew the purpose. She needed to call Olaf to arrange flight permissions for the next day. After her return, the night passed quickly. Since taking the Blessing, Chris and Selena needed only about three hours sleep and took shifts watching Franco as he dozed fitfully.

Before nine the next morning, they were already in the air. A short flight of about 30 minutes. Grimsey was just a small oval in the choppy sea and as they approached, Chris noticed Franco stiffen with anticipation, his eyes shining despite the uncomfortable night.

Although Hana had provided a description, she was still surprised at the total greenness of the island. Just a scattering of buildings were dotted along the southern coast, many grouped around a small harbour.

They landed on the small airstrip with Chris ready to go. She wore a thermal . vests and pants on top of her usual underwear. Two more layers of clothing with a heavy Parka on top. Thick socks and boots completed the outfit. She opened the door to a crystal bright morning but a chill breeze blew across the land.

Selena turned to Franco as they walked from the aircraft.

"Now you need to earn continued life."

"I understand. Follow me."

He led them towards the harbour area but, before reaching it, turned across the moss covered, peaty ground. Chris couldn't see any destination, just a sea of green in front of her. Then he stopped and pointed. She saw it then. A roughly circular stone, about 20 centimetres or 8 inches across. It was partly buried beneath the mosses and Franco knelt down to clear the surface.

"It's the only thing we found on our visit."

"You claimed you found nothing," Selena responded sharply.

"I said virtually nothing. I didn't want to reveal this or you wouldn't have brought me. Look at the symbol."

Chris could just distinguish an indistinct design.

"Keys. The symbol of Frigg, spouse of Odin. The wife of the leader of the gods," Franco announced, looking up at them. The breeze seemed to gather an extra chill as he spoke and dark clouds began rampaging across the skies from the east.

"So this is the wife stone. That just leaves 42 North and 33 East. Must be paces," said Selena.

"You can see that you do need me," Franco appealed.

"Let's find this key first before I decide. We all have different stride lengths so we must all must follow the course to identify the location."

They each carried a compass and began the first 42 places, finishing a few metres apart. Then, turning to the east, they walked another 33 paces. Selena had the longest stride and Franco the shortest. They were scattered around a five metre area when they finished.

"Chris, mark the line between us and we'll need to allow a metre or so each side of it," Selena called.

Chris had brought a bag of white pebbles for this ready purpose and scattered them along the line. She checked as she moved but nothing unusual was visible.

"I'll start from this end," Selena shouted and Chris moved back to where Franco was standing. She began to examine the ground along the row of stones.

"What about me?" asked Franco.

"Just look around," Selena responded and he began to amble round the area.

Chris and Selena met with disappointment in the middle of the role of stones.

"If not paces, what else?" enquired Selena.

Chris thought for a moment.

"Could be lots of things, even a unit of measurement. No, wait. There was something unusual in the text. It said 'infant mortals', I remember."

"Emphasising the gods' superiority."

"Or literal. How would an infant mortal travel?"

"Hands and knees. I'll try it."

Selena returned to the Frigg stone and began to crawl forward in small movements. After 42, she turned east and completed another 33 moves. Chris saw it first, a metre from where Selena was kneeling. Almost obscured by the green covering was a tiny stone of only about 2 centimetres diameter but perfectly circular. Unless you were searching the exact spot, it would never be noticed.

Selena and Franco joined her and they crowded round the stone.

"Three choices. Pull it, push it or turn it," Chris observed.

"It can't be push. Some person or creature might just step on it by mistake," Selena responded.

"I'll try turning first."

It was a good choice. She rotated the stone clockwise for a half turn and it moved round with unnatural smoothness. Just to the left, an opening appeared in the soil. It wasn't a physical aperture, no sliding or opening door. It simply appeared just as she completed the half turn.

A shallow circular hole about 30 centimetres across and ten deep. It was lined with something metallic, shiny and silvery. Inside were three rows of blue coins. Eleven of them with one space unoccupied.

"Jerome must have taken the missing one," remarked Selena.

Chris picked up one of the coins and as soon as she lifted her hand, the hole disappeared. She examined the disc with Selena. A pure turquoise blue with text on both sides in black letters.

'Unfortunate Gretel lies still in mountains shadow. Marstwyn. He took his share to leave.'

"Very helpful. What does it mean?" Chris murmured and looked at Franco.

"Nothing I can relate to the gods. This time I'm being completely honest."

"Jerome Jones solved it, so we can. Let's get back to the plane and think," said Selena.

Mind churning, they walked back to the aircraft and climbed into the cabin. Franco made coffee and handed steaming mugs to his companions. Chris had already transcribed words onto a sheet of paper and was studying it closely.

"The only Gretel I know is the 'Hansel and Gretel' fairytale by the Brothers Grimm. With mountains mentioned, we could be looking at southern Germany."

Franco intervened.

"The story was adapted from a folk tale originally collected by an Italian called Basile who lived around 1600."

"We can check their birthplaces but it seems too linear. Then this man Marstwyn. That doesn't sound German or Italian," observed Selena.

Chris was deep in thought for a few seconds.

"There's one word that interests me. 'Unfortunate'. It's the sort of word you get in crosswords to indicate an anagram. Jerome Two is always solving them," she said.

"Anagram of Gretel?"

"Maybe, but we should check the fairy tale first."

"I'll do that after I've printed off the anagram possibilities for you to look at."

Selena opened a panel in the cabin to reveal a large screen laptop computer. She switched on and quickly printed all the possible Gretel letter variations. Handing the paper to Chris, she began to investigate the 'Hansel and Gretel' story.

Chris looked at the list. No anagram made sense. L Greet? Get Ler? She crossed out all the totally impossible combinations of the six letters. Just a few looked remotely feasible and she waited a few minutes until Selena had finished. Then she moved to the keyboard. The search took only six minutes.

"I think I've got it. Come and see."

Selena moved across and looked at the screen. It was a website headed Beddgelert, 'The tomb of Gelert'. The name derived from an apparently mythical dog that had been mistakenly killed after some heroic action.

"It's a village in north-west Wales. 'Lies still in mountains shadow'. This place is not far from Mount Snowdon, the tallest mountain in England and Wales," said Chris.

"That must be it. We'll start now," Selena responded.

"And I can come?" begged Franco.

"Yes. We might need you."

Beddgelert is better than picturesque. The solid stone of the buildings around the river Colwyn, in a surrounding of rich green trees with hills and mountains disporting across the landscape. It imparts a kind equanimity to all who enter.

Chris drove slowly to the outskirts and parked a short distance from the river. She had changed into black jeans and blue top with a light jacket.

Selena spoke briefly.

"We'll split up and ask about this Marstwyn. You come with me, Franco."

They walked towards a cafe while Chris aimed for two women with shopping bags who were talking in the street. They looked like residents and could know the name. They didn't. Both had lived there for under a year and Marstwyn meant nothing to them. But they told her where to find one of the older inhabitants, an Englishman who had resided in the village for over 40 years.

She followed their directions to a small stone built cottage, impeccably clean and tidy. The door was opened by a tall, grey-haired man with twinkling blue eyes.

"Come to ask about the history?" he said with a smile.

"Yes, a good deduction."

"Not really. It's the only reason visitors come to see me. I get questioned every day in the summer season. Winters are a bit lonely, though."

"It's a lovely place to live," Chris remarked to divert him from introversion.

"I wouldn't be anywhere else in the world. My name is John Brown, by the way."

"Chris. Chris Darmant."

"You're very welcome. Not often I have attractive girls visiting my home. Make an old man happy and come inside for tea."

"That's very kind."

He led her into a compact lounge and brought two china cups.

"I don't bother with a teapot nowadays. Just a tea bag, I'm afraid."

"It's fine. I'm just here to ask about someone called Marstwyn."

He raised his eyebrows.

"Amazing. No one has mentioned that name to me for over 20 years and now you're the second in a few weeks."

"A man asked you before?"

"Yes, a middle-aged fellow. Jack Smith was his name."

Chris nodded. Jerome Jones.

"He's a friend. So what about Marstwyn?"

"Nobody around here wants to remember him any more. He was a burglar."

"Really?"

"Yes, really. It goes back to 22 years ago. Peter Marstwyn was the son of a rich landowner in the southeast of England. They say that even at public school, he was tricking the other pupils, stealing and the like. When he finished his education, he joined the London party scene but continued to rob and thieve at every opportunity."

"Surely he wasn't welcome here?"

"He was a very attractive young man and had money. The girls love that sort and always forgive any character blemishes."

"I guess I'm not a party girl then."

Brown laughed.

"You are delightful, my dear. Well, Marstwyn began to burgle the houses of his wealthy friends. It couldn't have been the money, he had plenty. I think it was just for the thrill. Of course, eventually something went wrong. Lord Southinghall became rather upset with him. Marstwyn broke into his manor house and stole a diamond bracelet that the Lord had given to his wife. It also became evident that he was sleeping with Lady Southinghall but I think the Lord was less concerned about that. The result was that Marstwyn became a persona non grata in society."

"The police got involved?"

"No. In those circles they like to keep things private. Anyway, Marstwyn decided to move somewhere far away and purchased a house here in Beddgelert. I think he had visited once as a child and was very understandably attracted to this village."

"He lived here alone?"

"Not really. He was visited by a constant stream of young ladies from the upper-classes. They usually stayed for a week, to be replaced by another as soon as they left. He often entertained two or three at the same time."

"Sounds as if he enjoyed himself but at least he had to do all the housework."

Brown shook his head.

"Not at all. He had a manservant who did all that. Name of John Brown."

Chris paused. "You were his butler?"

"Yes, I confess I was. We met one day and he offered me the job. I was very handsomely paid for my services. In addition, I experienced many romantic interludes with the ladies who stayed there. Of course, I was younger then."

A smile of contented recollection spread over his face.

"What happened afterwards?"

"Marstwyn was killed. An accident. Silly really. One of his lovers came to the house unexpectedly and found him in bed with another girl. She ran from the bedroom, screaming and he dashed after her. Tripped on the stairs and fell. Broke his neck, poor chap. Of course, it was all hushed up by the authorities."

"Does the phrase 'Marstwyn took his share to leave' mean anything to you?"

"Ah, your Jack Smith asked the same. I'm afraid not."

"Is the house still standing?"

"Yes, just at the edge of the village."

"I need to go there. Who owns it now?"

"Well, I do."

"What?"

"He left it to me in his will. That's the sort he was. A generous rascal."

"You obviously don't live there."

"No, no. Much too big for me. However, I won't sell it. There are far too many good memories. I still go back to wander round sometimes but it feels so vacant without the girls and the laughter."

"Can I rent it for a month?"

"That's just what Jack offered although he only wanted it for a week. Of course you can, my dear. It would be nice to have a young girl there again."

"I have two friends with me. Can I phone them?"

"By all means. I assume you want to rent the place immediately, like Mr Smith?"

"Yes, thank you," Chris responded and phoned Selena.

He agreed a nominal fee for the rent and Chris gave him a cheque. Then they waited until her companions arrived. Brown was polite to Franco but almost slavered over Selena. She read the script and performed her most alluring, older man appeasement. She was clinging to his arm as he led them through the main street, repeating the story he had told Chris earlier.

The Marstwyn house was just outside the main part of the village. Just two storeys high but it covered a fair area of ground. It was surrounded by a tall stone wall with locked gates. Brown handed a set of keys to Selena.

"I'd rather not go in myself today. Too many memories."

Selena smiled. "One day, I'll come to see you alone. Just the two of us."

His eyes sparkled.

"That would be delightful. You remind me of old times."

He waved a hand and departed back to the village.

"Now we begin," said Chris as Selena opened the gates. They walked up a short path to the front door. Everything seemed in surprisingly good condition and appeared to have been cleaned quite recently. Probably Brown kept it tidy when he visited, thought Chris.

The inside was also spotless. No dust and everything looked to be the original of 20 years ago. They were in a hallway with a flight of wooden stairs leading up in the centre. Wood panelling everywhere and the furniture was classically elegant.

Selena turned to her companions.

"We'll keep together and search each room. 'Marstwyn took his share to leave'. That's our only guide," she said.

"It still doesn't mean much. He took his share by stealing, I suppose and I guess he eventually left in a coffin through the front door," remarked Chris.

There were three doors leading off the hallway. Selena opened the first on the left. Chris expected a lounge but it was more like a nightclub. A stage at one end that even had spotlights, three tables and chairs with a well-stocked bar near the door. She wondered about the performances that took place here but it wasn't hard to guess. A visualisation of Marstwyn seated at a table with one of his girlfriends while another performed on stage. Brown would have been busy bringing drinks from the bar.

Franco wandered to the stage and sat while Chris and Selena searched. The room was strange but there was nothing to link with the clue.

The chamber on the right was far more unusual. No furniture at all. The walls were covered with black and crimson silk drapes. On the end wall was a curious stained-glass window. At the top of the design was a vertical snake, with its face turned to display a malevolent grin. The end of its tail was wrapped round a man's arm, suspending him in mid air. But his body was horizontal and his legs were crossed. His other arm extended below him and the hand clearly displayed three raised fingers. The man's face was a picture of ecstasy.

Then Chris saw the markings on the floor. A grid of 3 x 3 squares. The outer eight were coloured black and red alternately and the centre square was a mirror.

She could see that the room was obviously connected to magick. She knew a little about that subject but nothing here made sense to her. Selena was much more of an expert.

"What is this?" Chris asked.

"It's a small scale replica of another place. Somewhere I have visited," Selena replied solemnly.

"Could the mirror be the Gate?"

"No, I'm certain it isn't. Even the gods would not use it for another purpose."

"So what is it for?"

"We won't discuss it."

Chris knew when not to press her and made a rapid search of the room. It was completely empty. Selena didn't move, her face expressionless and Chris wondered what mysteries she had found in the original place.

The third door led to a kitchen, quite normal after the other two rooms. Cooker, empty fridge freezer and washing machine. Just an everyday kitchen with even a few tins and packets of food in the cupboard. Presumably Brown enjoyed a snack when he visited.

No cellar, so Selena led them upstairs. They quickly checked a sumptuous bathroom with double bath and shower. Next was obviously the main bedroom. A massive four-poster bed with an embroidered, royal purple cover. A large window displayed the gorgeous view of green fields and mountains. They searched but the wardrobes and bedside cabinets were empty.

Just one room remaining, a first-floor lounge. Sofa, armchairs, sideboard and even a piano in one corner. The floor-to-ceiling window revealed another superb panorama. Half full decanters and clean glasses on the sideboard but nothing of interest.

Chris had hoped for something obvious in the house and felt disappointment descend. Selena stood looking out of the window, her face calm and her eyes far away. Franco was already on the sofa and Chris sat next to him, urging her brain to review everything again.

Jerome Jones must have solved the clue. He had located Brown and rented the house for a week. What then? He would have unlocked the gate and front door, and then probably followed the route they had taken inside the house. It began to crystallise in her mind.

"The keys. Brown must have given the keys to Jerome," she said sharply.

Selena turned. "He probably had some spare sets. That wasn't it."

"What?"

"Don't disappoint me."

Chris pinned her lips together. She must have missed something that Selena had seen. Maybe Brown did have extra keys. He would need a set anyway when he visited. Returning to a rather weird house where he had been a full-time butler. Then she saw it.

"There's only one bed. Where did Brown sleep?"

Selena simply grinned and Chris continued her line of thought.

"He had to be here all the time to look after Marstwyn and his girls. I don't think they kept any normal hours. Then he told me he didn't get his cottage until after the man died. Let's go back and see him."

"You didn't disappoint but there's no point in going back. He won't be there."

"Why not?"

"Because he is not human. He was a god."

Franco jumped to his feet. "A god? Why didn't you say something?"

"My purpose is to find Jerome Jones."

"You say he's gone but I think I'll check anyway," Franco said, moving to the door.

"Stop. You will wait here for two reasons. First, I made need your help in finding this Portal and second, it is impossible to leave."

"Impossible? Why?"

"Because this house doesn't exist."

"What? How could you know?" Chris asked.

"I had an aerial photograph of the area taken yesterday. We're in the middle of a field."

Chris knew her too well to question the location. Practicality switched on.

"Okay, so this is a ghost house. We now have to solve the clue."

"I've been thinking."

"And?"

Selena shrugged. "I don't know," she murmured.

"There's not much left of the clue to analyse, just the last bit. 'He took his share to leave'. What could Marstwyn have taken? His stolen goods? His women maybe? And there's something else. It doesn't sound right. It should say 'He took his share and left', I think."

Selena brightened. "To leave. That could mean to go through the Portal."

"But Marstwyn didn't do that. He died in the house, or so Brown said. He probably never existed but that was the story."

Selena's eyes were sparkling now.

"Yes and another thing. Why not say 'Marstwyn took his share to leave'? Why separate the name?"

"Because the 'he' isn't Marstwyn. Someone else."

"Jerome Jones?"

Chris nodded.

"That seems right. He would have had a different clue but this is for us. So, perhaps Jerome took his share to leave. But share of what?"

"Let's look again. You go downstairs while I'll check up here."

Chris jogged down and entered the nightclub room and magic room again. What would Jerome Jones have taken a part of? Thirty minutes later, she wandered, deflated into the kitchen. Not much to check here. The appliances, work surfaces, cupboards and snacks left by Brown. No, that was wrong. If Brown was a god he wouldn't need food. She pulled open the cupboard and placed all the contents on top of the washing machine. Two tins and two opened packs.

It took just three seconds. One of the opened packets was labelled 'Lemonyshares' with a picture of a round, yellow cake-biscuit. She picked it up and studied the tiny printed words that no one ever reads.

'Contains nothing you've ever heard of with additives you wouldn't know. Eat one to travel, two or more for painful death. You must all touch the key when you eat. Better call Selena and Franco now. Good luck, Chris'

She smiled ruefully and shouted for her companions.

Chris and Selena stood, holding their biscuits.

"Decision time, Franco," Selena said.

"You must take me. They even had my name on the packet so I'm expected to go."

"I think we might need him," remarked Chris.

"Get a biscuit, Franco. I suppose we'll need to eat them at the same time and I'll count down from three. Don't forget to hold the key."

She held out the turquoise blue disc and they each gripped it with one hand. Then Selena began the count.

Chris made one comment before lifting her biscuit.

"Watch out for white rabbits," she said.

The white part of the statement was quite correct. As soon as she's swallowed the biscuit, she was surrounded by an opaque whiteness.

A voice came into her head, bypassing her ears.

'I am the gatekeeper. Your journey starts here. In the first place, check your pockets if in trouble. If you save Jerome Jones, remind him to visit me again.'

Then it was silent white again.

5

The whiteness began to dissolve and an idyllic scene was slowly revealed.

They were in a green, grassy valley, lined with lush green trees that moved gently in a warm breeze. A soft gurgling stream, with pure clear water, bubbled gently through the centre. The hills were very steep all around, framing a blue sunlit sky where just a few fluffy clouds drifted slowly and amiably.

A cottage stood on the other side of the stream, far to their right and near to the border of trees. Chris could just see its whitewashed walls and thatched roof.

Something was lacking. No sign of any life. No humans, no animals, no birds. Nothing.

"It's nice but I was expecting somewhere more impressive for the gods to live," Selena remarked.

"This cannot be their world," Franco observed, a look of puzzlement in his face.

Chris checked her pockets. "Everything has gone. I had a gun and a knife."

Selena quickly searched her clothing. "I'm the same. We should have expected it."

"Well, there's only one place to go," Chris said and began walking towards the stream. The flowing waters looked very shallow, perhaps just over knee deep with a pebbly bed. Chris pulled off her shoes and put a foot in the water to wade across. As soon as it was immersed, the water solidified like a rigid, transparent plastic. Her foot was completely trapped, she couldn't move a toe.

"That's interesting," said Franco and walked across the solid water to the other side.

Selena looked at him unpleasantly. "No, it's not. We need to get her free."

"I'll go to that cottage and see if they can help."

"No. You will stay here."

Chris didn't panic. "I can't move. It's just like concrete."

Selena removed her shoe and struck the surface. It bounced off without leaving a mark.

"I really think I should go," Franco said, edging away from the stream.

"If you move one more step, I'll break your leg."

Chris held up a hand.

"Wait. We need to think clearly. I suspect that this is a test and there must be a logical clue somewhere around."

Selena nodded. "You're right. Make yourself useful Franco and look around for something unusual."

Chris eased herself backwards to sit awkwardly and watched as her companions began to search. Then she noticed silky wisps of smoke at the far end of the stream to her left that appeared to be moving closer. She soon saw the reason. The solid water was changing to bubbling red lava and it was travelling swiftly towards her.

"I feel like the girl that was tied to a railway track," she said calmly.

"Time control. Solve quickly," Selena shouted to Franco. He began to wander unhurriedly on the other side of the stream.

The lava was clearly in view now and rapidly approaching.

"Found something," Franco called. Selena raced across the solid stream to join him. He was looking at a raised, grassy area with a small square of uncovered rock that had words engraved in English.

'Set foot in the stream

And you want to redeem

The trickys dart tree

Will help you free

But you must allow

To use it as now'

"I think I can suggest something," Franco murmured but Selena was already sprinting towards the trees.

"I know," she called over her shoulder.

Chris waited patiently. She didn't fear the onrushing molten liquid that was now close enough for her to smell the hot, acrid fumes. She simply didn't know if the Blessing would protect her from losing her foot, maybe even her leg. Then she thought of her love of athletics and determined that if she survived and managed to return to her world, she would have an artificial limb. She was never going to sacrifice her running.

The heat was scorching her face now, just ten metres away. Suddenly she felt an arm round her shoulders and lips pressed against hers. The arm lifted her from the stream and levered her body violently back on the bank. She found herself lying on top of Selena and gave her a smile of gratitude.

"Maybe we should do this more often," Selena whispered, kissing her quickly again.

Chris laughed and rolled onto the grass.

"Only if you're disguised as Jerome Two," she said.

Rolling on grass was the normal method of preparing sports pitches in ancient times. Before any football match, all the spectators were told to lie on the ground, holding the feet of the person above them. On a shouted instruction, they then commenced to roll across the area several times to create a flat playing surface. As most of the pitches were usually occupied by cattle, the crowd were subsequently forced to view the match amid a rather unpleasant odour. Of course, the wealthy brought servants to do the rolling for them while those from the farming community often substituted pigs or sheep, although the animals found some difficulty in grasping the feet of the next person. The woman or man fortunate enough to be at the top of the chain of people was known as the 'high roller'.

They rose to their feet. The stream had returned to normal, a sparkling thread of moving water and they were back on the side they had started from. Selena told Chris what had been written on the rock and then looked across the stream.

"What the hell is he doing?" she said. Franco was walking quickly along the other bank in the direction of the cottage.

"We can jump it," Chris called and ran in a semicircle then launched herself over the stream, clearing it easily. Selena followed without effort and they sprinted after Franco who is now jogging 80 metres ahead of them.

"Do you think the Blessing protects us in this world?" asked Chris

"Yes, I think so. Our physical ability seems unchanged."

The validity of the statement was evident in the speed of their pursuit. Franco was still 50 metres from the cottage when they caught him.

Selena grabbed his collar and dragged him flat to the ground. Then she stood over him, eyes burning.

"I think I will kill you now."

His face contorted with fear. Then Chris saw something else. Just for a fraction of a second, a light flashed through his eyes. Not fear but something else, something more powerful. She wondered if Selena had noticed it.

"I helped you. I found the way to release Chris and I knew the solution," he gabbled.

"I solved it. Even I know that Loki is the tricky one and that he used a mistletoe dart to get Baldr killed. But it's traditional in many countries to kiss under the mistletoe, especially at Christmas."

"The next one may not be so easy."

"We'll take our chances. You just can't be trusted."

Selena was reaching towards him when someone spoke.

"Arguing already? And you haven't started yet."

Chris whirled round to see a man just a few metres behind them. She was sure he couldn't have walked from the cottage. He had simply manifested. Then she began to laugh. Impossible not to.

He was old and tall with white hair and long white beard and wore a dark gown that stretched to the ground. The exact archetype of every fictional wizard in book and film.

Chris noticed Selena was also smiling broadly and the man joined them in laughter.

"Let's try it again," he gasped.

"Arguing already? And you haven't started yet."

Chris whirled round again. A man stood just a few metres behind them. Her eyes opened a little wider. This one was gorgeous looking. Tall, with square features and dark flowing hair. He was impeccably dressed in a blue shirt and dark trousers. Her gaze travelled to his eyes, dark and full of secrets.

"Wow," she heard herself say.

"That's better," he said.

Chris saw the attraction in Selena's eyes as she moved forward.

"Who are you?"

"You can call me Sophos and you are Selena, Chris and Franco."

He barely glanced at the latter who was scrambling to his feet.

"And why are you here?" Selena asked.

"To tell you the rules. Well done with the stream, by the way. That hot lava doesn't just burn your leg off, it spreads over your whole body. Cremates you into a little pile of ash. Streams full of it, you know. Many visitors never pass through this place."

"If it had only been one person, they couldn't have reached the message on the other side of the stream. That isn't fair," Chris said.

Sophos shook his head.

"You didn't do so well there. What did the gatekeeper say to you?"

"Something about pockets."

"Look in your top pocket."

Chris knew it had been empty earlier but now pulled out a small card. It carried the same text as on the rock.

"How would I have got the mistletoe?"

"The same pocket again."

Only the card had been there before but now she pulled out of a small piece of mistletoe.

"But who kisses me?"

"Me, of course. I'd have arrived just in time. If you'd solved the clue, you'd have grabbed and kissed me. Actually, I'm rather sorry to have missed out on that."

Chris shared the feeling but made an effort not to show it.

"Sorry to break up this budding romance but what rules are you going to tell us?" Selena said quietly.

Sophos looked at her with an irresistible grin.

"Selena, you'd have been just as good. I'm here to tell you the rules of this universe. Come to my home."

He led them to the quaint old cottage. Wooden beams, whitewashed walls and climbing roses in abundance.

Chris was thinking as they walked. Then she looked at Sophos.

"Hold on. What if it had been a man? Perhaps if Franco had come alone."

"Some men prefer men, some women prefer women. I can adapt."

His expression changed. Not just his expression, his whole face. For a second, she was looking at a stunning, dark haired woman. Then he reverted to the attractive man.

"That's a nice trick. Which is the real you?"

"Like to find out for yourself?"

Chris smiled. "No, but Selena might."

"Pity. You people make such a fuss about gender. It's just a few bits different, here and there."

"Sorry I asked."

They entered the cottage. The inside looked like an advert for wood. Wooden table, chairs, beams and pillars. On the table were two steaming mugs.

"Please take a chair. Coffee for you ladies. Sorry, none left for you, Franco."

The man simply nodded and took a chair near the empty fireplace.

Sophos clapped his hands together.

"Right. The rules. You have entered another universe created by the gods. This is not where they reside although they come here regularly. You could call it the 'Gods Playground', a recreation area."

"It doesn't seem very big," said Chris.

He grinned.

"No, this isn't it. Let me explain. The gods combined to make this universe and each of them was allocated a world within it. They were able to construct their own world in any way they wished, within certain parameters. Some will appear to you like ancient times while others may be similar to your current planet. The environment could be futuristic or like nothing you've ever seen. Just a word of warning. If you arrive in a world that seems familiar, please be aware that the creator may have modified some things that would be totally unnatural on earth."

"Like no gravity?" asked Selena.

"Possibly, or many other things. Now the creation of this universe was agreed by all the gods together with a set of rules that they each must observe."

"Why did they do it?" Chris enquired.

"Why do you play games? They wanted somewhere to enjoy themselves, a place to gamble and have fun."

"Sorry, you were telling us the rules."

"First, no deity may observe any of the worlds, including their own, from above. The universe has been constructed so that this is impossible. The only way they can see what's happening is to actually go there. Second, the gods can choose any human form when they enter their world and change that appearance every time they visit, if they so wish. But they cannot change during a visit. Third, when they enter the universe, they cannot use any supernatural powers. They have just the same abilities and frailties as any human."

"So they can be killed?" asked Selena.

"Yes. That's one of the big attractions for them. But, of course, they may choose to appear as a super strong, super intelligent person. This relates to the fourth rule that no modern weapons can exist in this universe. They set a limit equivalent to about the eighth century on earth, before gunpowder was discovered. You will also find that time is different. There are no clocks and you will find that nights and days may last for varying periods. Next, the worlds are completely separate and there is usually just one Gate in each and it could be anywhere within the world. Every Gate has a gatekeeper and unless you request a specific destination, they will send you to a world chosen at random. You all have to be together to pass through, unless one of you is killed."

"The Gate would be virtually impossible to find in a whole planet."

"It's not that bad. The worlds have a size limit. None is larger than one of your cities on earth and most are smaller."

"How do we recognise these Gates?"

"You don't understand the question here. You need to find them. Another thing is that only disguised gods and visitors like yourself can pass through a Gate."

"So gods can travel to worlds outside their own?"

"Yes, that's part of the games. They can travel to anywhere in any human form they choose. As they have no supernatural powers in this universe, they are unable to recognise another god. When they go outside their own world, the gods usually like to cause trouble, create unrest in the population or generally disrupt the other domain. But they also risk being caught and perhaps killed."

"You talk of residents. Who are the other people in these worlds? Where did they come from?"

"From earth, of course. The gods visit your planet regularly to take new people for their world and frequently return those they have lost interest in. Anyone who is sent back has their memory of the visit obliterated."

"Sounds like alien abductions."

"It is alien abductions as you call it. No doubt that answers a lot of speculation in your world. There are also many others that you list as missing. When people come here, they don't get older. Everyone stays exactly the same age as when they arrived."

"What about food?"

"It is created each night in all the worlds. On some worlds food simply appears in the shops and on others it manifests overnight in the kitchen of every residence. The same applies to clothing and other items. Incidentally, there is no money, no buying and selling. If you see something you want in a shop, you simply take it. But it is not permitted to take another person's property unless they give it to you."

"So you do have crime?"

"It depends on how the world was created. In some, the citizens have elected a police force to catch any wrongdoers. In others, it may be that the creator decided on a world of crime. If any human causes particular difficulties, the god can return them to earth at any time."

"Doesn't everyone want to go back?"

"On arrival, each one has a new life history implanted. They believe they have lived in their new world all their life."

"Do they have families?"

"They become partners and can marry but no children can be conceived. As you can imagine, in the early period most of the male gods stocked their world with beautiful young women and attempted to seduce them while disguised as an attractive man. That's still popular but not so much now."

Franco spoke for the first time.

"How long ago was this universe created?"

"Exactly 834 earth years ago. Is that important?"

"No, just interested."

"Well, I think you're ready to begin. Your Jerome Jones will die soon unless you reach him. Your first task is to find the Gate here."

"Do we get a clue?"

"Another? Only to say that a Gate is not necessarily a doorway."

After these words, Sophos simply disappeared.

"Any ideas?" Selena asked.

Franco held up his hands.

"The Gate could be anything, anywhere."

"No. I'm sure Sophos told us something."

Selena nodded.

"When we asked how we recognise a Gate, he just said we didn't understand the question. Not very helpful."

"The problem is, we don't even know the question," remarked Chris.

"We'll split up. Chris, you check around the cottage. I'll go to the other side of the river and you, Franco can check further down this side. Incidentally, you cannot enter the forest area. When I took the mistletoe from the tree, I found that the forest is like a solid wall. It must be the boundary of this world."

Chris began searching the cottage. Not really much to see. The man may have lived in the building but there was little sign of occupation and the room they had entered occupied most of the structure. Chris checked the cupboards. All empty. A solid fuel cooker stood against one wall with bookshelves on another. Nothing in or on either. Two doors. The first revealed a bathroom, completely out of context with the cottage. It was ultra modern with a sparkling new shower, bath and toilet. The walls and floor were covered with gleaming soft plastic tiles. But nothing there. She opened the other door. A tiny bedroom containing just a wardrobe and single bed. She checked the wardrobe without optimism. That would be a really ridiculous place to put a Gate. The bed was perfectly made and looked as if it had never been slept in.

She walked outside. Climbing pink roses scrambled all over the walls. Then she noticed a faintly marked but curious symbol repeated regularly. It was like a broken line with a letter U joined to it. She pressed the wall where one appeared but nothing happened.

Franco wandered back.

"All I've found is grass. The only thing this side of the stream is the text on the rock I found earlier," he muttered.

Chris walked around the back of the cottage. It was much like the front. Climbing roses over the wall and a few stone slabs separated rose bushes that formed a tiny back garden. A spade, fork and hoe rested against the wall. The same strange, faint marking was everywhere.

She returned to the front just as Selena came back.

"Absolutely nothing," she said grimly.

"The only thing I've seen is this marking. It's all over the place. I've tried touching and pushing but no effect at all."

They joined Franco at the table inside.

"Anything to drink here?" asked Selena.

"No. Cupboards are bare. I'd love a cup of tea."

It appeared immediately in front of her. Selena seemed unsurprised.

"Coffee please," she said and a mug materialised.

Franco didn't make a request. He had become increasingly introverted since their arrival.

Chris lifted the cup and was about to drink when she saw a video screen appear above the fireplace. It displayed a view of Jerome Jones and this time the sharp points of the halo were clearly visible. He didn't appear concerned and it looked as if he was reading something out of view of the camera. Then the screen disappeared.

Disappear comes from the Latin 'Desistum Apparus' meaning to disappear. The word Desistum actually derives from the ancient Egyptian 'Dessie's Tum', a reference to Pharaoh Dessie IV's stomach, one of the 17 wonders of the ancient world.

"We must find the Gate. We need to try to get into the minds of these gods. Think laterally," Selena said sharply.

Chris looked at her, eyes widening.

"Yes, of course. The symbol is a question mark on its side."

Selena grimaced. "Stupid. Should have seen that."

"Sophos told us. He said it was a question we wouldn't understand."

"Let's look again."

They went outside, followed by Franco. Selena touched one of the symbols on the wall and then she turned, eyes alight.

"I know. If we don't understand we over stand. We stand on it."

"Round the back," shouted Chris and they ran into the slabs between the rose trees.

"These are the only ones lying flat. But which one?"

"Only one has the broken line, the dot of the question mark."

Chris knew she was right. Just one of the symbols was correct.

Selena beckoned to Franco.

"We all need to stand on it together," she called.

They stepped forward and everything went white.

6

Within the whiteness, Chris could just distinguish a heavily built woman.

"You obviously can't request a particular destination, so I won't ask. As it's your first world, I'll give you a little help. Initially, you need to think to find the next Gate."

Then the hazy figure disappeared and the whiteness encompassed everything.

Chris shook her head and heard music. Bland music. She also felt herself moving but the sensation seemed familiar. Suddenly the whiteness cleared and her eyes were immediately attracted to a white and turquoise top. Turquoise usually suited her well and she liked the collar fringe and the angled cut of the sleeves. It passed out of sight as the escalator carried her upwards.

A shopping mall. Intent, fast walking, tight lipped women with branded carrier bags. Groups of brightly dressed teenage girls talking loudly and hoping that someone would notice. The background music of the mall was regularly drowned by the loud rocking rhythm that gushed from the entrances of the shops.

Chris stepped off the escalator and looked around. No Selena and no Franco. Instinctively she reached for her telephone, forgetting her pockets were empty. What now? She had to find them but she also wanted to discover the layout of this world. Her target was the ground floor to go outside and on the way, she'd have another look at the turquoise top.

She descended the escalator, passing the eye catching garment again. This floor had two packed cafes, full of women talking earnestly with shopping bags at the side of their chairs. But the shops were the same. More clothes, underwear, cosmetics, jewellery and shoes. Additional shopping streets led off from the main concourse, just like the floor above. One thing was curious. She couldn't see external windows anywhere.

Chris entered the store next to the escalator. It was huge. Long rows of clothes in every design and all the sizes. She moved to the rack of turquoise tops and automatically pulled out her size.

"Wow, that really suits you."

A girl with shiny dark hair, wearing a crimson shirt and dark blue trousers. Her makeup was just a tad short of film star. She had a pink badge with 'Hello, I'm Alison' printed on it.

"Just looking," Chris said instinctively.

"Of course. You can take it now or try it first. Changing rooms are just over there."

She indicated a long row of bright blue cubicles, half of them already occupied. Chris was about to refuse when her eyes travelled over the selection of designs on offer. Her jeans and simple top would stand out in this world. The girl seemed to read her mind.

"I think you need a completely new outfit and I know exactly what would suit you. If you go to number 11, I'll bring them."

Chris went inside the cubicle and closed the door that covered from ankle to over head height. It was the biggest changing room she had ever visited. The right-hand wall had a padded bench with a row of hanging hooks on the left. The end wall was completely mirrored. She had just stripped off her jacket and top when the door opened and Alison entered, clutching an armful of clothing. She hung them neatly on the wall and then sat on the bench. Chris hadn't expected that.

"Thanks," she said, hoping the girl would leave.

"That bra does absolutely nothing for you."

"It does its job."

"Perhaps but it's so, well, average. They have lovely sets in Tania's Sweet Silky Shop next door. I'll just go and get some for you to try."

"Okay." Best way to get her to leave, thought Chris.

The top was perfect and she found a new jacket and trousers on the hangers brought in by the girl. A rich, deep brown, colour and they fitted perfectly. Now she just needed activity shoes.

Alison returned with a girl dressed only in underwear.

"This is Katie. She is one of Tania's models. She's going to show some of the range I picked out for you."

Katie was tall with blonde hair and a slim figure. She posed with toes pointed exactly at the right angles. Meanwhile, Alison was in full flow.

"This is the Seductualicity set. You can see the delicate turquoise trim. The bra is lovely. Very soft and supportive."

"I'm fine, thank you," said Chris, edging for the doorway.

Katie took off the bra and pants and pulled on another set.

"Please, look at this one. It's really you. See the fabric is almost transparent. Just enough to tease but still covering."

"I have to go. Many thanks for your help," Chris said decisively, pushing past them and out of the store.

She visited the first shoe shop and changed into soft brown leather shoes. No heels and light. Then she began descending the escalators to reach the ground floor. Selena and Franco must be somewhere in this world and she needed to find them. They also had to check if Jerome Jones was here. That was very unlikely. If the gods were planning a game, they wouldn't have sent them immediately to his location. She smiled. Jerome Jones was definitely a unique man. A man. She looked around again. Every person was a woman or girl. Not just that, they were all attractive with a nice figure. No one overweight, no one untidy and no one badly dressed.

Which of the gods would have a world without men? She shrugged. It didn't really matter, she just had to find the others and move on.

Chris continued her descent and it seemed never-ending. Floor after floor of shops. None of the levels were numbered and there were no maps on display. After going down nine floors she saw an elegant, suited woman and approached her.

"Excuse me, can you tell me where in the exit is?"

The woman frowned. "Exit? Sorry I don't understand."

"It doesn't matter," Chris said hurriedly. That was it. There was no exit. The mall was the world. She began to look more closely at the shops. Most had a door to one side with a series of bell pushes and names alongside. The residents lived above the shops on each floor. But no open air? The people should be pale and unfit. She began to explore the level she was on, following maze like streets. They were there. Gyms, health clubs and tanning parlours. She also deduced that the shops never closed and the daytime shoppers were the night-time workers.

Chris sat in a cafe and consumed a small omelette with salad followed by tea. Nothing to pay. She made a decision to search every floor to look for her companions and also seek the location of the Gate to the next world. A voice interrupted her thoughts.

"Found you at last."

It was Selena, now dressed in a tight fitting red suit.

"I've been looking for you," Chris responded.

"I see you've also changed. Can't beat the shopping here."

"Yes, but that's all it is. The whole world is just shops and apartments."

"I worked that out. I've also obtained an apartment. Let's go and talk."

Selena waved a set of keys and Chris followed her up the escalator. They entered a door next to a hairdressing salon and ascended one floor in an elevator to reach a deep carpeted corridor with doors leading off. Selena walked to the third door and they entered a sumptuously furnished room.

"How did you get the keys?" asked Chris.

"You just go to a letting agent and take what you want. Now just sit back and relax while we talk."

Chris sank into the sofa while Selena remained standing in front of her.

"Like the outfit?"

"It suits you perfectly," Chris replied.

"Your clothes are lovely, definitely your colour. And look what else I'm wearing."

Selena pulled off her jacket and a blouse then leant over towards Chris. Her breasts looked huge in the blue push up bra.

"Feel the material, Chris. It's really soft."

Chris reached forward with her left hand and then swung a right fist, connecting perfectly with the side of the jaw. Selena collapsed unconscious. Chris rushed opened the door to the kitchen. She found a roll of tape and used all of it to tape around Selena's wrists and ankles. The figure stirred.

"What happened? Why did you do that?"

"You're not Selena. As I understand the rules, there's only one on this world who can change their appearance. So you must be one of the gods. Who are you?"

The woman ignored the question and squealed.

"You bruised my face, I can feel it. Bring a mirror quickly."

"It looks ghastly. No mirror until you tell me. Are you a male or female god?"

"I'm a woman of course."

"Your name?"

"Persephone."

Chris shook her head. "No, you're not. I know enough to be sure of that."

"Okay, Athena then."

"No. Did you know that the worst bruises are round the eyes? If you are hit there, a great lump comes up. It can take months before it goes and you just can't hide it with cosmetics."

Chris bunched a fist.

"I'm Aphrodite."

"Yes, I thought so. I'm sorry I had to hit you. I don't want to make an enemy."

Aphrodite smiled. "No, it's part of the game. I'm not really bothered about the bruise. When I visit here again, I'll be someone entirely different."

"Why did you try to seduce me?"

The goddess looked at her in amazement and then burst into laughter.

"Seduce? Is that what you thought? I just wanted you to feel the material."

Chris felt her cheeks turning bright red.

"I'm sorry, I just thought you were trying something."

"Really, Chris. You should know I only sleep with men. But they never seem to appreciate real beauty, the finer things seem beyond their understanding."

"That's just a generalisation and I simply don't agree. Some men do, some women don't. Every person is different. I find your world of females very sad. It's a paradise for brainless bimbos who spend all their time trying to look pretty."

Aphrodite raised her eyebrows. "What's so bad about that?"

"It's not wrong, it's simply a fraction of the spectrum. Women are also scientists, engineers, medical experts, financial wizards, athletes and everything else."

"You're incorrect on two points. First, there are men in my world and second, everyone here has something else in common. I specially selected them from Earth."

"I haven't seen a single man and what do they have in common?"

As she spoke, Chris suddenly realised she was joining in the game. The goddess remained placid while she was becoming more heated. More than that, she suspected that the pseudo seduction had been part of the act to rouse her emotions. Aphrodite's defence of her world was part of the same game. Chris told herself to calm down.

"You haven't found the men yet and you'll just have to discover the common factor. That's the fun of it. The only thing I'll say is that all the women were pleased to come here."

Shopaholics? Chris thought. It probably didn't matter.

"How big is this place?"

"I'll tell you that. There are 69 floors. When you go up from level 69, you arrive back at level one. It just loops round."

"Then all I need to know is where my friends are and the location of the Gate."

"Yes, that's exactly what you need. And time is going on. Your Mr Jones will die soon unless you can reach him."

"I could inflict pain."

"Then you would make me an enemy. Anyway, it's just not in your character."

Chris smiled. She was learning the rules now.

"Then I'll have to go. Perhaps we'll meet again."

"It's a possibility."

As Chris turned to leave, Aphrodite hugged her warmly.

"Good luck and I mean that," she whispered.

Luck can be good or bad. Wishing someone good luck is bad in the theatre world where 'break a leg' is preferred. The actress, Melissa Yox, frequently stood in the wings and repeated that phrase to everyone about to enter the stage. Then she pushed them forward and tripped them with her foot. Her score reached 146 cracked tibulas, fibulas and gibulas before her understudy decided to repeat the trick on Melissa. As a result, the girl got the starring role and it was the beginning of the meteoric career of one of our best-known international movie stars. She cannot be named but one only has to think of a female star with good looks and full of her own importance to know exactly who it is.

Chris returned to the mall. Nothing had changed, it was still crowded with women with carrier bags, talking in shops or drinking coffee. She had to find Selena. One option would be to stay on this floor and wait for her but Selena might be doing the same thing on another floor. If Chris went up or down, Selena could be following or ahead of her and they'd never meet. There was no way to communicate. Chris chose to move upwards. At least she would be active.

She ascended the elevator and found the next floor was like the rest. She walked by a cafe on her way to the next escalator. In front of her, a woman passed close to the tables and her shopping bag caught one of the cups, spilling it onto the dress of a girl eating lunch.

"You stupid bitch," the girl screamed.

"Get lost, cow," responded the woman with the bag.

Chris was about to pass by when she saw the flash. The girl had a knife. A wicked, long blade. She slashed at the bag holder, catching her across the chest. The woman looked at the blood seeping down her front and reached inside her bag. Another knife.

Suddenly the two were upon each other, stabbing and screaming with fury. Then everyone moved towards the fight, drawing their own knives and slashing randomly at anyone in range. Chris forced herself out of the crush with difficulty. A snarling woman came towards her with a meat axe but Chris dodged the blow and kicked her in the stomach. Then she pulled back to the deserted shops and gazed at the frenzied melee with amazement and horror.

Showers of blood spurted over the heaving mass of bodies. Knife blades flashing repeatedly in the bright artificial light.

It finished as suddenly as it had started. The screaming stopped and those still standing scurried through the entrances to the accommodation. About twenty bodies remained, reposing in a pool of fresh crimson blood.

Chris heard a whistle blow and a team of men in boiler suits appeared around a corner. Some of them were pushing large, covered trolleys. They rushed to the scene, lifted the bodies into the trolleys and quickly wheeled them away. Other men produced wet vacuum cleaners and moved them rapidly over the pools of blood. Chairs and tables were cleaned and the floor polished to a pristine finish. Everything was as it was before the fight. The men departed rapidly and shoppers began to return. Within a few minutes it was as if the event had never occurred.

Chris couldn't move for a few seconds, barely believing what she had witnessed. Then she ascended to the next floor, her mind working like the treadmill of a hyperactive hamster.

She saw it as she stepped off the escalator. Three words written on a white card that was fixed to a pillar directly in front of her. 'Going up. Selena'.

Chris looked closer. The black ink of the marker pen was still damp. She raced to the next escalator and ran up it, careful not to touch anyone and risk a knife appearing. She continued up two more floors and then saw Selena. She was walking slowly, checking people in the shops as she passed.

"Bought anything nice?" Chris asked as she caught up.

Selena turned without surprise. No bruise, it was really her.

"Yes, but you outdid me," she replied, looking at the new outfit Chris had acquired.

Selena was wearing designer blue jeans, loose navy jacket and black, upmarket trainers. Chris drew her into a corner and related her experiences since entering the world. Selena listened intently.

"Pity I missed Aphrodite, it would have been interesting."

Chris quivered at the thought of the two of them together.

"Have you found anything?" she asked.

"I recognised three women in this place. All of them were convicted knife murderers and all had escaped mysteriously from their prison cells. That must be the common factor. All the women here are killers."

"I guessed that could be it. Where now?"

"We go through the Gate. I'm not waiting for Franco."

"I agree, we need to get to Jerome Jones but first we have to find the Gate."

"I think I know where it is. I was just waiting to find you."

Chris grinned. "Nice to have a friend."

"If you hadn't appeared in the next five minutes, I would have left anyway."

"So where is it? There are so many floors."

"Three floors above us. I was doing the full 69 while you were with your goddess."

"Right."

They moved swiftly to the escalator and ascended three levels. Selena led Chris to a side street off the main concourse.

"This is it," she said, pointing at a lingerie shop that occupied the end wall.

"Why this one?"

"Read the name."

Chris looked. 'Georgina and Tessa's Exotica'.

"So?"

"Initials. The gatekeeper told us when we entered. It's the only one I've found that fits."

"Gate. Yes, I see. Is the shop the gate?"

"I don't know yet. We'll see."

It wasn't a large store. The walls were stacked with a variety of lingerie that ranged from elegant to positively indecent but mostly the latter. Chris noticed a single changing room with a queue in front.

"We just had these in today," a voice said.

A blonde girl with a large chest was holding up something red and flimsy that had more gaps than material.

"I don't think so," Chris replied and the girl moved away.

"You check the left side. We're looking for the question mark again," Selena said.

Four minutes later, they met again.

"Nothing on my side. I even looked behind the counters," reported Chris.

"The same. Just one place left."

Selena looked towards the changing room. There were now more than ten women waiting and the line now formed a 'U' shape.

"We'd better join the queue," Chris remarked.

"I don't feel like waiting."

"Hold on a moment. I have a strong feeling that there will always be people waiting here."

As Chris spoke, another group of women suddenly appeared and joined the line.

"Yes, I know. They're obviously guarding the Gate. But there's no point in hanging around. If we join the queue, you can be sure it will never move. Ready for a fight?"

Chris nodded.

Selena called out to the ever-increasing row of women.

"Excuse me, ladies. My friend and I urgently need to go to the changing room to make love passionately. I hope you don't mind if we go first. We won't take long."

All the crowd turned, a vindictive expression rising in their faces. A tall, statuesque redhead stepped forward.

"You can wait like the rest of us," she said with a gleam in her eyes.

"You're obviously not a romantic," responded Selena as her heel smashed into the woman's face.

Chris rushed forward and a woman blocked her path, brandishing a long bladed knife. Chris gripped her wrist, twisted it from her grasp and grabbed it with the other hand. Then she slashed in an arc, slicing the chest and arms of three more assailants. She didn't want to kill anyone but that was going to be difficult.

Piercing screams shredded the air but Chris couldn't tell whether from pain or frenzy. She moved continuously, never leaving a static target. Sometimes she crouched, sometimes twisted sideways but always swinging her knife in a curve in front of her.

Then she stepped in a pool of blood and slipped forward. Three women pounced towards her, eyes afire with bloodlust. Chris squirmed on the floor and kicked at their ankles and two of her assailants fell towards her. She tried to rise and miss the falling bodies but a shoulder caught her and she staggered helplessly towards the third woman, a well-built blonde who grinned savagely and turned her knife for an upward thrust. Then her head rolled to one side, probably due to the handle of a metal cleaver striking her neck. Chris briefly glimpsed Selena's arm holding the cleaver as she regained her balance. Not a second to think. She kicked two more to the floor and then was inside the changing room.

She just had time to notice an old woman with a headscarf at the end of the room before Selena burst through the door. She was covered in blood with the shining cleaver now dripping crimson.

"Let's go," she shouted, pointing at a large square tile in the floor with a question mark in the centre.

"Wait for me."

The old woman pulled off the scarf. Franco.

He joined them on the square and it was all white again.

7

The whiteness cleared and for a second, Chris thought they were back in the world of Sophos. Then she saw it was very different. She stood on a hill overlooking a green valley surrounded by tall mountains but this was much larger than the referee's domain. In the valley was a large village of about 100 houses, all constructed with stone blocks. She could see people in the streets and one or two in the green areas outside the village.

"Let's move," Selena called.

Chris turned to find her companion just behind with Franco alongside. He pulled off his old woman disguise to reveal his original clothing underneath. Then his eyes caught her and she looked at him for a few moments, held by something unusual. Then it was gone. She shook her head and began to follow Selena towards the village.

At first, Chris could see only women. Not just women but young and attractive and every one wore a short, low-cut dress although in a variety of styles and colours. Then she noticed two men, deep in conversation outside one of the houses. Both looked near middle age and their garments were conservative but casual. As they neared the edge of the village, a buxom girl with a mane of dark hair smiled cheerfully at them. Her eyes moved to Franco and then opened a little wider.

"Who are you?" she asked.

He smiled warily.

"I'm Franco. You look lovely. What's your name?"

A bright red blush crossed her face and she put a hand over her mouth. Then she ran back towards the houses. Chris saw a group of girls crowding round her, whispering and glancing towards them.

"I seem to have made an impression," Franco announced grandly.

Chris looked at him again. Strangely, his voice had changed. It was now deeper, more fluid and insistent. She wondered if Selena had noticed anything. One of the two men she had seen earlier walked towards them.

"Good morning, travellers," he said in a friendly tone.

The man was heavily built with receding, dark curly hair. Chris saw Selena perform her most ingratiating smile.

"Good morning. I'm Selena and this is Chris. We're strangers here and would like to know more about this world."

She pulled him in nicely and he returned the smile.

"Of course. We rarely get visitors and some of the princesses have never seen an outsider. My name is Horatio."

"Princesses? All the women are princesses?"

"Yes, of course you wouldn't know. They will have prepared your home now. Come with me and I'll explain everything."

"Our home?"

"We always keep a property vacant for travellers. It's one of our rules."

He led them down what appeared to be the main street where the houses were typical stone built structures of maybe the 16th century or earlier. The surface of the street was constructed of close fitting stone slabs. Everything was sparkling clean. Not a scrap of litter, not a speck of grime.

They reached a small square in the centre and the first thing Chris noticed was a life-sized statue. It was carved out of solid rock and depicted a tall, muscular man with shaggy hair down to his shoulders. Then she saw the village shop. Completely out of context with its surroundings, it was a replica of a small modern supermarket. Through the large windows, she could see aisles of metal and plastic shelving with shoppers carrying wicker baskets. No trolleys, no checkouts and no cash machines but otherwise it could have been in any present-day small town.

A group of girls were waiting outside a house at the end of the village and stared as they approached. Horatio led them through the group but Chris noticed Franco lingering behind, wallowing in the admiring glances. She stopped and herded him into the building. They entered a room dominated by a wooden dining table with six chairs and the blonde girl they had seen earlier was bringing cups to the table.

"This is Cleopatra," Horatio introduced.

"The tea is decaffeinated. I hope that's acceptable," she said timidly.

"That's fine," Chris responded, empathising with the girl's awkwardness in their presence. She was rewarded with a grateful smile.

The four sat at the table while Cleopatra busied herself preparing food. Horatio took a sip of tea and leant forward.

"Now I will tell you what I can but unfortunately there is little to say. Nearly 400 live in the village. Just 20 men and the rest are princesses."

"Why princesses?" asked Selena.

"Every one that arrives informs us she is the daughter of a king or queen."

"How often do they come?"

"One or two every week. Very occasionally, a man will arrive to join us."

"So the population keeps growing?"

"No. The same number is taken each week and our population never increases."

"Taken? What does that mean?"

Just at that critical moment, the screaming began outside and Horatio's eyes rolled with fear.

"Hide quickly," he shouted and sprinted out of the door. Cleopatra was frozen for a second and then pressed her arms to her chest and joined in the screaming. Selena grabbed and shook her, then slapped her face but without success. Her high-pitched wailing continued. Then it stopped as Selena hit her accurately on the side of the jaw. Disregarding the unconscious body on the floor, she ran out of the door. Chris followed but saw Franco climbing into a large food cupboard and closing the door.

They emerged into an empty street, all the doors and windows closed. The community screaming had ceased but then Chris heard a single shriek of horror from the other side of the village. She sprinted towards it with Selena alongside.

"I'll stop it somehow. I cannot stand squealing women," Selena shouted across as they ran.

They passed the centre square and ran towards the area where they had entered. Then Chris skidded to a halt, disbelieving her eyes. The source of the screaming was now obvious. It came from a girl who was facing her from a horizontal position. She was being carried under an arm. Not so unusual, particularly outside clubs on a Saturday night. What made it extraordinary was the woman who carried her. Chris could only see her back as she walked away but there were two significant factors. First, the woman was completely naked and second, she was tall, very tall. Chris guessed her height at 3.3528 metres or about 11 feet. The body appeared completely in proportion, just like the back of a nude model only twice the size.

"What the hell is that?" Selena shouted.

"A giant, I assume. Shall we try to stop her?" responded Chris.

"I don't know. Let's just follow."

The giant was headed for the mountains, covering the ground easily with long strides. Chris and Selena had to jog to maintain their distance. Fortunately, the girl had ceased screaming as she now appeared to have fainted.

They were halfway across the lush, soft grassland when the giant turned to face them. Chris gasped. She recognised her. The body and features were an exact replica of one of the best-known international celebrities. Dark, flowing hair, perfect blue eyes and rich red lips. Her body was also perfect. Chest large but not excessively so, slim waist and finely curved hips.

She looked at her two pursuers and then her lips parted in a brilliant smile. For a moment everything froze and then the giant turned and began running towards the base of the tall, craggy mountains.

"Come on," called Selena and they ran at top speed but still fell behind.

Then Chris saw the cave. An opening in the rock, about twenty metres above the ground. The giant ran swiftly up a wide pathway and disappeared through the entrance. As they followed, Chris saw a massive stone slab moving across the opening and by the time they reached it, the cave was sealed shut.

Selena looked annoyed.

"If we had enough explosives we might open it but I can't see any other way."

"Did you see her face? You know who she looks like?"

"Yes. Obviously she was copied. The only thing we've learned so far is that the god of this world is certainly a man."

They returned to the village where Horatio was waiting, his countenance a mix of sadness and fear.

"Another has been taken and this time, Galahad did not come to save her."

"You need to tell us the rest," Selena said firmly.

They accompanied him back to the house. Franco had climbed out of the cupboard while Cleopatra had recovered but still had tears rolling down her face.

"It's such a shame," she blubbed.

"Did you know her?" asked Chris sympathetically.

"Not really, but it's such a shame."

The tears began again but Selena was definitely not in the mood.

"Listen, either stop that stupid noise or go."

The girl stopped, forcing her lips together with her cheeks trembling.

"Right Horatio, now tell us."

"Now you have seen how people are taken. When they come, they choose one of our princesses to carry back to their cave and we never see the girl again. Unless Galahad comes to save her, of course."

"They? We only saw a woman giant."

"There is also a male in the same cave. We never know which will arrive but they never appear together, thank goodness."

"How often do they come? And is it always at the same time?"

"At least once every week but it could be on any day. We never know what time of the day or night. Sometimes they reach in to a bedroom and take a princess while she sleeps."

"Do you know what happens to the girls?"

"Not for certain. Some believe they are eaten by the giants and others say that they are tortured and forced to work as a slave. But most of us think they are taken simply for sexual delights and that there is an obscene orgy within the cave every night."

"Then who is this Galahad?"

"Our guardian. You saw his statue in the square. He often appears in time to save the princess."

"Often means not always."

"He comes in time to prevent more than half of the abductions. Sometimes he arrives before the giant has captured anyone and drives it away. Other times, he confronts the creature and forces it to leave the girl before scurrying back to its lair."

"How can he beat a thing that size?" asked Chris.

"He carries the great sword, Thorodin. He never needs to use it as its very presence fills the giants with fear. He has never failed every time he has come. After his victory, we express our gratitude by presenting three of our most attractive princesses. They spend the night with him and provide pleasure in every imaginable way."

Horatio choked back a sob.

"But there will not be a foursome tonight."

He burst into tears and Cleopatra quickly followed his example.

"I was chosen as one of the three but he didn't come. I was so looking forward to it," she wailed.

"Enough. Out, both of you," Selena shouted and herded the pair through the door, shutting it firmly behind them.

Chris could see Selena was becoming irritated and waited until she spoke again.

"Right. Now we know what this world is about. I can't say I like it. It's more of a male fantasy than a fairytale. We just need to find the Gate and get out."

"I think there are two possible locations and one is strong favourite," Chris observed.

"Yes, it could be somewhere in the village but it's almost certainly in the cave. Our problem is that we have no weapons. Even the cutlery here is wooden. That gives three choices. Use our brains to defeat the giants, make weapons of what we can find or get that sword when this comic book hero shows up."

"I think our best chance is to wait outside the cave until one comes out. At least then the door will be open and we'll only have one to contend with."

Selena shook her head.

"I think I have a better idea."

She went through the details. Chris wasn't too sure about the risk she was taking but had to agree it could succeed.

"What do I do?" asked Franco.

Selena looked at him scornfully.

"Keep out of the way. Do you have any idea of the god of this male world? Not that I really care."

"It seems obvious that the god is disguised as this Galahad. I can't be sure, of course but I think the most likely is Thor. This hero is armed with a great sword, equivalent to Mjolnir, his magical war hammer. Now, as you don't want me for the moment, I'm going to explore the village."

After he had gone, Chris left the house and walked to a grassy hollow, outside the village and in line with the cave. Selena joined her some minutes later. She had acquired the same style low-cut dress that the other women were wearing. This one was in bright crimson.

"Now we wait," she said.

Nothing happened the next day. Cleopatra brought food to them and they paid occasional visits to the village for bathroom purposes. It was mid-morning on the second day when Chris saw the slab moving from the cave entrance. She nudged Selena and they watched as a figure emerged. A man. A man she recognised.

He was a replica of a muscular TV and movie star, his picture adorning the walls of many teenage girls' bedrooms. But never naked, as he was now. As he came closer, Chris appreciated how big he was. About half a metre taller than the woman giant with bulging muscles everywhere.

"Yuck," she murmured. Like most women, she didn't find a completely naked man particularly attractive. Much better with shorts on. The sheer size of the giant accentuated the feeling.

"Let's just hope my hero comes," Selena said, rising to her feet, straightening her dress and walking a few paces towards the approaching giant.

"Hello, big man. I'm ready to be taken," she shouted, posing seductively. The giant stopped, and a look of puzzlement briefly crossing his handsome face. Then he began to inspect her, starting at the long, shapely legs and gradually moving up to her chest that Selena had accentuated by pulling back her shoulders.

"Oh my god," Chris gasped in horror, a sick feeling gathering in her stomach. The giant had become aroused, a vision of every woman's worst nightmare.

Chris looked at Selena. She appeared totally unconcerned by the ghastly thing in front of her.

"Well, bigger man. Don't keep me waiting. Let's go," she called and began to walk towards the cave. She passed beside him while he stood, raised and confused.

Then he turned and began to follow her. Chris looked around. No one yet. Then, as she started to pursue them, she caught a movement. A young man with a dark, shaggy mane of hair and suited in leather armour. In his hand he carried a long, heavy sword that glinted in a rainbow of colours. He ran with powerful, loping strides to stand in front of Selena and the giant.

"Stop and release the maiden," he shouted, holding the sword with both hands above his head.

Selena stopped, hands on hips.

"Get out of the way, you scruffy ape. We're going back to the cave to have some fun. Either come with us or go but in either case, I want that sword."

Galahad looked bewildered.

"Your mind is unbalanced by your capture. I will save you and you can bed with me to show your gratitude."

"Sorry, you're not big enough for me but my friend here just about qualifies. Will you give me the sword or do I have to take it?"

The shaggy hero was astonished.

"You are distraught, my sweet. Look at the creature. He is much too large for you."

Chris cringed. She knew what was coming. Selena's expression took a turn for the worse.

"It's obvious you are just envious of my friend's attributes."

Selena walked over to Galahad who had now lowered his sword. He was much taller but her very presence dominated him.

"And no one no one calls me 'my sweet'," she said and swung a foot directly into his groin. Fortunately, the leather armour prevented permanent damage but he doubled up in agony. Then she hit his exposed neck with the edge of her hand, the power and timing of the blow almost lifting her from the ground.

He went down, all two metres of him and the earth shuddered with the impact of his body. Selena picked up the sword and beckoned to the giant.

"Come on, don't keep a girl waiting."

She continued towards the cave, the giant following obediently with Chris trailing behind them.

Selena reached the cave and stopped in front of the entrance. She beckoned Chris to join her and then turned to the huge figure.

"My friend here is joining us. I'm not really interested, but which god are you?"

Chris was puzzled. The giant grunted and gestured towards the distant figure of Galahad.

"No, you are the god. The Gate is in this cave and you're the only one who ever enters. Just for variety, you appear as either a woman or man. I must say I feel a little cheated in this game. The referee said you gods are always here in human form."

A smile spread across the massive face and Chris was very relieved to see his passion had subsided.

Then he spoke in a quiet, soft voice.

"Selena, you're learning the game too quickly. I comply exactly with the rules. I am in human form, right down to the last detail. Just a little larger, that's all."

"You used film stars as models," Chris remarked.

"Yes but I change regularly. I always choose the most handsome man and beautiful woman I can find on earth."

"I rather like the real person you've copied now. Is the copy exact? I mean, the whole body?"

"Yes, it's a perfect replica and completely in proportion."

"Right."

Chris was still looking at his body but her mind had left on a fantasy trip.

Selena was becoming impatient.

"For god's sake, Chris. I've been to bed with the real one and I can tell you his performance is well below average. Can we finally get moving now? I just want to get to the Gate."

The giant smiled.

"It's just inside the cave. Metal plate on the floor with a big question mark. But of course you can't go yet."

"Why not?"

"Your companion must be with you."

"We don't need him. He can stay here and find the Gate for himself."

"Sorry, that's not allowed. The referee must have told you that all three of you have to travel together, unless you lose one."

"You mean unless one of us is killed."

"Yes."

Selena glanced at Chris who shook her head.

"We can't kill him, Selena."

"Maybe but I'll consider it."

"I think he's coming now."

Chris pointed back towards the village. A figure was running towards them, pursued by a large crowd of girls."

"I'm going. Can't let the villagers see me talking," the giant said.

Selena turned back to him.

"I still don't know who you are."

"Hermes. Before you go to the Gate, just press the big black button inside the cave. That moves the slab across the doorway."

"Okay. But what do you get from taking these women?"

"I get a kick out of all the screaming and carrying them off. You'll find that there's a nice place inside the cave where I keep the girls. Most days, I don't leave the cave and inside I appear as the same person but normal size. I have 30 girls in there now and we have some real fun together."

"Only 30?"

"I regularly send some of them back to earth and bring a fresh supply to the village. I'm never without a new variety."

Selena looked at him with faint disgust.

"I can't say it's been a pleasure but goodbye."

The giant disappeared into the cave and Chris turned to the chase scene below them. Franco seemed to be slowing and the girls were gradually getting closer. They didn't appear to be angry. It was similar to a posse of teenies chasing a rock group. A few had even stripped to their underwear.

"Damn. He'll never make it," Selena muttered and started towards Franco. Chris ran after her and they got to him just in time.

Selena held up her hands.

"Stop. Leave this man alone. He's going with us to fight the giant in his cave."

The crowd halted reluctantly while Franco sheltered behind his companions, breathing heavily.

"I must have him," a pink cheeked blonde shouted.

"We want him now to give our thanks," called another girl.

"It's not fair. Only 11 of us had the chance to show gratitude. I want my turn," came a voice from the back.

Selena didn't hesitate.

"He is only allowed 11 each session. He will return tonight to continue. You need to draw lots to choose the next lucky group."

The girls were silent for a moment and then turned among themselves, arguing loudly as to how to conduct the lottery. Selena grabbed Franco and pulled him up to the cave.

Chris was astonished when they entered. First came an area of darkness where not one particle of sunlight from the outside was visible. After a few steps they emerged into the bright light of what seemed to be a holiday resort. A clear blue sky above with a golden yellow sun beaming down. She was facing the entrance of a hotel with a large swimming pool at the front. A number of girls were splashing in the pool or lying on sun loungers around the perimeter.

Chris moved forward again and her nose hit something. A transparent wall. She assumed it must allow one-way vision as none of the girls had noticed their arrival. As she watched, a figure emerged from the hotel entrance. It was the giant, but not as she knew him. He was now normal size and wearing swimming trunks. The girls immediately ran to him, clinging to his arms.

He looked directly at Chris.

"Don't forget the door," he shouted. The girls briefly glanced in her direction with a puzzled look and then turned back. It confirmed they weren't able to see her. Chris waved a hand and moved away from the scene. The button was just inside the doorway. She ran across and pushed it with her palm. A grinding noise indicated that the slab was moving in place.

"Come on," Selena called. She was gripping Franco's arm firmly and they stood in front of a large square plaque set in the ground. A plaque with an embossed question mark.

Chris ran to join them and they stepped forward together.

The renowned cave explorer, Ron Inburrows, recently completed a solo exploration of the deepest pothole in Europe. On his return, the media gathered like a swarm of vultures and quizzed him for two hours on how much he had missed marital relations with his wife who was pictured in most newspapers with a short skirt and appealing smile. 'Caveman Craves Cuddle' was the headline the next day. A few minor details of his journey didn't make the story, including finding an underground civilisation and the origins of humanity.

9

The gatekeeper was old. Wispy grey hair over a heavily lined face. She had a bottle in her hand and took regular gulps of the golden liquid.

"Got addicted to mead," she croaked in explanation.

"We want to go to any world except the shopping mall and the giants," Selena requested politely.

The woman didn't seem to hear.

"This isn't much of a job, you know. I can go for aeons without seeing anyone at this Gate. Look terrible, don't I?"

"You look nice. Like a lovely grandma," Chris responded lyingly.

"Rubbish. The reason I look like this is lack of sex. That's the one thing that will make me youthful again. I just need a good session with a man. Hello, you've got one here."

Her beady little eyes fixed on Franco and he gave a polite smile.

"Want to give it a try? You won't be disappointed."

For a moment, he gazed at her gnarled countenance and then said something unexpected.

"Yes."

She took his hand and they disappeared into the whiteness. Selena was not happy.

"More wasted time. Why the hell did he say yes?"

Chris shook her head.

"Franco is changing. Remember all those girls chasing him in the last world."

"So he's turning into a sex addict. Why should I care? Our job is to find Jerome Jones."

"But there is something strange about his sudden popularity with women. Remember when we saw him in the shower and then on the bed. He seems to have grown into a different person."

"I just hope he isn't long now."

"Right."

Four seconds later, Franco returned. This time he was accompanied by a delectable, young, dark haired woman.

"Wow, that really worked," Chris exclaimed.

The woman smiled.

"No, I'm not the old crone. Silly old fool fell over drunk and I was sent to take her place. But just in time to enjoy Franco."

"He wasn't gone more than a few minutes."

"Don't be silly. There is no time in the Gate. We actually spent the equivalent of two days in bed together."

Chris was about to ask the 'what did you find to do' question but suppressed it.

"Can we finally get moving now?" Selena asked impatiently.

"Of course. Bye Franco. I really hope to have you here again."

"I'd be very pleased to come," he responded.

Then the whiteness thickened and they were through the Gate.

The first thing Chris saw was a man with a club. He was filthy. His body was caked in mud and grime and he had a mane of dirty, lank brown hair. He was beating the club against the ground near to a hole. Every 10 seconds, a creature pushed its hairy head out of the hole and he immediately swung the club at it but missed every time. The man grunted louder and louder with each failure.

He was standing in a barren, rocky area. Behind him, Chris could see several caves and above, were rocky peaks rising to the heavens. She knew it must be the edge of this world.

"Prehistoric," Chris muttered automatically. Then she heard a loud noise behind her and jumped forwards. She rolled over and her eyes widened in astonishment.

She had been standing with her back to a busy road with cars racing past in both directions. Beyond the road was an expanse of grass and then a modern looking town. Further back, she could see the tall mountains that surrounded the world.

No sign of Selena but she could see Franco rising to his feet on the other side of the road. An orange drove past at high speed. Yes, it was an orange travelling along the road. It had no wheels but made the exact sound of a car engine. Chris looked again at the vehicles. They had no wheels and none of them had drivers or passengers. As she watched, a frying pan, mouse, silver birch tree and negligee motored past her amongst the cars.

Chris shook her head. First thing was to get to Franco but it wouldn't be easy. The flow of vehicles, animals and objects was incessant. She edged forward and the traffic stopped immediately. As soon as her foot had touched the road surface, everything had frozen. She ran quickly across and the vehicles moved again as soon as she left the tarmac.

She looked around for Franco. He was now on his knees, looking intently at the ground in front of him. As Chris approached, she bumped into something. Something transparent. She reached out a hand to touch it and began to follow its outline. It was a dome, waist high, about two metres across and completely invisible. She followed the curve and reached Franco. He was staring into the dome.

"Look inside," he whispered without switching his gaze.

She turned and looked down. Then she gasped.

Chris could see a vast army gathering on the shore of a river. As she moved closer, the scene magnified and when her eyes were nearly touching the surface, she could distinguish the features of individual soldiers. It looked like the army of ancient Greece. As she moved round the dome she could see another army approaching the first but on the other side of the river. Ancient Persians maybe.

"This beats TV," she said.

"Incredible, quite incredible," Franco muttered.

"I think that's the rule in this world."

He turned to face her and his eyes opened even further.

"Do you realise you're naked?"

"What?" Chris exclaimed in horror. She looked down. No, she still wore the clothes she had obtained on the shopping mall world.

"That wasn't funny," she said.

"It's not a joke. You're completely nude. But it's fine with me if you're not bothered."

She saw his eyes travelling over her body and stopping at various points.

Instinctively she reached one hand downwards and the other across her chest. Then she turned her back to him and scrabbled in her pockets. No mirror but she did have a small notebook with a polished metal cover.

"Oh my god," she said. She looked over her shoulder at Franco.

"But I can see your clothes. Why not mine?"

"No idea," he responded helpfully.

"I want your trousers."

"Sorry."

"Take them off now or I will be very violent."

He heard the intent in her voice and reluctantly removed his blue trousers.

"Throw them over."

Chris took off all the invisible garments and picked up the trousers without turning. She had no scissors or knife and chewed a small hole at the top of each leg, then ripped the material. The result was a pair of shorts and two separate legs. She pulled the shorts on quickly and then tied the legs together and wrapped the cloth round her chest, tying it firmly on one side.

Relief coursed through her. Chris hated to be naked but it seemed to happen to her all the time. Before turning around, she checked the mirror to confirm that critical parts were covered.

Franco stood in his underpants and shirt, otherwise he still wore the same outfit as when leaving Earth. He didn't look embarrassed, maybe the opposite and Chris began to feel more comfortable with him. He hasn't demonstrated much courage but had not deceived her since arriving in this universe.

"Have you seen Selena?" she asked.

"No. I was fascinated by the armies until I saw you. It's a representation of a battle between the Greeks and Persians over 2000 years ago."

Chris pointed at the town in front of them.

"We need to go there. There are no people in the cars but there must be some residents in a place that size."

They reached the outer buildings after crossing two more roads. Again, the traffic was a mixture of unoccupied strange objects that stopped as soon as they put a foot on the roadway.

The first building looked like a three storey office block but there was no door, just windows and walls. Chris looked up. The entrance was on the top floor. Franco walked directly underneath it and she saw him rise suddenly. His body lifted from the ground as if in an invisible elevator. He looked down and waved to her. Then he entered the building. Chris moved to where he had been standing and found herself rising. Exhilarating. She opened one of the opaque glass doors and walked inside.

A small, modern reception area. Franco was wandering round the far corner but otherwise it was deserted. A desk stood on one side. Chris searched quickly. No documents anywhere. There was a computer keyboard and screen but it was lifeless. The place was like a museum exhibit.

"Let's look around," she said and Franco followed her down the stairs. Each floor was the same as the top. Offices with no paper, nothing working and no people.

Then she heard a noise, somewhere outside. The thick double glazed windows muffled the sound but she was sure it was a human cry.

"Come on," she called and ran up to the top floor then out of the door. She closed her eyes, took a step forward off the edge of the building and found she was descending to the street.

No one in sight and that made her uneasy. This world was beginning to trouble her. A silent malevolence behind the friendly fantasy.

Her concern was accentuated by Franco's scream. She turned quickly. He had fallen back against the wall, an arrow embedded in his shoulder. Now Chris acted instinctively. She ducked down, grabbed him and dragged his body round the corner. A row of six two-storey houses with the doors where they should be.

She ran to the second, pulling Franco by his uninjured arm. It wasn't locked and she pushed him inside, slamming the door behind them. They were in the hallway of a typical suburban house, framed pictures on the magnolia walls.

"Stay here," she said and dashed through to a kitchen where she found scissors, antiseptic and bandages. Franco was sitting on the stairs when she returned. She quickly cut through his bloody shirt and slapped his face hard just before she pulled out the arrow. Then she cleaned and bandaged the wound. It wasn't deep. Only the tip had entered the flesh.

The arrow itself was crudely made. A roughly finished wooden shaft with a sharpened point and feathers tightly bound to the end. Franco moved to sit on the stairs.

"How do you feel?" she asked.

He raised his eyes and smiled broadly.

"I feel absolutely fine," he said, reaching out a hand. She grasped it to help him to his feet and then felt dizzy. Not dizzy, something else. She looked at him. His eyes were deeper now, something mysterious and enticing there. The moment passed and she spoke quickly.

"We know this world is crazy. The only person I've seen is a caveman but someone else is trying to kill us."

"That seems to summarise it perfectly."

"Any ideas?"

"I can't identify the likely god of this world. I suppose you could say Chaos but that would be classified as a primeval spirit rather than a god."

"We simply have to find Selena and the Gate. But first I think we need new clothes and weapons."

"I'll go with that. I don't think these underpants are very practical."

A trip to the bedroom wardrobe provided trousers and then Chris visited the kitchen again. She took three table knives, handing one to Franco and tucking the other two in her belt.

"Let's go," she said firmly.

Chris opened the door slowly, looking up and down the street. Completely deserted.

"Come on," she called and sprinted to the end of the row of houses. As she moved, another arrow thudded into the door frame. She didn't wait and kept moving towards the road running across the end of the street, hoping Franco was following.

Chris turned the corner, hoping for safety but instead saw a man charging towards her with a long knife. He had short blonde hair over a pleasant face and wore only a pair of shorts. His muscular body was marked with daubs of colour.

As he neared her, his lips drew back in a snarl of fury and he swung the knife towards her throat. Chris ducked underneath, and then swung a leg at his ankles. It didn't stop him but he stumbled against the wall. She turned and kicked as hard as she could into his kidneys. It was like hitting bone. He simply grunted and turned back to her. No choice now, she had to use the weapons. She pulled out a knife in each hand and slashed towards his forearm. It cut a deep groove and blood coursed down his arm. The man howled with pain and levered his blade upwards towards her stomach. Chris jumped to one side and rammed her knife so deep into his shoulder that it wouldn't come out. It had little effect. He came forward again and this time she aimed her remaining knife for the heart. It sank into him and she felt his body shudder, then collapse to the ground.

She gasped for breath, slops of the man's blood smeared across her face and body.

"Very good indeed," said a voice behind her.

She turned to see a group of men, dressed exactly as the one she had killed. Two of them held Franco. Then something hit her head and she fell.

Chris met consciousness again upside down. She was tied firmly to two wooden planks joined in a narrow X shape. Her legs were above her head, one on each plank at the top of the X. Her head was near the ground with her arms stretched out on the two lower planks. The big relief was that she was still wearing the rudimentary clothing she had created from Franco's trousers. Her body was covered, that was the important thing.

She turned her head and felt a movement. The X shape had turned slightly. She was only able to move it a fraction but guessed that it spun round like a wheel.

"I see you are awake."

Chris looked up. Her head was close to the floor and she was staring at an expanse of ornamented silk material. Further up, it bulged out across the woman's bosom and she couldn't see her face.

"I'd feel better the right way up," she said.

"Very well. Vasco, turn her upright."

Chris glimpsed a man turning the X shape until she was vertical. She was in a small, brick lined chamber. In front of her was a woman wearing a long silk gown, decorated with beads and gems. It was exactly like the huge frame dresses worn by the aristocracy a few hundred years ago on earth, usually by females. She expected the woman's hair to be piled up on top of her head but it was shoulder length and finely groomed in a modern style. A large diamond necklace hung round her neck, over the top of the dress that had a neckline around the throat. Her skin was tanned and heavily made up with full red lips and accentuated brown eyes. She looked about 30. The man was dressed like the one she had fought. Short black hair, muscular body covered with coloured markings and wearing only a pair of blue shorts.

"What is your name, girl," the woman asked.

"You'll need to ask more politely."

She laughed and then slapped Chris across the cheek.

"A little spirit in her, Vasco. You'd like to tame this one, I'm sure."

The man grunted.

"If she doesn't satisfy me then I may give her to you."

Chris started to speak but the woman slapped her again.

"You will refer to me as Lady Borgia. You will be called Scorpio. A little dangerous unless firmly disciplined. First you need to be cleaned. Arrange that, Vasco."

She lifted the long gown and swept out of the chamber, followed by the man. A minute later he was back with three companions, similarly attired. Chris felt them turn the wheel sideways and release her arms but they tied them again tightly behind her back. Then they freed her legs and lowered her to the floor. Chris considered running for the door but her chances would be negligible. They bound her ankles just loosely enough to allow her to move her legs slightly. Then they lifted her to her feet and pushed her out through the door. She shuffled forward awkwardly.

She was hustled along a modern brick corridor then the men carried her up a flight of stone steps. They arrived in an elegant hallway with green marble flooring and carved stone arches along each wall. The doors rather spoiled the décor. They were bright red plastic with fluorescent green panels.

Chris was half dragged to a door on the far wall and the men pushed her inside, closing the door at her back. She looked around in disbelief. It was a forest. Unusual in itself to be found indoors but this one was even stranger. The trees, leaves and vines shimmered in every colour but none of them natural. Artificial purples, greens, blues, reds and yellows. The glare of this fiery spectrum hurt her eyes.

"Hello, I'm Nell. I'd love to kiss you but you're too dirty."

A pink girl had emerged from the foliage. Shoulder length hair, pretty face and a short white dress. And she was pink. Every exposed part of her skin was bright pink.

She took Chris by the hand and pulled her gently into the forest. After about ten metres of bending her head down to avoid the yellow and orange leaves and branches, Chris was led into a clearing. She shuffled forward to see a group of pink girls lounging around an amber coloured lake.

"We have a new one to clean. Her name is Scorpio," shouted Nell and the girls rushed towards them with little squeals of delight. They surrounded Chris and began touching her skin and squeezing any squeezable bits.

Chris wasn't pleased. "Stop that, will you. Haven't you grown up yet?"

This appeared to be the funniest thing they had ever heard. The group collapsed in uncontrollable laughter. It was a full minute before they recovered.

"To the pool," they shouted in unison.

Chris was helpless as six of the girls lifted and carried her to the edge of the amber pool. They untied her bonds but continued to hold each arm and leg. Their grip was much stronger than expected.

"Take off those horrid clothes," shouted a pink skinned blonde.

Chris squirmed frantically.

"Don't touch them, you stupid bimbos," she screamed but they simply laughed again and she felt the trouser legs round her chest being removed and then they pulled off her ragged shorts.

"You'll be sorry you did that," she shouted with venom. This statement had an immediate effect. They pushed her into the pool.

Chris found the amber liquid was thick, almost syrupy. She sensed it entering the pores of her skin, cleansing like an expensive body lotion. She pulled her arm out of the liquid. It had been covered with a large bloodstain but was now clean and glowing. Something else. It was also perfectly dry. She dipped her head down and felt the tingling touch of the liquid on her face. When she surfaced, she touched her cheek. Her skin was perfect. Then she ran her fingers through her hair. It had somehow been styled and the loose strands over her forehead were now blended perfectly.

"Look, she's the same colour," shouted Nell.

They stood around the edges of the pool, staring at her. She knew the reason. The liquid must make the skin pink but the Blessing had prevented her body changing.

Another girl spoke.

"It's a pity. Her body is reasonable but I don't think Lady Borgia will find her sufficiently enticing."

Chris was relieved at this comment. She could see a full-sized mirror on the far bank but to reach it, she had to get out of the pool. And she was naked.

"Can I have my clothes, please?" she called with as much amiability as she could gather.

"Don't be silly. You haven't been oiled yet," replied one of the onlookers.

Six girls entered the pool and although Chris struggled womanfully, they carried her to the bank.

"See how nice you look, apart from your colour," said Nell.

They stood her upright in front of the mirror and she gazed at the reflection. Chris couldn't prevent a glow of satisfaction as she saw her fresh, glowing look and her hair looked better than it had ever been. Hair. She looked down. Not one strand of hair on her body.

"Oh my god," she screamed, fervently hoping it was temporary depilation and not permanent epilation.

"We knew you'd be pleased. You look so much nicer."

"I need clothes. Immediately."

"After you've been oiled. Will you walk or do we carry you?"

No choice. Chris walked with them through the multicoloured forest. After two minutes they reached the bright orange trunk of a massive tree. Set into its base was a full-sized door.

"The Chief Oiler will be waiting inside. You'll really enjoy it, he's got wonderful hands."

"He? A man?" Chris exclaimed with horror.

"Of course. Lovely long fingers. I wish I was being done," Nell said with a smile.

"I'm not going in, so you can take my place."

The girls laughed again and then opened the door and pushed her inside.

When the door closed she found herself in blue, shimmering semi darkness. She was in a cavern lit by flickering blue candles down the walls. At the end stood a large couch, the size of a double bed and behind it was row of large cupboards against the wall.

A figure stood next to the couch, barely distinguishable in the hazy blue light. She could just see a loose robe with a hood over its head. Chris crouched forward slightly, her hands and arms occupied in covering positions. Just one man, so her chances were good. She glanced around, seeking clothing or a weapon but the rocky walls were bare.

She bent her knees a little lower and then launched herself at the figure. Just as her heel was about to strike his head, it moved and she landed heavily, directly on the couch.

"I'm assuming you don't want a massage then," Selena said, pulling back the hood.

"Selena. Why the hell didn't you say something? I could have killed you."

"I very much doubt that. I must say you're looking well exposed."

Chris covered up quickly with her hands.

"I want clothes. I'll murder if I have to."

Selena grinned.

"Try that cupboard," she said, pointing at one of the doors on the end wall.

Chris opened it in a flash. It apparently contained the clothing to be worn post massage and pre Lady Borgia. Definitely not practical. She eventually found a shiny black bra and pants, the only opaque set with no holes. A short blue dress and ankle boots were the sole choice this side of decent. She finished dressing and turned with a sigh of relief.

'Relief' was one of the secret code words employed by the Royalists in the English Civil War. They used it to mean alleviation or easement. Similarly, the word 'foe' was the code for enemy, 'plane' meant aircraft and 'leader' was the disguised word for their commander. The phrase 'assault at dawn' was the secret cipher for 'attack at sunrise' and 'male gathering shortly before a wedding' really meant 'stag party'. All of these formed an integral part of their military strategy. The code was never broken by their opponents, the Roundheads who still emerged victorious.

"Happy now?" asked Selena.

"I wouldn't have picked them but least they're clothes."

"So what have you been doing? Or shouldn't I ask?"

Chris related the events since she arrived.

"What's your story?" she asked Selena.

"Nothing so exciting. I entered the world just outside the town and kept out of sight while I checked the layout. I followed a man into a side street and saw him entering a door in a large advertising board. I followed him and I was inside this building. Most of it is a huge room like an encampment with tents. It's full of men like the one you fought. Muscular, brainless, half naked and covered in war paint. The place is enormous. There's even a stream running through the centre. I hid until night and then started to explore. I found a bright orange tree with a door and here I am."

"I can't see another door here," said Chris.

"It's inside the centre cupboard, next to the one with the clothes. When I opened the door, I met a pleasant young man wearing a robe who offered me a massage."

"I think I know why. Are you still wearing the clothes you got in the shopping mall?"

"Yes."

"They don't work on this world. They're invisible."

Selena pulled off the robe. She was completely naked underneath.

"You're wrong, I can see them."

"Only you and nobody else."

Selena reached behind the couch and picked up a metal massage oil container. She looked at her reflection for a second.

"That's interesting. I suppose I'd better look in the clothes cupboard."

Chris saw her remove the invisible garments and then dressed quickly in very brief scarlet underwear, barely covered by a stretchy dress of the same colour.

"Doesn't match my trainers but I'll keep them on. I guess it looks as if I'm hovering off the floor."

"Yes it does and you could make money in that outfit. What happened to the man who was here?"

"I reluctantly refused the massage. He's unconscious and in one of the other cupboards. I put on his robe and you came in soon afterwards."

"Any ideas where to find the Gate?"

"None at all yet."

Chris stopped. Her sensitive hearing had picked up a noise in the centre cupboard. She quickly slid under the couch while Selena donned the robe again. Chris recognised the new arrival from floor level. Lady Borgia in her long dress.

"I require a massage," she declared imperiously.

Chris saw her undressing and placing her clothes in the left-hand cupboard. Her view was limited but she assumed the woman was naked when she got onto the couch. Chris slid along the floor and rose behind the headboard. Then she stared in amazement.

Lady Borgia was a man. Unarguably. And he was young, no more than 25. But his face was most definitely female. Selena moved in front of him and pulled back the hood. The man squealed.

"Who are you?" he screeched.

"I'm certainly not going to massage you," Selena replied mildly.

Chris walked into his view and he squealed again.

"I know you."

"We met and I still don't like you. To avoid any violence you just need to tell us about question marks."

"Please don't kill me. I'll tell you anything."

"We need to know the location of any question mark symbols in this world. Maybe on the ground somewhere."

"I can help you escape if you release me."

Selena was losing patience.

"Answer now or I begin hitting you."

"There is one in a reception room at the Queens palace."

"Then you will take us there."

"No. The guards will kill us all."

"Where is the palace?"

"You can enter from here. I'll show you if you release me."

"We are also looking for a man who came with us. Another visitor," Chris said.

Borgia smiled curiously.

"Yes, I know of him. He is a special guest of Queen Celeste."

"Marie Celeste?" Chris asked.

"Yes, do you know her?"

Selena stood back from the couch.

"Put your clothes on. You are leading us to this palace."

The man gave a sly smile.

"Yes, of course."

He quickly donned the heavy dress and then led them to a corner of the room.

"There is the door," he said, pointing upwards.

Chris looked up at the roof of the chamber. It seemed exactly the same in the corner as elsewhere. Just a polished rocky surface.

"Just hold hands, then go to right in the corner and touch the walls. You'll be lifted through the door," said Borgia.

Chris reached for Selena but she shook her head.

"Grab his right hand, Chris."

Selena took his other hand and they moved forward.

"No. Stop," shouted Borgia.

Selena turned to him with a stony face.

"Thought so. It's a trap. Now I'll break your neck."

"No, please. We just need to stand on one leg before touching the wall."

"What?"

"Stand on one leg."

Selena looked at Chris who nodded.

"If it doesn't work, he'll be dead too," she said.

They moved forward and each lifted one foot. Then Selena touched the wall in the corner.

10

Chris felt a sudden gust of warm air and felt herself rising. The rocky roof disappeared and they passed into darkness. Then suddenly she felt a floor under her feet and the scene brightened. They were standing in a tiny cubicle, barely large enough for the three of them. The yellow walls were decorated with purple ducks of every imaginable shape and size. In front of them was a door, also yellow, with a huge embossed crown.

"The god of this world must be a kid who reads fairytales. The whole place is infantile," Selena remarked sharply.

"What do god and kid mean?" asked Borgia.

Selena ignored the question and opened the door, pushing him in front of her.

"Keep holding our hands and remember I can kill you with one blow."

He nodded and led them out into an ornate but haphazard room. It was a mixture of Chinese, Egyptian, 18th-century and ultra modern. A massive flat screen plasma TV was surrounded by Chinese tapestry with Egyptian figurines and gold porcelain vases at each side. Furniture varied from King Louis chairs to stone benches. The walls were bright green and blue stripes. The only thing lacking was people.

"They will come soon. A warning light appears in the servants' quarters when someone enters," Borgia advised.

He was correct. Under ten seconds later, the door opened and two dark haired girls entered. They wore near transparent white lace skirts and nothing above the waist except for a thick silver chain round their necks.

"Ask them where our companion is," Selena whispered.

Borgia beckoned to the girls.

"Inform me of the location of the man captured today."

"He is with her Majesty in her private chambers," responded one girl.

"Very well. We do not require you further."

The girls bowed their heads and left.

"Where are these chambers?" asked Selena.

"No one may enter unless instructed."

"Lead us to them."

"No, I can't."

Selena reached up and pressed two fingers into the man's neck. He gave little squeal of pain.

"If I add one more finger in a specific place, it will kill you."

His womanly face contorted.

"We will all be killed."

"Let's move."

He led them out of the door and along a yellow and orange corridor, lined with fluorescent paintings. More girls dressed like the ones they had seen were scurrying around. Chris shared Selena's desire to leave this bizarre place as quickly as possible.

After walking through two more corridors, they entered a wide chamber. Thick, bright green carpet with yellow and purple walls. At the end was a sky blue door with two large men standing directly in front.

"The Queens Chambers I assume?"

Borgia nodded nervously.

"You cannot enter. Those guards will kill us."

Selena ignored him and looked at Chris.

"Can you take the one on the left?"

"Think so."

Selena strolled sensuously towards the guard on the right, her tiny scarlet dress enhancing the attraction.

"The Queen desires our presence," she said breathily.

The man didn't turn his head. He just switched his eyes towards her.

"No one may enter."

Selena reached a hand to his shoulder and began to curve it round his neck.

Chris had never mastered the art of seductive movement but made every effort to use the areas exposed by her short blue dress.

"Hello," she said awkwardly to the guard on the left.

He simply held up a palm.

"You can not enter."

Seeing the opportunity, she grabbed his wrist and twisted it back and up. He stumbled back off-balance and she pulled a knee into his stomach. Then she rammed a fist directly into his throat. As he toppled forward, she cut into the back of his neck with the edge of her hand.

"You're obviously feeling violent," said Selena, standing over the inert body of the other guard. Chris knew she had simply hit the nerve points on his neck.

"Anyway, we're in," Chris said and pushed open the door. She noticed Borgia cringing against the far wall as Selena followed her through the portal.

They were in a small white room facing a large pink door. Chris moved across and silently pulled it open a fraction. A large woman lay naked on an ornate, orange bed. Her long hair was red, blue and yellow in equal parts and her body was expansively voluptuous. She lay on her back with her hair cascading over the pillows.

"Again, again please," she cried.

"I told you. First tell me how to find Poseidon's world."

Franco sat on the bed, fully clothed in a neat shirt and trousers. He appeared to be reading a document.

"I don't know what that means. Please, again."

"You must be the god here. Tell me."

"The question means nothing to me. I beg you."

Without looking, he touched her arm for a moment. Immediately, spasms ran through her body and she squealed with delight.

"More. Please more."

"No. Tell me first."

"She doesn't know, Franco or whoever you are," Selena said, pushing past Chris and entering the room.

He jumped up, pushing the document into his trouser pocket.

"Selena. I've been trying to find you. They captured me when I've been asking this woman how to get us out."

"Hold my hand."

"What?"

"Hold my hand." Selena grabbed Franco's palm and stared hard into his eyes. Chris saw her body begin to shudder, quivering like a tiger on the edge. Her face began to moisten and her lips were squeezed together. Then she noticed Franco's eyes. The small light she had seen in them before was now a rich golden glow.

"No, you won't do that to me," Selena whispered.

The shudders intensified. Beads of sweat rolled down her face and her eyes were wide with ecstatic determination. Chris started to move forward to separate the agonised embrace but suddenly Selena laughed and pushed Franco back on to the bed.

"You were not strong enough," she said quietly but triumphantly.

Franco looked anguished and exhausted, symptoms shared by the woman on the bed who was now sitting up with a mystified look.

"What's happening Selena?" asked Chris.

"Later. First we find the Gate."

"Do you think it's here?"

"Yes, it's here."

The answer came from the doorway. Chris whirled round to see a pink figure. Nell, the woman she had met at the pool.

"Has anyone told you that you're pink?" asked Selena.

"Yes, it's a lovely colour."

"So I presume you are the god here?"

"One of them. I am Leto."

"I'm confused. I understood that each world has only one god," Chris said.

"I created this world but you brought another god with you. In the next room, I have a large screen with a perfect view of this bed. Welcome back but I'm not sure everyone will be pleased to see you."

Chris saw she was looking at Franco.

"He's a god?" she exclaimed.

"Yes, and as before, he's not observing the rules," Leto observed.

Selena nodded. "I knew it. Saw it in his eyes and when he touched me, I was sure."

They all looked at Franco who had been silent during the conversation.

"I want to go now," he said uncomfortably.

"You should tell your friends who you are. If you won't then I will," Leto said in a firm voice.

"I was tricked."

"You are very fortunate to be in my world. It would be very unpleasant if the other gods found you."

The ample figure of Queen Celeste rose from the bed and wrapped the sheet around her substantial body.

"Excuse me everyone. I don't know what you are all doing in my Royal Chambers but I do not wish to stay and listen to all this nonsense. My guards will be here shortly and I suggest you depart before they come."

She marched to the other side of the bed and pressed a large panel on the wall, which opened like a door. With a final, imperious glance she walked through and the panel closed behind her.

"Wait," shouted Chris and rushed to the wall, searching desperately for the hidden switch.

"Let her go," the pink woman declared.

"No. I saw something in her eyes. Like Franco."

"Are you sure?"

Leto rushed to the wall and pressed the switch. Inside was a small chamber with two doors. Chris followed her through one of the doors into another tiny room. Another Queen Marie Celeste was lying against the wall, her arms and legs tied tightly and tape across her mouth. She rolled her head and grunted violently.

Franco rushed in behind them.

"I knew the one on the bed was a god. I didn't realise it was a visiting one."

Leto laughed. "Now you are in trouble. You need to get away quickly before she tells Poseidon or perhaps even Zeus."

Franco was now in a panic.

"The Gate, quickly."

"I may tell you at a price."

Selena interrupted.

"The safety of Franco doesn't concern me but I want to know who he is."

"There's no time. We must go," wailed Franco.

The pink woman ignored him.

"He is the god of sexual desire."

She told them his name.

"I'm not repeating that. It's obscene," Chris said emphatically.

Selena nodded.

"We will continue to call him Franco."

"I thought Aphrodite was the god of desire?" Chris asked.

"No, she covers procreation, love and beauty. This one is in charge of pure lust. As you can imagine, he was very popular with the other gods, particularly the male. If they desired a human female, they simply requested him to help in the seduction. Usually he created an item, perhaps an ornament or precious stone that generated uncontrollable desire in the recipient."

"A while ago, I touched a large diamond he created. For Poseidon, I think," Selena said thoughtfully.

"Yes, I've heard of the diamond. Poseidon gave it to his Atlantis people after using it a few times. Most of the gods used Franco's services but then came the problem. Zeus demanded his help to seduce a young woman he had developed a desire for. Franco refused. You must know that no one does that to Zeus and escapes unscathed. Immediately afterwards he also defied Poseidon in the seduction of another girl. The brothers are perhaps the worst enemies he could have made."

"He doesn't seem to have the courage," Selena observed.

"Maybe all those centuries in human form have changed his character. To return to the history, Zeus summoned a meeting of all the gods and Franco was put on trial. It wasn't really fair as the verdict was never in doubt. Several others related that he had not complied with their requests. Aphrodite was one and she announced that he had given her a golden heart that had no effect at all on a man she was trying to bed. Just a handful like me that didn't care either way but the majority was against him. It didn't really matter what they thought, as Zeus and Poseidon had already made their decision."

"So what did they do?" asked Chris.

"They placed him in a human body and sent him to earth. While he was there, he was unable to use any of his powers and could not return. He was just like any other human except he would never grow older and couldn't die."

"How long ago was this?"

"About 1600 of your Earth years. A long time Franco?"

She looked towards him but he simply grunted.

"And when does his sentence finish?" enquired Selena.

"You definitely don't know Zeus. It's forever, of course. He does not forgive easily."

"I thought the powers of the gods didn't work in these worlds but he seems able to use his abilities."

"This universe was created after he was banished to earth and he wasn't party to the rules and structure of this universe. So he's the only god who can use his powers here."

"Perhaps that was Zeus impersonating Queen Celeste?"

Leto smiled broadly. "Yes, it could have been, couldn't it Franco?"

His fear was very obvious now. Eyes wide and panicky and perspiration appeared on his brow.

"We must go quickly. He will send me to the underworld or worse. What is your price?" he asked.

"I think I would like to sample your powers again. It's been a very long time since I last experienced them. I want the maximum, of course. I created this body to withstand any level of ecstasy."

"It will take too long," he wailed.

"Then good luck in finding the Gate."

"Very well. Where?"

"Back in the bedroom."

He followed her through the door.

"I'm not watching that," Chris said decisively.

"One of us has to go to get directions to the Gate. We certainly can't trust Franco to tell us," Selena responded and walked into the bedroom, closing the door behind her.

Chris looked across at the real Queen, still struggling with her bonds. It would be silly to release her as she would just begin screaming. Time to think. This universe was becoming more uncomfortable by the minute. They were using up valuable time and still had no clues to the location of Jerome Jones. Now they had discovered that their companion was an ex god. An unpleasant thought entered her mind. The referee had said that the Gate would only work if all three of them went together. The only exception was if one of them was killed. So they had to take him with them unless he died. The thought crystallised. Perhaps that was Selena's plan. To kill him in the bedroom as soon as she found the location of the Gate. Chris had no great liking for Franco or his powers but couldn't be involved in cold-blooded murder.

She rushed through the door to the bedroom. Franco was lying naked on the bed with Leto's pink body on top of him. She glistened all over with perspiration.

Selena was leaning against the wall, her face emotionless.

"You missed it," she said.

"It's only been two minutes."

"I think Franco was rushing. Imagine everything in extra high-speed. That was her third and I don't think she can take any more."

The comment was accurate. Leto rolled off onto her back, completely drained. Franco rose and dressed quickly and Chris saw Selena move towards him. She grabbed her arm.

"I'm not going to kill him. Not yet, anyway," Selena smiled without humour.

"Sorry," Chris replied. Selena always seemed able to read her mind.

Many will have heard of the tradition of three villages situated in the far north of England, where any couple who were found to be indulging in an illicit affair are taken to the village square to be criticised and condemned for their behaviour. This is known as the 'Shaming Of The Two' and was recorded in history by Shakespeare's play of the tame sitle.

Leto stirred, her eyes dreamy.

"That was the best two hours I've had for a long time," she murmured. Chris realised that Franco had made it seem fifty times longer to her.

"The Gate?" Selena asked.

"I'm not sure now. I could return here in another body and repeat the experience."

"You can't break your word," Chris said firmly.

"But I'm human here and you do it all the time."

"As you're human, I can kill you," observed Selena coldly.

"You'd never know then. I'll go part way and give you a clue so if one of you starts again, you'll beat it."

"Okay. What is the clue?"

"I'm sleeping now," she replied. And she was.

"Sleeping? What does that mean?" asked Franco.

"Perhaps it's where she normally sleeps. You said you saw her by a lake, Chris?"

But Chris was silent for a few seconds.

"No. I know the place. We need to get outside the town."

She led Selena and Franco out of the Queens Chambers. The two guards still lay unconscious on the floor and Borgia had disappeared. The only person inside was an old man in a purple robe who stood facing them. His gnarled face and white beard made him look about 140.

"I have come to help you escape," he croaked.

"Who are you? asked Selena.

"You may call me Sylphgratiat, or Sylph for short. Take this talisman and wear it at all times."

He produced three loops of cord with a glittering stone pendant on each. They reluctantly donned the necklaces.

"What does it protect us from?"

"Absolutely nothing. It just looks nice, except on the man of course."

Chris could see Selena's patience diminishing rapidly.

"I think we'll find our own escape."

"I can show you the way out of the palace. Follow me."

Moving more swiftly than could be expected at his age, he touched one of the walls and a door appeared. Then he opened it and they cautiously followed him inside. The four were squeezed in a small cupboard-size room and Chris found herself pressing against the old man's arm.

"Look," he announced and opened a panel in the wall to reveal a row of buttons. Each had a label, 'Guardroom', 'Cafeteria', 'Women's Quarters', 'Top Of Tower', 'Outside The Town and 'Certain Death'.

"Is this like an elevator?" asked Chris.

"Yes but it goes in any direction. Clever idea."

Chris reached over to press the button for outside but he stopped her.

"It may not be that one."

"We want to go outside."

"The labels are not accurate. The destinations change randomly each time. You'll go to one of the places shown but never know which one."

Selena squeezed past him.

"Six buttons so it's a five to one chance."

She pressed 'Guardroom'.

A slight humming noise for a few seconds and then silence.

"We're here. Who wants to be the first to go out?" asked Sylph.

Selena glared at him and opened the door. A wild eyed creature with a white, smeared face and erect pointed hair screamed at her. Slamming the door, Selena hit another button.

"Certain Death?" she asked.

"No, Women's Quarters. Just doing her hair with face cream on."

Another hum, another silence.

"I think Franco should go this time," Selena said.

She grabbed his collar and pushed him through the door. It was obviously the Guardroom but could have been Certain Death. About 20 warriors were standing in a group and produced their weapons as soon as they saw Franco. A knife hit the door just next to his head and he jumped back inside the chamber.

Selena barged past him.

"Why did we get burdened with a god who has useless powers," she muttered and pulling the knife from the door, she threw it directly into the sword arm of the leading warrior. He dropped his weapon and clutched the arm with an anguished cry. His companions looked at him for a few seconds, then turned to Selena and burst into applause.

"Let's go," Chris shouted. She waited until Selena had closed the door and pressed the button marked 'Outside The Town'. If the chances were equal, it didn't matter which one. As soon as the hum finished, she opened the door. Then she smiled. A caveman was striking the ground with a club.

"This is it," she called and the others followed her outside.

She was in exactly the same place as when she entered the world. The road, with its fantasy traffic, was just behind her.

"So where's the Gate?" asked Selena.

"I think it's just where the man is striking the ground. Leto did give us the clue. She said that if one of us starts again we'll beat it. That must mean my entry point and this man striking the ground with his club."

Selena nodded.

"He really needs a good wash. I'll just move him out of the way."

Chris watched as she approached the grubby figure. He didn't seem to have noticed them, continuing to beat on the ground and then swing the club at the creature that popped its head out of the hole.

"Stop that," Selena shouted above the thuds.

He stopped and looked up. A strange confrontation between a filthy, near naked prehistoric man and a smart woman in a tiny scarlet dress. The only equivalent would be a groupie meeting her rock star idol.

The man grunted and swung his club directly at Selena's head. At the last second she moved to one side and it smacked into the earth. As he lurched forward, she joined her hands and slammed down hard on the back of his neck. With a final grunt, he slumped unconscious in a grimy heap.

Chris walked over to them. It was there. A square of about a metre was marked in the rocky surface with a question mark embossed in the centre. Remarkably, it seemed completely undamaged by the blows of the club. She felt Franco grip her hand and a small spasm of desire ran through her. Selena took her other hand and Chris turned to Sylph.

"Thank you. We really appreciate your help."

"I hope you'll express your gratitude more physically next time we meet," he replied in a young man's voice.

"What?" Chris said, but Selena had already pulled her on to the square.

The whiteness came again.

11

Chris came out of the whiteness and tripped over into soft earth. From her position on the ground she looked up to see three pairs of legs with the remainder of the bodies in the usual position above. The three women wore what appeared to be animal skins, bikini like and each had short fur boots in the same colour as their two-piece. The first was similar to a deep brown shaggy bear fur and well suited the tanned skin of the woman. It was cut perfectly, not too small but styled to accentuate her long legs and firm cleavage. The others were not so well matched. One was in a light grey fur that did nothing for her muscular torso and the other was frankly appalling. It looked like a zebra skin with tie-ups on each side of the pants and at the back of the bikini top. The girl who was wearing it was pale skinned and instead of enhancing, the outfit seemed to dominate her body. It would have been perfect as a man's loincloth but on her, it gave the impression that it was two sizes too large.

As fashion designers will know, there is a golden mean, a perfect symmetry in the design of garments. Clothing is a tool. For example, a man's clothing can emphasise masculinity or sensitivity, strength and sociability. A woman's garments may present her as businesslike, exotic, erotic or represent stylish unavailability. Colours and texture are so important in this art form and the myriad of combinations can never be fully comprehended in any lifetime. Most unfortunately, Chris could not spend further time to consider this fascinating subject before she even had the chance to explore the effect of unseen undergarments on the psyche of the wearer.

The reason for this sudden disruption to her train of thought was a sword poised 3.9 millimetres from her eyes. She looked up again. All three women looked fit and amazingly strong with a complete absence of make up. Of course, cosmetics can also significantly affect the appearance, even character of any individual. Many of these secrets have long been known to women but now men are becoming more regular users with an ever expanding range dedicated to the male. How long before eye shadow is a required, post morning shave application? Rouge and lipstick will unquestionably be in every man's suit pocket, almost certainly in purpose designed containers to avoid smears or marks on jacket and trousers.

"Who are you?"

The zebra woman inconsiderately interrupted these new and important considerations running through Chris's brain.

"I'm Chris. A visitor."

"You are wearing strange garments. Like one of the Eves. We need to be sure you are an Adam."

"I don't understand Eves and Adam."

The woman grimaced. "It's very simple. Take off your clothes."

"What?"

Before she could react, the other two women had grabbed her arms and the zebra woman pulled out a knife and slashed vertically through her short blue dress. Chris struggled but the women were as powerful as they looked. Two more slashes and the dress fell to the ground.

"Oh my god, that is so Eve," declared the muscular woman in the ghastly grey fur outfit. Her face contorted with disgust as she stared at the shiny black underwear Chris had acquired in the last world. Zebra skin didn't hesitate. Four slashes with a knife and Chris was not only completely naked but still hairless.

"She's definitely an Adam but we needed to check," said grey fur.

They released Chris's arms and took a pace back, allowing her to look around for the first time. They were in a small clearing in a forest, the thick trunks and foliage making it impossible to view any further. Above was a blue sky with a beaming sun. It could have been on earth except for the three women. She looked at them again. Surprisingly they were not at all grimy. They looked as if they had just left the shower and their skin gleamed in the sunlight.

Raunchy Roberto, the cartoon character so popular in the early 1800s, is now seldom remembered. Only a small number who were children at the time, are still alive. One of them, Dorothy Mammaria, still has videotape recordings of his shows (they were broadcast before the invention of DVDs) and she frequently entertains other members of the fan club at her house. Roberto was, of course, an aardvark best known for his favourite trick of biting the hem of a woman's skirt and ripping the garment from her. With his friend, Bobby the boa constrictor, Roberto got up to all sorts of hilarious japes that mostly involved the female leg area. As a finale to each meeting, Dorothy pretends to be a woman and allows one of the fans to tear her dress off with his teeth. However, most of the male members prefer to impersonate the snake.

Chris analysed the situation. All she knew was that the women referred to themselves as Adams but there were apparently others on the world they called Eves who clearly wore more up-to-date clothing. Her major concern was that she was naked again and hating it. She reached down for the slashed garments but the brown fur spoke for the first time.

"You cannot wear these things. I think leopard would suit."

"No, definitely llama," said zebra woman.

"Yes, llama," agreed grey fur.

"I suppose you're right."

"Stop. I want clothes now," Chris shouted.

"That's better. Showing some fire. I will test her," said grey fur.

Chris saw the fist swinging towards her face and ducked beneath it. Then she kicked for the knee. Her foot connected just at the top of the shin bone and grey fur fell forward on to her bunched fist. She slumped unconscious to the ground. Chris grabbed the knife the woman had dropped and turned to the other two.

"I said I want clothes now. I'll kill if necessary."

For a second, they stared at her and then collapsed in laughter.

"You're a real Adam. Come with us. We'll find you a new outfit," zebra skin shouted between giggles.

"What about your friend?" Chris asked, pointing at the unconscious woman.

Zebra skin looked puzzled.

"We leave her. She'll return when she wakes."

Chris noted that compassion did not appear to be common on this world. She picked up a piece of her dress and tied it round her waist to give minimal cover. The remainder of her clothing was in fragments and she attempted to keep an arm across her chest as she followed the two women towards the trees.

It took just a couple of minutes to walk through the forest and Chris emerged to an amazing scene.

The trees were on top of a hill and the hill was on one of a pair of islands. Bright blue-turquoise waters all round that extended to the horizon that must be the limit of this world. The islands were almost identical in size, about eight kilometres or five miles long in an oval shape. They were only about one kilometre apart and joined by a stone bridge, wide enough for three people to walk abreast. A walled city occupied about a third of each island with the remainder covered with forests and cultivated fields.

The similarities ended there. On her land, Chris could only see buildings of dour, grey granite. The high walls of the city, the dwellings inside and a larger structure like a castle. Spread evenly around the walls were small stone guard posts where she could see women patrolling, each clad like her companions. Outside the walls on the coast near to the bridge, was a small harbour with a turreted building. No one was on the bridge and all the boats were in the harbour.

In contrast, the other island was a mass of colour. The city walls were constructed of white and red stone and Chris could see colourful murals almost covering the surface. The buildings were also multicoloured, either from the stone or painted. Flags and bunting were everywhere with figures in brightly coloured garments just visible. The harbour was directly opposite the one on her island but the boats were in bright reds, yellows and blues. The port building was in an attractive pattern of red and white stone.

Chris didn't take long to draw conclusions. The two islands must be enemies and the obvious difference between the two was the drab utility of her land compared with the bright colour of the other. Presumably, they were Adams and the other land were Eves, although it seemed unlikely that snakes or apples played any part in this world.

"I thought you were in a hurry for clothes?" asked brown fur.

Chris realised her arm had dropped from her chest and quickly replaced it. She saw that the two women were almost ten metres ahead of her and quickly caught up. They continued towards the walled city, arriving at a closed, heavy wooden gate that was reinforced with metal struts. A woman looked down from the parapet above.

"Identify," she yelled.

"Adam 393 and Adam 241 with a visitor," zebra skin shouted back.

"I you sure the visitor is an Adam?"

"We have checked."

"We must be sure."

Another four women had appeared on the parapet and all were looking towards Chris.

"What?" she asked.

"They have to verify before you enter," said brown fur.

Chris sighed, dropped her arm and pulled off the piece of cloth around her waist.

"Satisfied?" she shouted angrily.

"Yes," the crowd on the parapet yelled back in unison. The door swung open and Chris quickly tied the cloth back again.

They entered a narrow street full of activity. A number of women were talking, walking or marching. All wore a similar animal skin bikini outfit but in a huge variety of designs. Leopard, lion, tiger, squirrel, panda, camel and more. But Chris couldn't see a single man. She remembered the shopping mall world where the men appeared only as cleaners. Maybe this place was the same. She followed her companions along the street to a two-storey building. The ground floor was open, just a massive pillar at each corner. Inside was a communal shower. Water cascaded down from the matrix of holes in the ceiling and flowed to a drain in the centre of the area. About half of the showers already had a woman standing underneath.

"You must shower before clothing," said zebra skin.

Chris didn't hesitate. She walked on to the nearest hole and felt the water splashing over her. Maybe not water. It was warm and felt slightly thicker. It appeared to follow the curvature of her body, cleansing deeply. She noticed the other women were using a small block of stone to rub their bodies and saw a similar piece by her feet. She rubbed her leg gently and found the stone was soft, like a sponge and wherever she rubbed, her skin tingled. Chris was beginning to enjoy the experience and she remained there for nearly 10 minutes. She stepped out and looked for a towel but then realised her body was completely dry. She grabbed the cloth again and tied it round her waist.

"Clothing?" she demanded.

Brown fur smiled and led her to the next building, a large single storey structure. It was the epitome of a 14th century fashion store, completely full of rows and rows of the animal fur outfits. They were on long wooden poles with hangers made of wire.

"I don't wear animal skins," Chris said coldly.

"Animal? What does that mean?" responded zebra skin.

Chris picked up the nearest costume. Of course, it was synthetic and the insides were lined with a soft cotton fabric.

"Llama. Try this set." Zebra skin was holding out a furry outfit.

Chris pulled it on quickly and sighed with relief that she was covered again. The bikini was superbly comfortable. Both top and pants were elasticated and seemed to mould themselves to her figure. Now she felt comfortable and could begin to consider a plan. First, she needed to ask about Selena and Franco.

"Have any other visitors arrived here recently?"

"No, only you. We continuously patrol every part of the island."

That wouldn't prevent Selena hiding from them, thought Chris and she could conceal Franco if he was with her. But it made it more likely they were on the other island.

"Do you have anything with a question mark here?"

"A question mark? That's a strange thing to ask."

"I mean on a plaque or stone set into the ground perhaps."

The women shook their heads.

"In that case, maybe I need to go to the other island."

"To the Eves? Don't be silly, you will be killed. We must take you to the palace, to our Queens. All visitors must be presented to them immediately."

Chris was guided through the streets to the large building in the centre. Another heavy door, another shouted conversation but this time Chris didn't need to strip. Like the other buildings she had seen, the palace was frugally appointed. They entered a bare stone passage lit only by a row of torches on each wall and pairs of women carrying swords were patrolling up and down. They turned left into another corridor with a large wooden door at the far end. Standing motionless in front of it was a line of six guards. Each held a sword vertically in front of them. One stepped forward as they approached.

"The visitor will enter. You others will wait."

Chris was motioned forward while her two companions stepped back. The two guards in the centre moved to the door and knocked three times in unison. It opened and Chris was escorted inside, hearing it close behind her.

She had expected a large chamber with a crowd of people in front of raised thrones but found she was in a compact room with three guards standing on each side against the wall. No thrones, just a long block of granite where three women were seated. Despite the spartan surroundings, they dominated the room. Identical triplets. Each with long black hair and strangely seductive dark eyes. Their expression was unreadable. No smiles but no sign of animosity. They wore different clothing. Leopard skin effect, greyish tunic dress and a loose white garment but all finished at mid thigh.

"We are the Queens Arthur. I am Arthur 2 and these are my sisters Arthur 1 and Arthur 3," announced the one in white, and indicating her left and right respectively.

"You will tell us why you have come here," added Arthur 3.

"I'm just passing through. I am looking for my two friends and also the Gate."

"I don't understand Gate and we have no news of other visitors. The Eves will show us soon if they are with them. Now you must stand on the red stone," the Arthur 2 said.

Chris looked down. A large square of red rock was embedded in the floor, the first colour she had seen in the architecture of this city. She stepped forward and a picture appeared in front of her. She was looking at Selena and Franco standing on a similar red slab. Nothing was visible to her outside the square. There was no sound but she could see Selena smiling broadly at her while Franco simply looked a little lost and fearful. She waved at them and the picture disappeared.

"Where are they?" Chris asked but already knew the answer.

"In the throne room of King Mavis of the Adams. This stone is our only communication. Both sides must always show any new visitors when they arrive."

"I have to get to them."

"You will die if you go alone."

"We'll see. Do I go over the bridge?"

"No one has crossed the bridge for 37 years."

Chris sighed.

"I need to know more. What exactly is this Adam and Eve thing?"

Arthur 1 responded.

"We will tell you our history and hope you comprehend. The previous 17 visitors have listened but not learnt. All are now dead, consigned to the fires. We are the Adams. We all possess the correct body design as was intended. The Eves who dwell on the other island are grotesquely deformed. Sadly, they are deficient in the line and presence of the chest and carry a gruesome disfiguration in the groin."

"You mean they are men?"

"I don't know that word. Perhaps it is Eve in your language. We have no records of when and how these creatures came into being but legends tell us that long ago, we Adams occupied both islands, living in perfect harmony with nature and ourselves. Then some evil force created these Eve abominations. Some say they came from the bowels of the earth, others that they had travelled across the great sea and there are a few who believe they came from the skies. The legends then relate that the creatures murdered all the Adams on the other island. We had no weapons then to defend our lands but captured some from the invaders. We quickly trained ourselves for battle and managed to retain our island, annihilating a number of Eves who had encroached here."

"So I guess the bridge was already there?" asked Chris.

"Yes, from the time both islands were ours. After we retained our land, we saw the Eves building a great walled city and our ancestors did the same for our protection. Since that time we had been at war with the creatures."

"Do you have battles with them?"

"We know they are desperate to conquer us. They send small groups in boats at night to test our defences. They even attempt to murder some of our people but we always find and exterminate them."

"Do you also send groups over to their island?"

"Yes of course, almost every day. We need to reconnoitre and look for weak areas. Some return as heroes but others sadly do not."

"How many are killed?"

"We lose perhaps one every day on average but we kill at least that number of Eves. We believe that our population is gradually increasing while they are becoming less. Soon we will cross to their land and finish them forever. Detailed plans had been made and we just await the right time."

"So there are no men, or Eves, living on this island. Not even prisoners?"

"None. We do not take prisoners."

Chris hesitated for a moment.

"Then how do you procreate? I mean, how does your population grow?"

"Other visitors have used that word and we still do not understand it. Every ten days, new Adams arrive in the Birth Room of this palace."

"I would like to see it."

"You can look but not enter. It is a sacred place."

"I suppose you don't know about sex either?"

"That is another word we have heard but do not comprehend."

Chris felt she now knew all she needed. Women versus men with the missing ingredient of sex. Then a thought hit her. The Adams didn't take men prisoners. If the Eves were the same, then Selena was in big trouble. She needed to get out quickly but first she had to locate the Gate.

"Can I see the Birth Room now?"

"Remember that you cannot enter."

The three Queens rose and led her to a door behind the rudimentary throne. Chris was disappointed when it was opened. She stood in the doorway and looked round a small room, even bending her head inside and peering at the inner wall. It was simply a polished stone chamber with no markings visible at all.

"Thank you. Now maybe I can help you."

"How?"

"I will go to the Eves island and try to talk to them."

"Talk to the vermin? No, we cannot allow it. Anyway, they would kill you immediately."

"I'm planning to disguise myself an Eve."

Their majesties looked blank.

"What? Deform yourself to the shape of the enemy?" asked Arthur 3.

A brief pause before Arthur 1 spoke.

"Actually, that's a good idea."

"You never thought of it before?" Chris asked disbelievingly.

"Umm, no. It seems so, well, gross."

Chris sighed. "I just need to know what Eves normally wear."

"Gaudy garments that pain the eyes and offend the senses.

"Yes, but what do they look like?"

"If you are sure you can retain your sanity, we have a casket of their clothes."

"What?"

"We need to remove the clothing of captives before they are burnt in the Charring Room."

"Can I see? Perhaps I can stop this war forever."

"We will show you ourselves. Follow us."

The Queens walked to the door of the throne room, exactly in step with each other. Chris followed them out into the corridor. They walked to the end and entered a small chamber. It contained just one item, a massive wooden chest. Arthur I pulled open the lid and immediately shielded her eyes. Chris pulled out a pile of garments and laid them on the floor. Like the Adams, the Eves seemed have only one style. A loose shirt and baggy, knee length trousers. The styles varied only a little but the colours were extraordinary. Far more than could ever be found in a high street on earth.

"This is all I need. I will disguise myself as an Eve and go to the other island," Chris said decisively.

"You cannot go alone," Arthur 1 responded.

"Yes I can. It would be easier for one person to infiltrate. I want to go immediately."

The three Arthurs looked at each other.

"We will accompany you," announced Arthur 2.

"No. You are the rulers. It's too risky."

"Queens do not reign long here. We have been on the throne for only 28 days."

"What happened to the previous leader?"

"Queens. There are always three identical Queens. New ones arrive in the Birth Room as soon as we perish."

"What if only one of you dies?"

"The other two disappear. No one knows where they go. If one dies then we all die. We will go with you together and succeed or depart this world as heroes."

Chris didn't want to be burdened by these warlike women but needed their help to reach the island.

"Very well, but there can only be one leader. You are the rulers here but I lead this expedition."

The Queens exchanged glances.

"We agree. When do we begin?" said Arthur 3.

"Tonight."

"Then we must prepare. Come with us for the sacrifice."

"What?"

"Come."

Chris followed them back to the throne room and heard Arthur 1 give instructions to one of the guards. A few minutes later, three naked women entered the room and their faces were wreathed in joyful smiles. They knelt in front of the Queens who had returned to their seats on the stone block. Arthur 1 rose and stood over the women.

"You are honoured to be chosen to bring fortune and success to our assault on the evil ones. By your blood, we will gain vitality and strength for the dangers ahead."

She pulled out her sword and lifted it over her head.

"No, stop," Chris shouted, jumping across and blocking her arm.

The Queen's eyes flashed.

"You must not interfere."

"It's madness to kill. That won't help us."

"It is tradition. These girls must die or we fail."

"No. You'll have to kill me first and there won't be an expedition."

One of the kneeling girls looked up at her.

"No, please. I want to be sacrificed."

"Don't be stupid."

"Then kill us instead," begged the other two.

"No. There will be no sacrifice."

Arthur 3 came forward, drawing her sword.

"This must be done," she said.

Chris saw the six guards approaching and somehow herded the naked women into a corner. They pushed and jostled her. One dodged under her arm and stood in front with arms outstretched.

"Kill me now," she screamed.

Chris grabbed her by the hair and dragged her back just as Arthur 3 jabbed a sword at her heart.

"Throw me a knife and I'll do it myself," the girl shrieked.

Chris was losing and needed to change the rules. Spinning round, she rapidly struck all three of the sacrifices with a mixture of fist and finger jabs. They fell to the floor, silent at last.

The Queens appeared disappointed.

"We cannot leave without the sacrifices," Arthur 3 said.

"That's fine with me. I'll go by myself."

"Unless we burn the twig," remarked Arthur 2, her face displaying an agonised expression.

"No, that is sickening. We must sacrifice," responded Arthur 1.

Chris held up a hand.

"What is this twig?"

"I cannot speak of it as the bile rises in my stomach," replied Arthur 3, looking as if it had already risen.

"We have to take a fallen twig from the forest and place it in the Burning Room. Then we must remain to observe the cremation," said Arthur 2.

"Is that the place where you burn your dead?"

"Yes it is."

"And what happens then?"

"The twig is consumed by the flames."

Arthur 1 tottered to the wall and began to retch violently.

"Don't speak of it. We must sacrifice the women. The guards will hold the visitor while we kill them," she cried.

Chris heard a feeble moan behind her.

"Kill me first, please."

This was becoming ridiculous.

"Enough. Stop," Chris shouted, holding up her hands. Everyone was frozen by the intensity and anger in her voice.

"Now listen. These girls will not be sacrificed. Go and get this stupid twig and bring it to me. I will personally put it in the oven of yours. Then we will go. Is everybody clear on this?"

A brief silence before Arthur 2 spoke.

"You would make a great Queen. Pity there's only one of you."

"Just get the damned twig. I am not moving until it is here."

The Queen nodded to one of the guards who rushed out of the door. Then Chris waited, maintaining her position in front of the naked women. They had all regained consciousness and begun a communal weeping session.

"I was so looking forward to it," sobbed one.

"I may not get another chance to be sacrificed," added another.

Chris turned her head.

"Shut up, you stupid bimbos and stop that wailing."

Relative peace descended or ascended, if it happened to be below ground at that moment. To pass the time, the Queens began to throw daggers at the guards, aiming to miss their head by the smallest margin possible. They then chose the girl with the bushiest hair and competed to cut off the longest strands with their throws. The other guards played a similar but simpler game. They drew their swords and aimed over arm slashes at each other's chests in an attempt to shave some fur from the bra. Chris sighed and waited.

Eventually, the door opened and the guard returned with a closed wooden casket.

"Do you wish to inspect, your majesties?"

They quickly shook her heads in horror. The box was then presented to Chris and she opened it immediately. She half expected to find the twig was a wriggling creature but it wasn't. Just a twig. A piece of dead wood only a few centimetres long.

"Don't let her do it, kill us quickly," came a shout behind her.

Chris turned and hit the speaker on the jaw with the casket.

"Anyone else want to object?" she asked.

A murmur of reluctant negatives.

"Then show me this incinerator."

The Queens moved to the door.

"Wait. I don't trust these stupid girls."

She herded the two conscious ones to carry the one she had hit and they followed the Queens with Chris in the rear.

The burning room was simply a large, windowless, door less box, about three metres square. A silvery metal plate occupied most of the floor.

"What now?" asked Chris.

"The body or item must be placed on the plate. Then we wait outside the room," Arthur 3 said with horror in her eyes.

Chris didn't bother to remove the twig. She just placed the casket in the centre of the plate and returned to the doorway.

"I don't know if I can stand it," squealed Arthur 1.

Suddenly a cube of light formed around the square plate. It was then that Chris understood the reason for the general apprehension. A scream of anguish filled her, like nothing she had experienced before. It burned into the brain, sharp thorns of agony piercing every receptor on her body. The intensity grew until her head was bursting with distraught grief like her hundred worst fears all happening together. Her knees buckled and she fell to the floor, head against the ground. She could feel her face contorting in the most painful torment that hacked and scraped at her mind, body and soul. It seemed to continue forever until she felt death offering a welcoming arm and gladly reached out for it. Just before she touched, the pain stopped.

She rolled onto her back, sweat rolling down her face.

"We told you. You wouldn't listen," Arthur 2 murmured.

"Okay. Next time we'll kill the bimbos," Chris responded, only partly in jest. The pain had subsided but it was an ordeal she never wanted to go through again. One good thing was that the three sacrifices had lost consciousness during the event and their constant bleating had mercifully ceased.

They returned to the room with the clothing and Chris showed the Queens how to flatten their chests with cloth binding and change their hair to a rough, masculine mane. When they had finished, they could all pass as men from any reasonable distance. Someone looking from a window, for example.

The word window derives from the old Anglo-Saxon, win meaning win and dow or dough. Starving peasants competed to throw stones at the narrow slit windows of castles. The first to get a stone through the opening without touching its sides was rewarded with a loaf of oatmeal bread. The losers were also given bread but then were drowned in the castle moat (this word being an abbreviation of murdered with oats).

12

"So, can we start now?" asked Chris.

"Darkness is with us. We will go to the boats," responded Arthur 2.

Chris was led to a doorway and the Queens descended a flight of stone steps. Just as she was about to follow, a movement made her turn. Nobody in sight but she was sure she had glimpsed a figure, tall and dark haired with a long sword glinting in his hand.

Slightly concerned, she descended and quickly caught up. They emerged outside. It was gloomy but a faint glow seemed to emanate from the stone of the buildings to give partial visibility. Within a few minutes they were at the shore. The row of boats were little more than wooden rafts, crudely constructed by binding a row of logs together. The four climbed on board one of them and used short, wooded planks as oars.

The water was smooth and Chris observed that they were headed for a landing on the other island, well away from the flickering lights of the buildings.

"Do they have guards?" she asked.

"Yes. We may need to kill many before we reach the city," replied Arthur 1 with a wide smile.

"No, that's stupid. Listen, all of you. We're not invading the place. We are supposed to be four men returning from a reconnaissance trip. Keep your voices as low as possible and let me deal with any problems."

Chris was becoming increasingly irritated by their lack of intellect or even basic common sense. If all the monarchs were like this then it was unsurprising they were killed so regularly.

About ten metres from the shore, Chris motioned for them to stop rowing. The three women were already in male garments but she had kept her llama skin bikini and carried a bag with men's clothes and another llama outfit. Her idea was to swim ashore and make sure it was clear before they landed. Then she would change into the dry outfit with the male clothes on top.

Telling the Queens to wait for her signal, she levered off the raft and swam with one arm, keeping the bag above water with the other. She pulled herself slowly and quietly onto the rocky shore.

Two men were standing no more than five metres away. Fortunately, they were half turned but her sharp hearing picked up the quiet murmur of their conversation.

"I hope there's turquoise blue in the next consignment. It's definitely my colour," said one.

"You've got at least six like that."

"Yes but I've worn them to death."

Chris moved slowly towards them and then froze as she heard a sound behind her. One of the Queens was emerging from the water. She drew her sword and moved alongside Chris, a strange fervour in her eyes.

"Wait here. I'll kill them," she whispered.

Chris grabbed her by the collar. She recognised Arthur 1 from the yellow shirt.

"You will not. Go back now."

The words were wasted. The bloodlust in the woman's eyes could not be stilled. She struggled with Chris, desperate to reach the men. They wrestled for a few moments and then heard a voice.

"Two Adams. A nice catch."

The men were standing over them, swords poised. Chris rolled to one side swinging a kick at the legs of the left-hand man. With a cry, he fell backwards into his companion and they both finished on the ground. Then from behind her, Chris heard a scream.

"Kill the creatures."

Arthur 3 with the crimson shirt was leaping towards the men, her sword arcing down. It struck the rocks with a clang as her target moved to one side. Then Chris saw that Arthur 1 had risen to her feet.

"Kill, kill, kill," she yelled and joined her sister as they hacked at the prostrate men.

Chris rushed forward and hit Arthur 1 with a fist to the jaw. Then another fist into the face of Arthur 3. They both fell unconscious. Now the men were reaching for their fallen swords.

"Kill the Adams," they yelled, blades now swinging.

Chris spun on her right leg and cracked her left heel into the jaw of the first. Then she struck the second with a double fist Khitanzu blow. This had become a disaster. Four unconscious bodies and enough noise to alert everyone on the island.

Arthur 2 ran up from the shore.

"If you try to kill anyone, I'll hit you too," Chris said, grabbing the woman's shirt to emphasise the point.

"They'll be coming soon. I must save my sisters."

She grabbed Arthur 1, slung her over a shoulder and moved off. Chris tied her bag of clothes to her waist and picked up Arthur 3. She followed the Queen to a small forest adjacent to the walled city. Chris could already see flickering torches moving towards their landing place but fortunately, her route skirted around them.

They entered the dense forest and found a hollow area surrounded by a mass of tree trunks. After laying the bodies on the grass, Chris turned to Arthur 2.

"You are the most stupid people I've ever had to fight alongside. Do you have any brains at all?" She spoke softly but carried a big brick.

"They cannot control themselves when the bloodlust is within them."

"I've decided we will part. You carry on with your suicide attacks and I'll find my friends."

"It's nearly morning and my sisters will awake soon. Wait for a few moments and talk to us all."

"It can't be morning, it's only just gone dark."

"The night last only for two hours."

"Thanks for telling me now."

The two queens were regaining consciousness.

"Kill, kill, kill?" said Arthur 3 quietly, looking round with wild eyes.

"We must slaughter these abominations. Death is the only solution," Arthur 1 added.

"No killing," Chris said firmly.

She opened her bag of clothing and asked the women to look away while she turned her back and pulled off the now soggy llama suit. She replaced it with the dry version and then put on the men's clothes. Blue shirt and green, knee length trousers. When she turned back, the three women were looking at her intently.

"I told you to look away."

"Why would we do that?" asked Arthur 1, puzzlement in her eyes.

Chris sighed. In a world without sex, it probably didn't matter but she still felt uncomfortable that her naked rear had been viewed by three pairs of eyes.

"Right. I just told your sister that I am splitting up. You crazy trio can go and get killed while I accomplish what I came to do."

Shimmers of light began to poke through the foliage. Morning was working as badly as ever today although Chris wished it hadn't broken. She couldn't afford to wait until the brief night-time, certainly not in the company of these idiots.

"I'm going now. Good luck."

Three faces turned towards her and nodded dumbly.

Chris crept silently from the hollow and moved quickly to the edge of the forest nearest the walls of the city. She could see the gaudily coloured buildings with flags everywhere. Figures moved about, very visible in their bright clothing. Now she had to take the chance that her disguise would work. She recognised the danger. The Blessing would not protect her against a sword in the heart or anything immediately fatal but she had to reach Selena.

Rising to her feet, she stepped into the open and marched forward with as much manliness as she could manage. Then she froze. Horrendous screams came from behind and two figures rushed past, shrieking loudly enough to jar the eardrums. Arthurs 1 and 3, brandishing swords. Immediately, a large group of men emerged from the town, matching the screams with their own shouts and yells. By the time the women reached them, the group had grown to over a hundred.

It was a bloody encounter. The women hacked and slashed like the rotor blades of a helicopter. Heads rolled to the ground and bits of arms and legs flew around. Blood gushed in torrents, along with various body parts. After the initial onslaught, the two Queens were gradually surrounded but continued to scream and swing their blades. Eventually, Chris saw them fall, still yelling for blood. Their bodies were chopped and sliced unmercifully by the crowd. Then all was silent. About thirty Eves and the two Queens lay still on the blood drenched ground. More men ran forward to gather the corpses in shrouds that they then carried back to the town.

Chris heard a figure walk up beside her. Arthur 2.

"My sisters died like heroes," she said quietly.

Chris was about to respond when a group of about 20 men came towards them. They all looked rugged and muscular, the bright reds, yellows and blues of their clothing now carrying blotches of blood.

"Don't speak. I'll do the talking," Chris whispered quickly.

A smooth shaven man came to the front. He had long blond hair, carefully styled in neat curls.

"You did not join us in the battle," he said, stony faced.

"Couldn't get there in time," Chris responded in the deepest, hoarse voice she could attain.

"What are your names?"

"I am Adam 439 and he is Adam 488."

Chris had already randomly picked the numbers to use.

The blond man nodded. Suddenly, from behind, a thick net was over their heads. A heavy steel mesh that resisted Chris's struggles.

"I am Adam 439," she heard the blond man say and then something hit her head. Insensibility took over.

Chris awoke in a sweat. The Blessing allowed her to recover quickly from illness, cuts, abrasions and even unconsciousness. It was hot, very hot. She was in a stone chamber with several large, flaming braziers that gave out a flickering light and burning heat. Perspiration was rolling down her skin and even the walls were sweating. The men's clothing had been taken and she was in her llama bikini but still had a strip of cloth tied across the front of the bra to flatten her chest. She was lying on some sort of table with her wrists and ankles held tightly in iron clamps. She could see Arthur 2 in the same situation on a table next to her. The Queen's outer clothing had also been taken and she wore just a pale, furry twin piece. Chris saw her head turn and a smile cross her face.

"How are you?"

"Annoyed. If your brainless sisters hadn't gone mad, I wouldn't be here."

"They've left us to sweat before they begin the torture."

"Sweat is right. We're cooking in this place."

"Do you want to escape?"

"Even for you Queens, that is a stupid question."

"I assume that's a yes."

Arthur 2 sat up and Chris saw the iron fastenings of her wrist shackles being ripped from the wood. With one hand, the woman then snapped each of the manacles around her ankles. She swung down to the floor and cracked open the bindings that held Chris.

"Ready?" she asked.

Chris couldn't respond for a moment.

"So you're the god here?"

"Yes."

"But you seemed so stupid."

"I had to act the same as my sisters."

"You let them die."

"Of course. They were a big mistake. I find a pair of identical twin girls on earth and bring them here. Then I appear as another sister to make triplets. Like everyone who comes to the universe, we replace their memory so they believe there were always three of us. Now I'll need to find another set of twins to take over as Queens."

"You could be killed here."

"Perhaps. That's the fun of it but it will also be enjoyable to follow your adventure."

"You cheated by giving yourself superhuman strength."

"Not really. I make myself as powerful as the strongest human but encase it in a young woman's body."

"So tell me who you are?"

"Perhaps you'll find out. I suggest you get moving now. Someone is sure to come soon."

"You're not going to help then?"

"I've already helped by freeing you. I'll come with you but now you're on your own. Your life is in your hands."

"I understand. That's fair. But now you must do as I say, not like the other two."

Arthur 2 simply smiled. Chris checked the chamber, finding a number of iron tools hanging on the walls, presumably reserved for torture. There were six braziers burning merrily and the two tables where they had lain. Nothing else. The chamber was built of heavy stone blocks that glistened with condensation. Just one door, small and locked.

Chris moved to the wall and grabbed an iron bar with a sharp tip. She forced it into the edge of the door and after a few seconds levering, it swung open without too much noise. She was looking down on a short corridor. Two men with swords were standing at the far end. They saw her emerge and ran forward.

"You take the right," Chris shouted and launched a flying kick at the left side man. It connected perfectly and he fell unconscious. She looked across in time to see the other man swinging his sword. Arthur 2 brushed her hand against his forearm, diverting the weapon and then hit him with her fist. The blow didn't seem to carry a lot of power but his head rocked back violently and he crashed to the floor.

Chris ran to the end where another corridor joined from the left. Empty but something moved. A section of stone wall was swinging open. She motioned the Queen to silence and edged back behind the corner. A figure was emerging from the new doorway. It was a young man in a long, purple robe. He had a design cut into his hair and as he turned away she recognised it. A question mark.

Now Chris made a quick decision. She could see him pushing the doorway closed with his back to her. In four strides she reached him and sliced her hand across his neck. Then she caught the door and dragged him inside. Arthur 2 followed and pulled the door closed.

They were in a long passageway. It was dimly lit but no apparent that source of illumination. She turned back to the unconscious man and searched his robe. It contained just one item, a circular metal object about the size of her palm. Etched in the centre was a question mark.

"This doesn't take much reasoning. This man is obviously part of some sect that has a question mark as an icon. Their headquarters must have a larger version somewhere on the floor and that will be the Gate."

Arthur 2 grinned. "I'm saying nothing. It's your adventure."

"This is a secret passageway. Hopefully, it will lead me to Selena and then to the Gate."

"You've just got to hope."

Chris removed the man's robe and pulled it on. No hood, but she already had her hair and face as masculine as possible. Then she headed down the corridor with the Queen following.

After only about 10 metres, she saw a window and quickly pulled back. A little laugh came from behind her.

"I'm not stupid. It's almost certainly one-way but I'll take a second to make sure," Chris whispered tersely.

She moved her head forward and found herself looking down into an empty room. The window was right at the top of one of the walls. As she observed, the door opened and a man entered. Tall, muscular with long black hair. The same one she had glimpsed earlier.

She heard Arthur 2 inhale sharply.

"Who is he?" Chris asked.

For the first time the woman looked disconcerted.

"You need to move quickly now. I must leave you immediately."

Then she was gone. The man looked up at her and then he smiled. He raised his sword and Chris could see blood dripping from the blade. She didn't wait but sprinted off down the passageway that began to curve round to the right. More windows, displaying various scenes of men drinking, sleeping and talking but no Selena. Her spirits fell as she saw a dead end ahead.

Then something of greater concern. The whole passage shuddered and she heard a noise like a huge nutshell breaking, probably walnut. A large crack appeared in the roof of the corridor and sped towards her. Chris thought quickly. An earthquake? But why should a god want to destroy its own world? This was something more sinister and she knew it was connected to the muscular man she had seen.

Looking around desperately, she saw a mark on the end wall. It was barely visible, the embossed design looked as if it had been worn down over many years. A question mark. She ran across and pressed it. Part of the wall swung open and she dived inside just before the crack reached her. A small, empty chamber with a window and through it, she could see Franco.

He was standing on a raised stone platform facing the window. In front of him, with their backs to Chris, was a gathering of over 20 figures in purple robes. Selena was at his side but she was uncomfortably tied to an upright stone slab, her legs and arms outstretched.

Chris could see that Franco was speaking but the window was soundproof. She looked around for a door. Eventually, she saw the question mark at knee height on a side wall. She pressed it and the wall opened as before. Now she was in a larger room with a curtain at the end and could hear Franco's voice coming from behind it. Chris lifted the edge slightly and found she was at the back of the audience with Franco and Selena on the stage in front.

"Listen, my fellow Eves. I tell you again that this Adam is special. He is the God of Query and has come to you in the form of an Adam as a test. If you take any action against him, your whole civilisation will be destroyed. For the last time, I say to you release him."

The robed figures turned to each other in heated discussion. Then Chris felt the floor rocking. The movements increased until cracks began to appear in the walls and ceiling. One of the robed figures rushed onto the stage and began to untie Selena.

"Forgive us. We obey you until death," he screamed.

She was free but the tremors continued. Blocks of stone began to fall and a large split appeared in the floor. Then the door burst open to reveal the dark haired man. He didn't hesitate, swinging his mighty sword with a guttural yell. It wasn't a fight, it was a massacre. Blood flew everywhere. Heads and limbs were mercilessly hacked to the floor.

Chris couldn't move for a second, appalled by the horrifying scene. Then she heard a shout.

"Quick, here."

Selena was beckoning from the stone platform. Chris raced across the edge of the blood spattered throng and joined her. At the back of the raised area was a little circle with a large, embossed question mark. Franco and Selena grabbed her hand and they moved onto it.

Just as the whiteness began, she glanced back. The big man had stopped hacking and was looking at a figure in the doorway. Arthur 2 but now in golden armour, resting the point of a long sword between her feet. She was smiling.

The scene dissolved into pure white.

13

Chris could feel something was wrong. The Gate seemed unstable and the solid white seemed easy and insecure. The gatekeeper suddenly appeared, her face wide-eyed and panicky.

"It's breaking up. No time," she shouted and they fell into whiteness again.

Chris emerged in a toilet cubicle with the throb of music in her ears. Routine 21st-century rock music. She opened the door to see a brown haired girl in a green party frock applying lipstick in front of the mirror.

Logically, lips should be constructed of some rough, serrated material to allow better gripping of food such as spaghetti. It would also provide robust edging to the oral orifice and provide an alternative method of securely holding items such as pens and pieces of string. There can only be one reason for the soft, moist red lips we have been issued with. Well, maybe two.

"Hello love. You a nun or something?" asked the girl.

Chris realised she was still wearing the purple robe from the last world.

"No. It's for a joke we're playing on someone."

Not a bad instinctive response, she thought. She couldn't take the robe off as she only had the llama bikini underneath. Chris decided to take advantage of the girls open conversation.

"Actually, I'm a stranger here. I don't know this place at all."

"Wot, the CubbleCubble club? I'm here most nights 'cause I think it's the best place to meet men. Do you usually go to the Tabbinskila place then?"

"Sometimes. I can never remember all the names. I was trying to think how many clubs there are."

The girl looked puzzled.

"There's only four. You are a bit mixed up. See ya later."

She left and Chris checked the mirror. The robe looked ridiculous in this environment. She untied the cloth that she had used to flatten her chest and lifted the hem of the robe around her waist. Then she used the cloth as a belt and the result was a knee length, baggy dress but it was an improvement. She opened the door.

The scene was just as expected. Flashing lights, an ever moving jumble of dancing bodies and loud, overexcited chatter. Noisy, crowded clubs were not her favourite domain and she left quickly.

The street outside was bright neon lit. Gaggles of gaggly girls squeaked in excited conversation. Glare faced young men looked around, ready for anything except the embarrassment of approaching a girl individually. The typical picture of a weekend night at almost any town on earth. Except no vehicles. The wide street had no roadway and there wasn't a taxi, bus or car in sight.

Chris walked slowly, looking carefully at her surroundings. The first task was to gain some idea of the size and limits of the world and to do that she needed to get high up. The architecture of the buildings was compatible with present-day England. Brick built, three or four storeys high. At ground level, there were bars, clubs, restaurants and shops and all were open. Clothes. First, she needed to change.

She crossed to a large store packed with every style imaginable. The people she passed stared with amusement at her clothing but she ignored them and entered the shop. In a few minutes she had grabbed underwear, blue trousers, a white top, khaki jacket and comfortable, flat shoes. After a quick visit to the changing room, she walked to the door in her new attire. Three girls were arguing in the doorway.

"Those shoes are sick. You look like an old woman," shouted one, a lean faced, dark haired girl.

"You say that once more and you'll be sorry," responded a pretty blonde.

"They're sick, old woman," taunted the first.

Suddenly, the blonde pulled out a knife and rammed it upwards into her tormentor's chest. The girl gave a loud cry and fell to the floor with a crimson patch growing around the embedded blade.

Chris grabbed the blonde.

"What have you done?" she called, shaking the girl.

"Killed her, I hope," came the sullen reply.

"I should break your arm for that."

Chris knelt by the body and then heard the laughter. The corpse opened her eyes and joined in. Chris reached for the knife. A dummy. The plastic blade had retracted that she could see the holes in the knife handle where the red liquid had emerged.

She rose and walked away quietly, ignoring the mocking laughter behind her. She cursed herself for being so stupid and getting involved. She needed to find out about the world first, not rush into situations. Back to plan one. Find somewhere high. She looked up to the top of the buildings and then saw the route. A fire escape zigzagged up the wall of an alley next to a four-storey building and she crossed back over the pedestrian street and entered the alley. Four young men were leaning against the wall. Chris sighed. Nothing was easy.

"Hello girl. Come to play with us?" called one.

Chris ignored him but he moved in front of her.

"We can do it the nice way. Just give a price for the four of us or we'll have you anyway."

Chris was about to react when she realised something was wrong. Price? There was no money on these worlds.

"How much can you afford?" she asked to test.

"We can't afford nothing. Haven't got a packet between us."

"What is a packet?"

He looked astonished.

"You a bit simple, girl? C'mon men, let's have her."

The next 43 seconds were unpleasant. Three boys unconscious on the ground and one that had spoken had a broken, bloody nose.

Chris gripped his collar.

"What is a packet?" she asked again quietly.

"Packet of Tirgixx," he murmured.

"What is it? What does it do?"

The astonished look again.

"You eat it. Gives you a day in paradise. You gotta be a visitor?"

"Yes and you need to treat guests more politely next time. What is paradise?"

"Yeah, you wouldn't know. I've only been twice. Can't explain, you need to see it yourself."

Chris rammed three fingers into his neck and his head slumped forward. She didn't want him to see her climbing the fire escape.

The metal ladders were old but in good condition and she reached the roof in under two minutes. Although it was night, the glow of the city lights showed her all she needed. The city was the world. It stretched maybe eight kilometres across or about five miles and around the boundary she could distinguish a sort of white net, like a metal mesh fence.

Chris sat cross-legged in the centre of the roof. The normal city with a variation. The difference was money, or the fact it didn't exist. What could be the motivation of the people, if not wealth? Many seemed to be working in the shops, at the clubs and restaurants. Why? What was their reward?

Then she considered this Tirgixx stuff mentioned by the boy. It had to be a drug. He said you reached paradise for a day. Probably a type of hallucinogen that lasted 24 hours. Maybe that was the currency to pay wages and salaries? But people had been working on the other worlds. Why? She considered what life would be like without money. Would everyone just lounge around all day? Some perhaps but not the vast majority. They'd be doing something. Working. Not necessarily turning up at an office every morning but occupied somehow. What else would give them a reason to live? One other thing. They'd also be fighting. If only three people existed then two of them would find a reason to join together against the other.

Philosophy over, Chris noticed the sky was brightening. Perhaps this was another world with short nights. She climbed down the fire escape into the alley. Of course, the boys were gone and she walked through the main street.

"I need help."

The old woman with grey hair. Clean, tidy and sincere.

"I'll try. What's the problem?"

"I'm being thrown out of my home. I'm so scared."

"Can't you just take another house?"

Tears welled up in the grey eyes.

"I can't move, I've lived there all my life. It's this gang of boys. They come every day. I'm sure they want to kill me."

"Why not tell the police?"

"Police? What's that?"

Chris sighed. "Where do you live?"

"It's not far. Please come."

Her face beamed with gratitude and she led Chris into a side street. Two more turns and they were in a road with a row of semi-detached houses on each side. The morning sun gleamed on sparkling rooftops and immaculate gardens. She accompanied the woman to the third building on the right.

"Please come in and have tea. I'm so grateful."

Sitting in a spotless kitchen and sipping the beverage, Chris asked for more details.

"It's a gang of six young men. You'll see them soon. They shout and threaten me, knock on the door and windows. It's terrible."

"Do they have weapons?"

"Yes, they all have knives. They said they will cut me open."

The old lady burst into tears and Chris placed a comforting arm around her shoulders.

"It will be fine," she said with certain determination.

She heard a clack at the kitchen window. A shaggy haired face peered at her and Chris returned the stare with cold fury. Two more faces joined the first, smiling and waving long bladed knives. One made a cutting motion across his throat.

"It's time to learn, boys," Chris muttered as she opened the kitchen door. As the woman had said, there were six of them, grinning and leering at her.

"A bit of younger meat to cut up," shouted one.

"We could have her first," added another.

The shaggy haired one moved to the front. He seemed to be the leader.

"Get your kit off, darling. We'll let you go if you're nice to us. That's all six of us, you understand."

Chris regarded him mildly, one hand on hip.

"You know you're scum, don't you?"

His eyes flashed. "Careful, darling. We might cut you up afterwards."

He glanced right and left and his five companions edged round her in a semicircle.

"Who goes first?" Chris asked with a slight smile.

The two at the points of the semicircle jumped forward, swinging their knives low. She jumped up and slammed her foot into the forehead of the one on the right. As she landed she swung a fist to the stomach of the other followed by a knee into his jaw. Four left and three of them came together, the shaggy haired one holding back. They were only average but spread out and attacked at the same time. Chris used the best counter to this movement. She jumped to the side of the one on the left and before he could turn, planted a fist on the back of his neck. The other two were felled by kicks. She hadn't even been touched yet.

Only one remaining, the leader. He waited for her, brushing back his long hair and crouching low. He began to move the knife from hand to hand. Chris stood still.

"Listen. I can easily break your arms but I'll give you a chance. I'll let you go if you never come near this place again."

His eyes widened slightly. Then he laughed.

"But I live here," he said.

The laughter was repeated behind her. The old lady stood outside the door, shaking with mirth.

"Well, lover. She was too good for you," she shouted.

Chris looked at her without amusement.

"What the hell is this?"

"Fooled you, little girl. That was great," the woman burbled.

Chris gestured to the shaggy youth.

"So who is he?"

"He's my partner. Still good between the sheets, aren't I Tom?"

He returned her smile.

"Yer not bad for an old woman."

Chris didn't waste time. She left the house and walked quickly back to the city centre. The event had annoyed her but she had trained never to dwell on unpleasant matters. She was conscious that time was getting shorter to find Jerome Jones and was concerned about the apparent breaking up of the last world with the muscular man who seemed to be the cause.

The feeling was confirmed by a sudden shuddering and a small crack opened in the pavement in front of her. The people in the street stopped for a moment and then continued on their business. The event birthed an unpleasant thought in Chris's mind. Perhaps the gods had decided to end the game and destroy the universe. She and her companions would never return to Earth. No future for her with her lover, Jerome Two. She shook her head. Action was needed. She would find Selena and Jerome Jones then return to her house in England.

To avoid another trick, she wasn't going to wait for someone to come to her. She would select a person to guide her around the city. A smart, thirtyish woman in a businesslike blue suit walked past her.

"Excuse me, I'm looking for directions."

"Certainly. I expect you're a visitor."

"I am and hopefully just passing through."

"How can I help?"

"First, I'm looking for two friends who came here with me."

She described Selena and Franco.

"I'm sure I saw the woman. She was in the south side at a cafe this morning."

"Can you tell me where it is?"

"Easier to show you. It's only five minutes walk. My name is Mary, by the way."

"Chris. I appreciate your help."

She walked with the woman and took the chance to talk.

"I've been tricked twice since I arrived here."

Mary smiled. "Charaders, we call them. They like to play little games."

"What's the point?"

"It's just their way of having fun."

"I think some are on drugs. A gang I met asked for a packet of Tirgixx. I guess it's hallucinogenic."

Mary looked across at her.

"There's no such thing as Tirgixx. That was another Charader."

"How do I know you're not tricking me?"

"Obviously, you can't be sure. We can go back now if you like."

"Sorry. Let's go on."

After a few twists and turns, they reached a small cafe tucked away between two shops. It was clean and bright with about half of the ten tables occupied. Mary led the way to the counter where an attractive young woman greeted her with a smile.

"My friend here is looking for her companion. I'm sure I saw her here this morning."

She gave Selena's description.

"Of course I know her. She's still in the back room."

"She's here?" Chris said with surprise.

"Just through there," the girl responded, pointing at a door to the left of the counter. Chris walked over and reached for the handle.

Then someone gripped her arm.

"I don't think that's a good idea."

Chris turned quickly. Selena.

"So you are here."

"No. I've been following you from the town centre. Let's just clear this up and then leave."

She picked up a large cardboard box from behind the counter, kicked open the door and threw it inside. Immediately, a set of massive blades swung down from above the door slashing the box into small pieces.

"Another trick," Chris muttered.

"It gets boring, doesn't it?" Selena responded. She grabbed Mary and the girl then threw them inside the room.

"I could break their necks but it'd be a waste of time. Let's go."

Chris recounted her experiences as they walked and Selena did the same. She hadn't been deceived herself but had witnessed several others.

"Surely the people know everything is a hoax by now?" Chris asked.

"No, they don't. It seems that every time they are tricked, it's wiped from their memory. I saw one man being fooled twice within five minutes."

The elephant is well known for its good memory. Everyone will know how this animal was first used in warfare by Queen Annabel of the Alps to attack the Goths and Picts. Coincidentally, Annabel was a close friend of Cleopatra of Egypt and they shared a mutual lover, Martin Antimony, an ancient Roman warlord. Of course, he wasn't ancient at that time and retained sufficient vigour to satisfy the two women. History does not record his relationship with the elephants.

"More importantly, what about these earthquakes and cracks appearing?"

"Something is happening. It could be that we're nearing the end of this universe," Selena responded.

"That was my fear. Did you notice the big man with the sword as we left the last world?"

"Yes. He's definitely linked to it."

Selena lapsed into thought but Chris didn't want her in passive mode.

"We've got to get out fast or Jerome will die. We need Franco and the Gate. Any ideas?"

"None," Selena replied morosely.

"Come on, Selena. Time to think. Start with Franco. He may well have gravitated to a place he could associate with."

"All he knows is sex."

"Exactly. Any brothels, sex shops or strip clubs here?"

"I saw a place. Some sort of club with plenty of flesh on the boards outside."

"Let's go."

Chris was determined to drag Selena into action. There was no time for idle contemplation. They walked quickly across the town centre and into a side street.

Several large posters of near naked women alongside a single entrance door. It was locked but Selena was now in active node. She kicked it three times.

After a few seconds they heard a voice.

"Go away. We're closed."

"New staff," Serena called.

"What?"

"New staff. We were told to come today."

The door opened and a wizened old man peered out.

"No one told me."

Selena pushed past him.

"We'll just check what needs to be done," she said.

Chris followed her into a typical strip club. Small stage with a walkway into the audience, cosy tables and a long bar. Only the old man in sight. Just two doors, one at the back of the stage and the other near the bar.

"You do the stage," Selena called and walked towards the bar, ignoring the protests of the little man.

Chris jumped up to the raised area. The door led to a small hallway with two rooms. The first was a dressing room, or more accurately, undressing room. A row of lit mirrors, lockers for clothing, chairs and sofas. But devoid of people.

The other room wasn't. There were four bodies mingled together on a large sofa. Franco was sleeping peacefully amid a jumble of naked female legs, arms and other parts. Just the sound of contented slumber.

Chris heard Selena enter behind her.

"Get him out and let's go."

At the sound of her voice, Franco's eyes opened and Chris was transfixed for a second. The pupils were pure, glowing gold. She had seen a flash of the colour before but never held for so long. His expression radiated power.

"I assume you want to go," he said. His voice was deeper now, full of assurance.

"Yes, time is getting short," Chris responded.

He extricated himself from the tangled bodies and dressed quickly.

"First we have to find the Gate," said Selena.

He looked at her, faintly amused.

"You are a strong woman. Fortunately for you, I admire that. Otherwise you would suffer."

"It sounds like you are regaining your powers."

"I am and in these worlds, my fellow gods are without their abilities. I must be the most powerful here."

"What of this big, muscular man who keeps appearing and these upheavals we experienced? Was that your work?" asked Chris.

"No, I have no desire to end this universe or even harm any of the other gods. I feel I have served my sentence and just want to regain my place in the hierarchy."

A loud rumbling noise and Chris felt the building shudder. Cracks appeared in the walls and ceiling.

"We need to hurry," she shouted.

"Find the Gate quickly," Selena responded and started for the door.

"I can sense its location," Franco said calmly.

Selena stopped.

"What? You know where the Gate is?"

"I know the area. But there is a price for this information."

The room shook again as Selena walked back to him, eyes afire.

"Price? What do you want? Sex?"

"That sounds like a good offer."

"An offer I'm not making. I will not be coerced like that."

Franco turned to Chris.

"Absolutely no chance," she said coldly.

He laughed, long and deep.

"I would have been very disappointed if either of you had agreed. Follow me."

He led them out of the building and continued a winding course through the streets. Chris could now see cracks in many of the buildings and fallen pieces of masonry lay on the ground. They reached a small cul-de-sac. Two compact houses on each side and one at the end.

"It's somewhere here," Franco announced.

"Start on the left, Chris," Selena shouted, sprinting to the other side. Chris completed her search in rapid time. The tremors had returned and she had to avoid falling furniture and wall hangings as she raced through the two houses. No question mark. She ran back to the road and Selena joined her, shaking her head.

A crowd had gathered at the entrance of the cul-de-sac and they looked angry.

"There they are. They brought the earthquakes," shouted a red-faced man.

"We're going to die but we'll kill them first," a woman's voice yelled.

Chris could see knives being brandished and the mob edged forward. Over fifty of them with more arriving all the time. She looked for Franco. He was standing in front of the end house, eyes glinting golden in the sunlight.

"Come on," shouted Selena and sprinted towards him with Chris following. The crowd yelled with anger and stormed after them. A knife flew through the air and grazed Chris's shoulder. More followed but they had now reached Franco. Then Chris heard a roar.

She turned quickly. The big, dark haired man was charging towards the back of the crowd, his sword swinging around his head. The yelling stopped and screaming began. The sword sliced through the mob like a messy lawnmower. Great geysers of blood flew up as he slashed through soft flesh. Another sickening massacre.

Chris felt Selena grab her arm and yell in her ear.

"Get inside now."

Franco had already entered and she was pulled into a hallway behind him. Selena kicked the door closed. Chris couldn't think for a moment, her mind was filled with the horrendous scene outside. She felt Selena slapping her face and returned to reality.

"Quickly, find the Gate."

Franco held up a hand.

"Try that room," he said quietly, pointing at the second door on the left. They entered a comfortable lounge with silver, chairs and TV in the standard arrangement. Chris looked quickly. No question mark. She hesitated but Selena didn't, pulling the chairs to one side and then the sofa.

It was there. Concealed under the sofa was a circular metal plaque with a question mark. Chris heard the outer door crash open as she held hands and stepped forward.

Then she was immersed in the tranquil silence of the whiteness.

14

There was no gatekeeper. For a few seconds, everything was white and then Chris emerged. She was in a green field with a river crossing her view about 100 metres ahead. Beyond it was another 100 metres of grassland and then a bright blue sky with small white clouds.

She turned and hit her elbow on something hard. Directly at her back was the same blue sky with clouds. It was a wall, extending infinitely upwards. The edge of the world.

'There are still those who are convinced that the Earth is a sphere shape. They have been disgracefully misled by photographs from space and a vast amount of so-called expert evidence offered by geographers, physicists and the like. You can easily prove this is nonsense. If the earth is a globe then the ground should slope away from you in every direction. But everyone knows that it often slopes upwards, particularly when you are walking or riding a bicycle.

The truth is very different. The world is actually a large, undulating, circular plain surrounded by a void. Places such as California, Scotland and New Zealand on the boundary, the edge of our world. Anyone who has visited John O'Groats, on the far northern edge of Scotland, will confirm that the place represents the outermost limits of civilisation and there is absolutely nothing lies beyond it.'

Extract from the booklet on 'It's Flat, I Tell You' by Counson Westlo.

Chris looked to her left and saw Selena staring at the river and followed her gaze towards a boat approaching the bank in front of them. A figure jumped out and strode rapidly towards them.

"It's her," Selena said without moving her head.

Chris deduced.

"Athena? How do you know?"

"I know."

The woman was tall with flowing brown hair and a pleasant but not beautiful face. She was dressed in a one-piece outfit, like a ski suit but looser. The top was amber and the legs a light green. In her right hand was a golden sword.

"Hello again," Selena said in a shy voice that Chris had never heard before.

The woman stepped in front of them and Chris could feel the power emanating from her.

"I remember you, Selena and your companion is Chris." She spoke in a deep breathy voice but no smile and Chris could sense Selena's disappointment at the formality of the greeting.

"This is your world?" she asked to break the tension.

"No. I will explain quickly. You need to hurry."

"I wanted to see you again, Athena," Selena said quietly.

"Perhaps we will meet later. Now you must go as I have to stay here."

"Something is happening to the universe," Chris said.

The woman turned to her, eyes shining with intent.

"There is a problem. You have been advised how this universe was formed and the agreement of the gods to the rules. You were not told that one God did not participate in this."

"You mean Franco who came with us?"

"No. He disgusts me. There is no need for a deity to control the animal urges. I am talking of Hades, brother of Zeus and ruler of the underworld. He decided that the concept of this recreation area was inappropriate and would not involve himself in the plans. For many of your centuries, he was content to remain outside the game. Then you came with that creature, Franco. Hades despises him for reasons I will not discuss now. He is furious that this universe provided the vehicle for Franco to return and has now vowed to destroy it."

"Is he powerful enough?" asked Selena.

"Yes. The universe was not created to withstand attack by one of the gods. That was never anticipated when we created it."

"We've seen a big, dark haired man with a sword. Is that Hades?"

"It is him. His rampaging through the worlds, demolishing everything as he travels."

"Can he do that by himself?"

Athena's expression turned even grimmer.

"He is accompanied by his servants, creatures of the underworld. They take many forms and be wary that not all are unpleasant to your eyes."

"What can we do?" asked Chris.

"Nothing except reach your Jerome Jones and leave as quickly as possible. I must wait and attempt to defend this world against Hades. He will travel through the Gates but I warn that his minions are able to enter through the cracks and holes he has created. They may already be here and you must be on your guard."

"What can these creatures do?"

"They have only one function. To kill without emotion. Your only consolation is that they are mortal when in these worlds."

"Tell us what to do."

"The Gate is at the end of the river. You must take the boat I brought and travel quickly. The craft moves by your willpower. Just think of a direction, fast or slow and it will comply. I have left a sword and knife for each of you on the boat. You have so little time now. Being watchful of the natives who live on the banks."

"We need Franco to pass through the Gate."

"He is already waiting for you at the end of the river. Now hurry."

Selena started to reach towards her but Athena turned away.

"Come on," Chris called and ran towards the river with Selena following reluctantly.

The craft was compact, like a small motor cruiser with a two person cabin. Chris waited until Selena climbed on board then thought forward at full speed. The boat quickly surged through the waters. Maintain speed and keep to the centre of the river was her next mental instruction. The craft dutifully obeyed.

Chris saw Selena was near the stern, looking back.

"Selena, forget her. She's just not a sociable type. These are gods we are talking to and they don't have our feelings."

"I know. It's not a sexual thing, Chris. I just wanted to know her, to somehow share between us. It's hard to explain."

"Don't try. We've got plenty to do. Athena warned us to watch the shores. You do that while I keep us on course."

Chris could easily have done both jobs but wanted Selena back in active mode. For 20 minutes all was perfect. The boat sped swiftly down the centre of the river, the narrow grassy banks on each side were clear and the sun shone brightly.

Chris sensed it first.

Something had moved on the stern. She turned quickly, pulling the knife from her belt. A heavy glob of dark red slime was edging over the hull. As if it recognised its discovery, the thing suddenly leapt over the side and slobbered into the boat. A fat, squidgy body with four globular appendages as legs. It was completely featureless, no eyes or mouth and was covered with a layer of shiny mucus, like thick saliva.

Selena didn't hesitate. She picked up a sword and took a pace forward, swinging the blade at the central body. The blow didn't fall. One of the legs shot forward and circled her ankle, pulling it forward. She fell back, the sword striking the deck. Chris grabbed the other sword and hacked at the part that held Selena. Sickly orange gunge oozed out from the cuts and the grip relaxed enough to free the leg.

Selena got to her feet, picked up her sword and began to slash repeatedly at the creature. More orange spilled out on the deck and Chris felt her foot slide from beneath her. She fell forward, directly into the slimy body. A sickly smell, like stale vomit, overwhelmed her and seemed to paralyse her. Then she felt her arm being pulled and came away from the creature with a sticky squelch.

"Don't ride it, kill it," shouted Selena.

Chris began the attack again, now thrusting the sword rather than slashing. At last, her blade entered the central body and she pushed it deep, right to the hilt. The sword clattered to the deck. The thing had gone, disappeared and so had the orange gunge. All was as before it came.

"I'm guessing that came from Hades," Chris remarked.

"It wasn't pretty," responded Selena.

The journey continued and, in retrospect, Chris wished she had asked Athena the length of the river. It was now winding dramatically, some turns more than 180 degrees and the banks were frequently covered with trees. After one right angled turn, Chris felt Selena nudge her and peered ahead towards the right bank. She could see movements of blue and grey figures near to a forest. As they approached, she became increasingly aware of something strange about the movements of the people. They just travelled smoothly with no jerkiness as they walked. Then one moved to the bank and stared at them. His legs moved but he was a few centimetres off the ground.

"Hover people," Chris observed.

"They don't look unfriendly."

The inaccuracy of this statement was underlined by the arrow that thudded into the cabin roof. It was followed by many more but by then, Chris and Selena were sheltering inside the cabin. Chris looked through the porthole at their attackers. They were dressed in suits. Real suits as in high street tailored. Pinstripe, tweed and plain in the most conservative dark blues and greys. Almost identical dress for women and men, the only difference was that the men all had striped ties over white shirts and the women wore open collars.

It could have been a banker's convention except for the bows and arrows. These people carried them openly but bankers would certainly have concealed the weapons in their briefcases.

Chris sent a message to the boat to move to the other side of the river but maintain full speed. Another two minutes and they would be past the suited archers. Then she noticed the net. It extended across the whole width of the river and she could see it was made of metal, like a fence.

"We'll have to stop," she called to Selena.

"Pull over to the bank."

Chris messaged the craft and they berthed gently on the grassy bank opposite their attackers. A thick forest offered shelter but there was a five metre gap across the grass and the fusillade of arrows was unceasing. Chris looked at the suited crowd again. Some had drawn swords and were coming across the river, floating over the water.

"No choice. We've got to go for the trees. Then we either make friends or fight them," Selena said.

They sprinted for the forest. A storm of arrows followed them but miraculously, they missed. Taking shelter behind a thick trunk, Chris watched the people approach. After reaching the bank, they assembled in neat rows and waited. Then she saw a solitary figure crossing the river. A short, chubby man wearing an impeccable blue pinstripe suit but he had an ornate, heavy gold chain around his neck.

"The leader, I guess," she muttered.

The man reached the shore and floated past the lines of silent figures. He took position at the front, facing directly towards the tree where Chris and Selena were concealed. Then he took a sheet of paper from his pocket and began to read.

"The management committee welcomes you to our settlement in accord with section 23, subsection 18C of our Constitution. My sisters and brothers have unanimously participated in the informal greeting ceremony, notwithstanding and without prejudice to any future actions that we may initiate, whether individually or corporately. It is my duty, as an elected representative of oral communications media and on behalf of the Corporation, to make the following announcement."

He paused in a well practised manner before continuing.

"Subject to your compliance with our statutory regulations, including but not limited to sections 1 through 397 and in the spirit of goodwill to all, providing the said all observe and conduct themselves in strict obedience of codes of practice 149, 221 and 683, we greet you. This greeting should in no sense be regarded as subservient acquiescence, whether implicit or explicit with regard to present or subsequent acts of any person or persons in our domain. We also unreservedly reserve the right, both moral and legal, in respect of any past, present or future mental, verbal or physical actions as specified in the appendices to section 821 of the statutes."

He paused again and looked expectantly towards the tree.

"Follow me," Selena said and walked out to face the man. Chris noticed she kept her knees slightly bent to minimise her height advantage. He still barely reached her shoulders.

"On behalf of my associate and myself, I express sincere gratitude for the spirit of goodwill embodied within your greeting. It is both an honour and privilege to visit such just and amicable peoples."

The chubby man smiled officiously. It was what he wanted to hear.

"Whereas this multilateral discussion may not be considered negotiatory, the Corporation are disposed to accept your verbal gesture as both an acknowledgement and understanding of our initial position."

Chris was becoming frustrated with the conversation.

"I'm Chris and this is Selena," she announced.

The chubby man's expression turned to displeasure.

"It is unfortunate that you retain the antiquated, elitist fashion for individual names. However, we are inclined to embody the fact that, as strangers from a less developed civilisation, your education has been inadequate. Such ignorance of the formal regulations is understood but will be recorded."

"May we be advised of your appellations?" asked Selena carefully.

The smile returned.

"You are permitted to conduct communications both orally and in written or printed script, using the appellation So."

"So?" Chris couldn't help repeating.

All the people looked at her.

"You wish to pursue interrogatory communication?" asked the chubby man.

Chris shook her head and adopted Selena's conciliatory approach.

"We are most honoured. May I inquire the appropriate method of ensuring initiation of intercourse with a specific individual?"

"There are 13 methods specified that include eye contact during the verbal phase and physical contact, providing this is conducted on certain points of the arm below the elbow. The contact must be momentary and any gripping or clasping will be considered invasion of personal space or indeed, common assault."

Chris could feel her brain bursting and kept silent with difficulty but Selena seemed calm as always and spoke again.

"We are traversing this liquefied thoroughfare, hereinafter known as the river, within the small craft you see behind you. It is our earnest and fervent wish to continue our journey at the earliest convenience. We express our wholehearted gratitude for your frank and open welcome but appeal to your goodwill in respect of temporary removal of the barrier that precludes our continued progress. Thus the stature of your already esteemed civilisation will demonstrate its munificent benevolence towards all peoples."

The man responded cautiously.

"You have submitted your request in accord with subsection 84, section 9 of the statutes. Consequently, it must be discussed by the section 9 Subcommittee and is subject to a mandatory voting procedure at the finalisation of their considerations. Meanwhile, for the duration of this period you are required to remain within a 20 person radius of the position where your request was made."

"What chronological value could be estimated as the highest probability before the ballot is concluded?

"The average period is three hours but this statement may not be taken as a formal declaration. It is provided purely for indicatory purposes."

Selena nodded and the man gave an almost imperceptible bow. He then returned across the river, followed by all but four of the assembled people. Chris saw one of the remaining men fix his eyes on her. He was young and good-looking with longish brown hair and wore a plain grey suit. He walked away from his companions and sat in front of the trees. Chris followed and sat next to him but was unsure why she did it.

"You didn't think much of us," he said.

"Normal speech at last. Your leader couldn't stop the words coming."

"I'm afraid I'm the exception. I only arrived here a few days ago."

"Where from?"

"Another community down the river. I got bored there and decided to walk upstream."

"Why did your people try to kill us and then offer a welcome?"

He laughed and rose to his feet, picking up his bow. He took a small yellow ball out of his pocket and handed it to Chris.

"Throw it high in the air."

She hurled the ball skywards. In a flash, he pulled an arrow from his quiver and shot. It pierced the ball exactly in the centre. He sat down again and she rejoined him.

"Everyone I know here can shoot like that. The arrows were their expressions of welcome. They could easily have killed you."

"We just want to continue our journey. What are our chances with this committee?"

"Absolutely none. They always vote to defer a decision. Then they meet again and refer the question to another subcommittee who consider it for a week or two before passing it on to the next committee. This continues for years until it reaches the ruling tribunal."

"What then?"

"They invariably agree to appoint a special subcommittee to look into it."

"Do you have any ideas about how we can get away and remove that net?"

"Yes, I can help. At a price."

"How much?" Chris asked automatically.

"You owe me already. Remember Sylph, who helped you escape from the palace?"

"You?"

He smiled.

"Yes, in another guise. You can call me Mark now. Remember what I said when I helped you?"

Chris felt her heart sink.

"You wanted a physical reward," she murmured, feeling queasy.

"I'll reward you."

Selena's voice. She was standing just behind them and now sat on the other side of Mark, placing her hand on his thigh. He looked at her.

"I had set my sights on Chris."

Selena gave her most lurid look.

"She's not very passionate. You wouldn't enjoy it. I can offer you something special."

She squeezed against him and whispered in his ear. Chris couldn't hear but he seemed convinced.

"It's a deal," he said and taking Selena's hand, he led her to the trees calling to the other three guards.

"So, So and So. This visitor must enter the arboreal vicinity for reasons of personal hygiene. In accordance with clauses 92 to 97 of Custodian Protocols section 332, I shall accompany her but will strictly observe clauses 114 to 137 in my observance procedures."

Chris watched the pair leave with a feeling of relief but also a little guilt, as if she had let Selena down. It was also irritating to have her passions described as inadequate. She didn't enjoy being regarded as a junior partner. Chris weighed up the two sides and relief won emphatically.

It was nearly an hour before they returned by which time the other guards had become edgy.

"That took a long time," called one.

"Not long enough," responded Mark, with a grin.

The couple rejoined Chris who wasn't going to ask.

Mark looked at Selena.

"I can understand now why Poseidon is so keen on you," he said.

She smiled. "You have a lot more to learn. For a god, you're pretty innocent."

"Okay, do we have a plan?" asked Chris, barely concealing her impatience.

"I'll do my part," said Mark and walked towards his companions, calling out to them.

"I have to make a verbal declaration under section 53, subsection 23."

That got their attention.

"Without prejudice to any personages within our community, it is my grave duty to impart the information that certain individuals, unnamed at this point in time, have conducted deliberate and specific actions that contradict statutes 439, 492 and 748."

The three men gasped and he continued.

"The implicit target for this unprecedented and scandalous aggression is our river fence. Under statute 19, I assume delegatory rights to initiate a comprehensive and immediate investigation. Furthermore, in conditional compliance with the regulations, I can now provide definitive titular appendages for the miscreants. I name them So and So."

Expressions of horror crossed the three faces.

"So?" exclaimed one.

"Yes?" his companion responded.

"No, So!" he cried.

"It can't be So," shouted another.

Mark nodded with grandeur.

"So and So," he repeated.

"But if it wasn't So, would you say so?"

"Only if it was So."

"So sad."

"Me too."

Mark held up a hand.

"So I delegate. So, So and So will accompany me to the river fence.

"So, these two?"

"The statute overrides, so they will accompany."

"So it is written."

"I know so."

"So's off we go," instructed Mark and marched along the bank towards the fence. Three others continued their conversation as they followed.

"So we must follow?"

"I believe so."

"Do you? What in?"

"So, what?"

"No So. In what do you believe, So?"

"So you reap what you sew So."

"I fear so."

"Yes he could be dangerous."

They reached the edge of the river next to the fence. Chris could now see it was a thick steel mesh, impossible for a craft to pass. Mark lifted open a square metal plate in the grass to reveal a red lever.

"So, So, So. We must lower it."

"Why So?"

"To determine the extent of potential navigability malfunctions implicitly initiated by the detractive incapacitation consequential to the intrusive accomplishments of the saboteurs. And So?"

"Yes, So."

"My empowerment requires it so."

"I'll remember you said so So."

"I will return to the aquatic vehicle and commence forward propulsion in the direction of the submerged fence under the terms of the Safety and Hazardous Circumstance Protocol, part two, paragraph 18. In recognition of my behoven requirement for visual supervision of these two personages, they will accompany me. So is that clear?"

"So, it is."

"Then it shall be so."

Mark guided the two women back to the boat. Chris thought the craft forward slowly while they watched the fence. One of the guards was pulling the lever and it began to slowly descend. Just as it disappeared below the water, there was a shout from the other bank. The chubby little man was moving across the water towards them, calling loudly.

"So, So, So, So. Under section 38, subsection 19 and section 14, subsection 23 and section 15, subsection 12 and …"

The voice grew faint as Chris moved the boat into full speed and shot over the submerged fence. When they were well away from the settlement, she coasted to the bank and Mark jumped ashore.

"I must leave you but I hope to meet you again, Selena. You repaid for my help as Sophos but you still owe me for this assistance."

"I'm looking forward to continuing your education," Selena called back.

Chris simply waved and then moved the boat forward at full speed again.

"Do you want to ask?" enquired Selena.

"No," Chris responded quickly.

"Then I'll just tell you one thing. We didn't even touch each other."

"What?"

"How can I be more exact?"

"I'm still not going to ask."

Selena simply smiled.

The blue sky glowed with pleasure, teasing little sparkles from the river whilst the slushing of water across the bow imparting a soft tranquillity to the scene.

Then the wall came into view. A tall, stone wall that stretched across the whole world, blocking the river and the two banks completely. In the section that crossed the river, there were three large doors, wide enough for the boat to pass through and in front of each stood a spindly stick like figure. The lower halves of their bodies were below water and the exposed area above was a bright, almost fluorescent green colour. The three were virtually identical, with long, bony faces.

As the boat approached, they smiled broadly and the centre figure spoke.

"This is a test. Behind two of these doors is immediate, certain death and the other is your safe route. You can ask any question but I warn you that two of us always answer with lies and only one of us replies with the truth. That starts from now."

Chris could see that Selena was somewhat impatient.

"We are in too much of a hurry for this game. I want all of you to go through the door behind you and come out again."

The stick figures appeared disconcerted.

"No, two of us would die," said the one on the right.

Selena turned to Chris

"Take us to the bank," she said and jumped ashore. She ran to the nearest tree, jumped up and grabbed a thick branch. She pulled downward with all her weight and it cracked at the trunk, and then broke free. Quickly stripping off the side shoots with her knife, she returned to the boat.

"Move next to the centre one," she said.

The figure looked bemused by her actions and stood with a puzzled look.

"Right. Go through that door behind you," Selena shouted.

"I said we can't do that."

The impact of the heavy branch on the side of its head was immediate but it didn't fall before she swung again and the body slumped against the stone wall, totally unconscious.

Chris steered to the figure on the left.

"Same question," shouted Selena.

Its eyes were wide with fear but it shook its head.

Two thudding swings of the branch and its head rocked back on the blows. Another stick body against the wall.

The one on the right began to look desperate as Chris moved the boat next to it.

"It's a simple request. I just want you to go through one of the doors."

The creature waded across to the door on the left and walked through it. Chris told the boat to follow and they passed the spindly entity on the other side.

"Very grateful for your help," Selena called and threw the tree branch into the water.

Venturing forth once more amid nature's dreamy soliloquy, the vestiges of human deceit and corruption fell away like shadows from the perfect peaks of the mother world's bosom. The singular concordance of mellow inspiration indemnified the errant spirit in comforting compassion. Slipping sweetly within the stream's sibilant caresses, the spirit was slowly and surely refreshed.

In distant sight did appear a knight, a paladin of virtue with immaculate purity shining from his steel blue eyes. And his gaze was righteous and true. And his silver armour shimmered with glory. And in his grasp was a mighty weapon, the Sword Axbeluric.

A glow of immaculate integrity gleamed like stars around the figure, casting to the grimy shadows those that serve the tortured path of evil. As if in knowing obeisance, the very ground trembled beneath his feet and the heavens glimmered with innocent piety.

"That looked like a knight," Chris remarked after they had passed him.

"Yes, I think so," responded Selena.

They reached a turn in the river and he was soon out of sight.

15

After travelling for another ten minutes, they saw a giant video screen on the bank and a picture appeared as they drew alongside. Jerome Jones. Just his face and Chris could see the spikes were very close now, perhaps only a few centimetres from his head. More disturbing was the look in his eyes. For the first time they displayed what seemed to be fear. The critical urgency of their mission focused again.

"Can't we move faster?" asked Selena.

"I've already asked for top speed."

They began to see settlements on the banks. Clustered groups of buildings with people moving around. No one seemed to be particularly interested in the small craft churning along the centre of the river. One or two glanced across and then continued what they were doing. The houses and clothing of the inhabitants ranged from 16th century to the present day but they had no time to investigate further.

"How long can this river be?" Chris remarked.

"Nothing we can do. Just keep going."

The group of settlements disappeared behind them and now the banks were largely forested. Suddenly the boat struck something and bounced backwards, throwing Chris to the deck. She scrambled up and joined Selena to look ahead. The river seemed clear. No obstructions.

"What was it? Could this be the end of the river?" asked Chris.

"It can't be. We can see a long way ahead."

Selena fetched a pot from the galley and threw it forward. It rebounded back on to the deck.

"Invisible wall. Follow it across the river to make sure there are no gaps," she said.

Chris instructed the boat and it tracked from one side to the other, nudging into the wall. No spaces.

"Having trouble?"

The voice came from a man who had appeared from the thick forest on the right bank. He was average size with short blonde hair above a round face with friendly brown eyes.

"There's an invisible barrier across the river. We need to get past urgently," called Chris.

"Too much urgency in the world. Too many have to be doing something. You need to relax and match your time with nature. Peace is all we need."

Chris saw Selena's lips tighten and feared the worst.

"I'll be peaceful if you reply to the question. Can you remove this wall or not?"

"That depends."

"On what?"

"On my judgment of your worthiness."

Chris felt Selena start forward and pulled her back. She steered the boat across and jumped onto the bank, next to the man.

"You'll have to explain what this worthiness means."

He smiled at her cheerfully. From close-up, he looked about twenty and not unattractive.

"Nothing to explain. I make a judgment and only those that succeed may pass."

"I'm surprised you're still here. Surely some of the people you refuse would have become violent?"

"Hit me," he said.

"If that's what you want."

Chris aimed at gentle slap at his face. The impact jarred her hand. She hadn't hit his face, just another transparent barrier around his body, maybe three centimetres thick.

"Nothing can pass through. Fists, swords, knives, nothing at all. Unless, of course, if I want it to," he said cheerfully.

Selena had joined them on the bank and Chris could see her making the amiability effort.

"So what criteria do you use in your judgment?" she asked.

"I despise aggression and violence. People with those characteristics will never pass. Otherwise it's purely my subjective assessment."

Chris recognised the need for subtlety.

"I'm Chris and this is Selena. We don't know your name."

"Peter."

"I'm intrigued by your lifestyle. Do you have a home here?"

"Yes, a little cabin in the forest. Would you like to visit?"

"I certainly would," responded Chris with added enthusiasm.

Selena was back in smart mode now.

"Sorry I was little abrupt earlier. We thought you could be another attacker. It's not easy for two young women to travel this river," she said, smiling as influentially as possible.

"That's okay. Come and see my place."

He led them along a narrow channel through the thick trees and, after about 20 metres, they entered a clearing. A small log cabin with a colourful flower bed in front. They followed him through the door into a cosy room with rustic wooden furniture and burning logs in the fireplace. Two half open doors revealed a bathroom and bedroom.

"Please sit down and have tea," Peter invited.

Most people will have been invited for tea in a log cabin but only a handful will have been offered 252 Tingo Tea in that location. This beverage is a blend of the finest herbs found only in a small area on the face of a mountain in a wild and remote area of northern Mongolia.

A cup of the liquid, which must be taken with 7.3 millilitres of milk from a Saharan yak, is reputed to guarantee prevention of hair loss, wrinkles and varicose veins. Additional benefits include the ability to attract incomparable wealth, enhanced brain power to genius level and immunisation against all disease and illness. The only negative effect is that death follows 252 years after drinking, hence the name. Unfortunately a fire has destroyed the crop forever and now only three packets of this Tea remain in the world, all in the hands of a secret supplier. Being forgetful, I wrote his name and contact details on a scrap of paper that I placed in my trouser pocket but it was consumed by my dog in one of his more playful moods. The good news is that my trousers were almost completely undamaged and I don't need to buy a new pair.

They sat at a table created from cut through logs and he boiled water in a pot on the glowing fire. Soon they were sipping from wooden mugs of tea.

"Are you alone here?" asked Selena.

"Yes, there's only me but I see people on the river almost every day."

Chris was ready for Selena's strategy and saw her widening her eyes and parting her lips slightly as she spoke.

"Don't you get lonely?"

"I understand the question but loneliness is unknown to me. I'm always in nature's company. I have a thousand friends among the trees, plants, flowers and grasses."

"You never feel the need for a woman?"

"You mean sex? You're wondering if I indulge in self gratification? Or perhaps that I don't like women?"

Selena smiled. "You're avoiding the question."

As she spoke, there was a great shudder. They ran outside to see the world crack. Literally. A fissure opened in the blue sky at the edge of the world behind the trees where they stood. Then things began to crawl through the opening. Things that were an animate but were impossible to describe. Shapeless globules of virulent aggression in the colours that didn't exist. They exuded evil, inducing feelings of loathing, disgust, hatred and mostly fear.

Peter viewed the scene with equanimity.

"The world has cracked," he said calmly.

"What are those things?" Chris asked, keeping her voice steady.

"They would appear to be denizens of the underworld. It seems that you two are now in mortal danger. Does death frighten you?"

"It can be a little inconvenient. Will you let us past the barrier now?"

"I haven't decided yet."

Chris could see Selena making a supreme effort to control her emotions as she spoke.

"Peter, we would be happy to comply with any of your requirements. We must reach a friend who is trapped in this universe with a very limited time to live. Will you help, please?"

Her words were spattered with cracking noises from the trees. The things were coming. Peter was silent for several seconds, gazing up at the sky with a smile on his face. Chris already knew there was something incorrect about him. His invisible barrier represented superhuman powers, something that the referee had described as not permissible.

"Run for the river," shouted Selena.

As Chris sprinted after her down the path, she glanced back to see something unnatural appearing through the trees. She increased her pace to join Selena and they quickly emerged on the grassy bank.

"What now?"

"We'll try to get past the wall on the bank. Maybe we can climb over or find a gap."

They ran across and felt the invisible barrier. It was as solid as on the water and stretched up further than they could reach. Selena was just about to climb on Chris's shoulders when Peter emerged from the trees. Then they saw the things come out behind him. They had no features that could be recognised but carried an aura of voraciousness, a desire to kill, desecrate and devour.

Chris felt a nagging nausea building up as she watched them. But they didn't come beyond the edge of the trees. Peter lifted his palms on outstretched arms for a second and they stopped. Then he began to change. His outline became hazy and started to reform. A few seconds later she was again looking at the hairy, muscular figure she had seen before. His black mane of hair cascading over his shoulders, his eyes dark and merciless. A callous grin spread slowly over his rugged face.

"I have decided you will not pass," he announced in a hoarse, deep voice bursting with implicit hostility.

"I assume your name is not Peter. You are Hades," Selena responded with no fear in her voice.

The man gestured to the things clustered behind him.

"My companions are desperate for blood. Before satiating their thirst, they will ravish your bodies until you are pleading for death to release you."

The creatures began to edge forward, unspeakable relish exuding from their foul bodies.

"They will not touch these women."

The words came pure and clear through the scene, like a crystal in a muddy pool. Athena was running up the bank, still in her amber and green suit and wielding the golden sword.

"Go to the boat now," she shouted.

Selena was reluctant, her eyes fixed on Athena but Chris grabbed her arm and half dragged her to the craft. As they jumped on board, she saw the woman move to the barrier and swing the sword. The crack of the impact shook the ground and suddenly the wall was visible, shattering and collapsing. Through each crack, gushed a yellow-green fluid, discolouring the river water as it dribbled out. Suddenly, it was gone and Chris told the craft to move forward at full speed. Only then did she join Selena to look back to the bank. The things had emerged from the forest and now surrounded Athena who clasped her sword in readiness. Just as the first of the loathsome creatures leapt forward, the river turned sharply and the view was lost.

"I wanted to stay," Selena murmured.

"Forget it. It's between the gods. We just need to get to Jerome Jones and leave this universe."

Selena turned away and all conversation ceased for 15 minutes as the craft continued down the centre of the seemingly unending river. They passed several more settlements but the people made no attempt to contact them. Fortunately,

Chris could see no further signs of any cracks or splits in the fabric of the world. Then, far ahead, she glimpsed a golden tower and called to Selena.

"That could be the river's end," she said.

"We'll soon see. Sorry about earlier."

Chris was pleased but didn't want to show it. An apology from Selena was rare.

"It doesn't matter. I'm just concentrating on Jerome now. Look ahead. I knew it."

She had seen a welcome sight. The river had straightened and the golden structure was fully in view. The best news was that it stretched across the whole world, from wall-to-wall. The river's end, at last.

The building was magnificent. A solid gold palace with towers, windows, balconies and turrets. The sun glanced brilliantly off the walls and sparkled in the eyes. A large number of people were visible in front of it. Men in trousers and loose shirts and women in knee length dresses. The garments were plain and simple, very much 16th century peasant wear.

The river finished in a stone built docking area, presumably flowing under the ground from that point. A few boats were already moored there and Chris guided their craft to a vacant space, before following Selena onto the dock. The palace was set back about 80 metres from the river's end and towered some five storeys high. Everything was golden, the walls, embellishments and ornamentation and right in the centre were double doors. A stone paved road led to it from the dock area.

"Follow the brick road to the yellow," remarked Selena and began to walk forward. The inhabitants strangely paid little attention to them. They scurried busily, many carrying boxes, sacks or bags. Some talked in groups and others simply walked quickly and intently.

"Franco should be here somewhere," Chris said as they approached the golden door.

"He'll be inside, probably with a bunch of women but he should know where the Gate is by now," responded Selena.

No guards at the door but also no obvious means of requesting entry. The golden panels were etched with a series of delicate patterns. Selena kicked it. The dull thud of the impact was barely audible and Chris was surprised when the door opened. She was more amazed at the sight of the figure that opened it.

A girl with bright blonde hair, tight dark leather-look jeans and a loose waistcoat in shiny black, that hung loosely over her chest. Panda eye makeup and bright crimson lipstick completed the effect.

"You are welcome here," the girl said in a soft voice. She stood back, beckoning them to enter.

Chris had expected the interior to be impressive and certainly wasn't disappointed. She stood in a square entrance hall, dominated by an ornate stairway facing the door. The walls and ceiling were a mix of gold and silver panels, each encrusted with rubies, emeralds, diamonds and other precious stones. The floor was composed of slabs of solid gold. A row of jewelled chests stood against each side wall.

A group of five women were slowly descending the staircase. Their clothing and makeup was identical to the girl at the door and their long hair was dyed a variety of colours. The one in the centre moved ahead of her companions and Chris saw she was wearing a gold tiara, decorated with gigantic rubies sitting amid impeccably groomed long black hair.

"I am Governor Moistlips of the Celibut Sect. You are welcome here while you abide by our laws."

"I am Selena and this is Chris. We are looking for a man called Franco."

As she described his appearance, the women began to look at each other with concern.

"This person is undergoing his penal servitude. You may not contact him either physically or verbally until his penance is complete."

"What was his crime?" Chris asked but already had a good idea.

The woman's face contorted with disgust.

"He made tactile contact with the lower extremity of one of the acolytes."

"He touched her foot?"

Little squeals of horror from the women.

"That word is not permitted here. You are forgiven this first blemish but you will serve penance if it is repeated. To stay here you must wear the garments of the Sect and comply totally with our regulations."

"Okay, where do we get the clothes?" Selena asked impatiently.

Moistlips motioned to her escorts and the four women led them to a room at the end of the hallway. It was full of racks of the black garments. Chris confirmed it wasn't real leather but an excellent imitation. She carefully selected loose fitting jeans and the largest jacket she could wear, very conscious that it was the only covering for her chest. There was no changing room and she moved to the end of the racks for some privacy but noticed that Selena was already dressing in open view. As she stripped off, Chris saw two of the escorts walking towards her.

"I'm changing."

"Yes," one responded with a puzzled expression.

Chris sighed, turned her back and quickly pulled on the new outfit and joined Selena. One of the escorts, a tall girl with long brown hair, stepped forward.

"I am Mistress Slipthigh. You will be in the Emerald Boudoir. Please follow," she said.

The girls led them up the stairs and turned right at the top. Another gold, silver and precious stone corridor. They opened the third golden door on the left. Eight large single beds with ornate silk sheets and covers. One was occupied. A naked girl curled up on top, sleeping peacefully. The room was liberally decorated with emeralds. Huge green stones that glowed and shimmered across the walls, headboards and on gold chests beside each bed.

"You will occupy these," Slipthigh said, pointing to the two beds nearest the door.

Chris began to move into the room but the woman stopped her.

"First you must undertake your duties. I will show you," she announced.

They were escorted down a flight of silver stairs and reached a communal shower room. The whole interior was lined with platinum with a layer of soft, transparent material over the floor. A couple of girls were showering but Chris paid them little attention. She stared with horror at a man in the corner holding a pile of folded towels. He wore a red waistcoat and nothing else.

Slipthigh followed her eyes.

"That one is serving penance. Therefore, he must wear the red coat."

"His penance is to stand here nearly naked?" Chris asked.

"It is an ordeal he has to pass. There must be no sign of arousal."

"And if he fails?"

"He's executed, of course. Decapitation by axe conducted by the Governor herself."

"You kill him?"

"What else?"

Chris looked again at the man. He was studying the ceiling and desperately avoiding looking at the naked females showering in front of him. Then she thought of Franco.

"What of the man we were with? He is also serving penance."

"His duty is night servant in the Ruby Boudoir. He has only seven more nights to complete his ordeal."

"What about the women who break the rules? How are they tested?"

"Oh, we just stab hot pokers into their epidermis. If they display any pain, we execute them."

"Right."

"Your duty is to clean this room."

The four girls left and Selena helped Chris in the task. It was already virtually spotless and they completed the job in a few minutes. Chris wasn't concerned about Franco. Now he was recovering his godlike powers, he could look after himself. But they had to find him to get through the Gate.

"Ruby Boudoir?" asked Chris.

"Yes and we can look for the Gate on the way," Selena replied.

They left the room and climbed the silver stairs. Chris noticed that most of the doors they passed were decorated with diamonds that formed a name. They continued to be unusual. Mistress Softlimbs, Mistress Sweetbosom and more like that.

"I remember there was no name on the Emerald Boudoir so the Ruby should be the same," Chris remarked.

They followed countless golden corridors passing several uniformed women and then one approached them. A short girl with dyed blonde hair.

"The Assembly is in two minutes. You need to hurry. Come with me, quickly."

She bustled to a door at the end and they entered a large hall, festooned with gold, silver and gems. Rich purple velvet hangings covered the walls with a gold stage at the front. Governor Moistlips stood alone on the stage, completely naked. So were all the women gathered in front of her. Each had their clothing in a neat pile on the floor at their feet. The blonde quickly stripped and Selena followed. Chris reluctantly pulled off her jacket and jeans, and then stood next to Selena at the back.

Moistlips raised her arms.

"This is the eighth Assembly and the mighty god Olivia comes to us once more. We renew again our unfailing obedience to her."

She turned her back and knelt. The audience all went to their knees, heads lowered and Chris followed but kept her eyes on the stage. Something was materialising there. A tall woman with flowing brown hair in a long, diaphanous pale blue dress. The form crystallised and the girls began to chant together.

"We obey. We give our lives, our bodies and our spirit to you."

The woman smiled serenely then descended from the stage. She lightly touched two other girls on the head as she passed and spoke in a soft but commanding voice.

"You are chosen today. The rest must leave immediately and seal this room until these two leave. Thus will you serve me and bring fortune and spiritual wealth to your Sect."

Moistlips picked up her clothes and walked out of the door, and the rest of the gathering began to follow. All except the two girls who remained kneeling. Chris rose to her feet and looked at Selena.

"Back to the search?"

"No. Dress quickly and come with me."

They pulled on their clothing and Chris accompanied her into the throng around the doorway. As they reached it, Selena pushed her to the side, behind one of the huge purple hangings. There was just sufficient space to stand between the velvet cloth and the wall and Chris pulled the edge around to mask them from the departing crowd. Finally, the last girl left and the door closed. All was silent for a few seconds and then Olivia spoke.

"Come to me to receive your bonding and obey everything I say."

A pause before she spoke again but this time it was in a new voice.

"You will forget everything that happens from now until you leave the room."

Franco's voice. Chris looked at Selena. She must have known already.

They waited for another few seconds and then Selena nodded. Chris moved out from behind the curtain. Franco was looking directly at her, a broad smile on his face. He was on the stage with the two girls standing to one side.

"If you'd waited any longer, I'd have had to call you," he said, his now powerful voice and golden eyes dominating the room.

"Still playing games?" Selena responded coolly.

"I was occupying myself until you arrived. This ridiculous Olivia doesn't exist, of course and they had quite a shock when I first appeared at one of these Assemblies."

"But they said you were doing penance. How can you accomplish both?" exclaimed Chris.

"When I first came, that frigid Governor tried to resist my advances and it suited me to be sentenced to penance. I've simply implanted the idea in their brains that I am dutifully standing in the showers or bedroom but I actually spend most of my time here."

"With your worshippers?"

"Of course. These poor girls really need some enjoyment in their puritan existence. I'm freeing them from their restraints and I can assure you, they very much appreciate it."

Selena wasn't smiling.

"We have to leave now. Time is critical to save Jerome Jones. Have you found the Gate?"

"Yes but I'm not sure I want to leave. This is fun."

"Then I'll have to kill you."

"You can't do that."

Selena glared at him and pulled out a knife.

"Just watch me."

She climbed onto the stage and moved towards him. Then she stopped. Franco's eyes were glowing brighter now. He smiled brilliantly and the knife fell from her hands. She pulled off the waistcoat and shiny black jeans and stood naked in front of him. Chris started forward but his gaze flicked briefly to her and she couldn't move. Not a muscle obeyed her and she could only stand and watch.

Selena went to her knees but as she reached her arms out towards him, there was a sudden crash as the door flew open. Chris felt movement returning and turned to see Athena striding past her to the stage.

"You sicken me, Franco. I should give you to Hades. He plans to castrate you before imprisonment in the underworld."

Franco looked fearful in her presence and began to mumble an explanation but she cut him short.

"You will go through the Gate now with these women. I will defend it for a time against Hades and his minions but you must leave immediately."

Franco nodded obediently. Chris noticed that Selena had already dressed and her gaze was now fixed on Athena although the god seemed to avoid her eyes.

"Good luck," she said simply and then reached out and briefly clasped Selena's hand before hastening from the room, sword raised.

"Come with me," called Franco and Chris shepherded Selena to follow him.

As he led them to the back of the stage area, Chris noticed the smile on her companions face but said nothing. They came to an apparently solid gold wall. Franco touched one of the ruby rose embellishments three times and a door opened. No gold, silver or jewels in the room beyond. Only velvet. The walls, ceilings and even the floor were covered with plush, soft mauve velvet. The same material was on the only item of furniture, an over large bed.

"I assume this is where you bonded with your followers," Selena remarked sourly.

He grinned. "It's very comfortable. The Gate is in the next room."

On the far wall was a single door also covered with padded velvet. Franco strode forward and opened it. Then slammed it shut quickly. But Chris had already seen inside. Hades was there, facing the door and resting the point of his sword on the floor. The room shook and the fabric on the walls began to rip apart. Selena grabbed Franco as he ran back towards the stage.

"We must go through. I'll distract him while you to get to the Gate. Then I'll join you. Hide your face with this, Franco."

She ripped off the bed cover and handed to him. He pulled it over his head and Chris gripped his arm. Then Selena opened the door.

Unlike the rest of the building, the chamber was simply finished in white paint with plain stone flooring. It was narrow but long and at the far end, Chris could see the Gate. A metal plate in the floor, embossed with the question mark. The massive figure of Hades barred their path.

Selena pushed Chris and Franco to the right hand wall and then walked towards the giant figure.

"We need to pass to rescue our friend. We have no wish to fight," she said.

The man's eyes turned to her and tracked up and down her body, like a customer checking a streetwalker. For a moment there was absolute silence. Then he swung his sword towards her neck. She crouched under the blade and it struck the wall, shattering splinters of white paint and stone. Fortunately, the textured finish of the walls would allow simple repair of the mark using an epoxy based filler, preferably in a white or pale colour. After careful repainting, it would be virtually impossible to distinguish that any impact had occurred.

Chris saw that Selena was trying to draw Hades away from them by moving against the far wall. He edged towards her and now almost had his back to Chris who grasped Franco's arm, ready to run for the Gate. Hades swung his sword again in a downward arc but again Selena was too quick. She dodged to her left and was now almost in the corner, next to the entrance door.

The massive man began to attack with fury, his heavy sword swinging unceasingly. Chris understood Selena's tactics. Fighting him was a sure way to lose, his strength would be too great. Instead, she used her main advantage, mobility. Constantly moving, feinting to one side or the other. The sword rang incessantly on the walls and floor as his blows missed her. The strategy was short-term. At some point he would connect and then she would be finished. Now was the time.

Chris dashed to the Gate, pulling Franco behind her. As he moved, the cover fell from him and he nearly tripped on it as they reached the edge of the metal plate. Chris lifted him by the arm and looked back. Selena was still standing against the entrance wall with a wide grin on her face.

Hades swung another mighty blow. Chris saw the thick muscles of his back straining to put every ounce into it. Selena dropped into a low crouch then sprang forward directly between his legs. She rolled once then was up and running to the Gate.

The man turned but too slowly. Then he saw Franco and his eyes changed. The pupils expanded and turned bright crimson. He gave a roar of fury and hurled the great sword at Franco's heart. Just as it left his hand, Chris felt Selena grab her and heard Franco scream.

Then it all went white.

16

The whiteness seemed to last a long time. It shrouded Chris like a shroud, numbing all the senses. She thought of Franco. Had the sword of Hades hit him before the whiteness came? Then she considered a more serious possibility. Perhaps the universe had finally collapsed and she would be trapped here forever. There was no sign of a gatekeeper and time continued to pass.

She breathed with relief when the blank white began to dissipate and found herself on a long, empty stairway. No sign of Selena, Franco or anyone else. The stairs were built of stone and covered with a thick layer of dust, as if unused for a very long time. Just above her, at the top, she could see a large wooden door while the foot of the stairs was lost in the semi darkness below. She mentally flipped a coin and ascended. No windows, just solid stone walls like the inside of a castle. At the top, she came to a flat area with plain wood double doors to her left. There was no lock but the doors were covered with grime and the iron handle looked as if it had never been used. It took a deal of effort to force it to turn gradually with a loud grating noise. She expected more filthy stone walls inside but found something entirely different.

The décor was ultramodern. A blank wall in front and to her right while on her left was a corridor. Smooth walls and ceiling, finished in a soft pastel blue with neon lights and a row of scenic pictures stretching as far as she could see. She walked forward and found another corridor leading off to her left, same decoration and just as long. The only thing missing were doors. One other noteworthy point was that all the side walls sloped inwards, as if she was in a massive attic room. She decided to follow the first corridor and, after a few minutes, found another passage on her left. This one was quite short and beyond the end, she could see people.

As Chris moved forward, the view clarified. It seemed to be a massive open plan office. A maze of partitions, about shoulder height and she could see desks with computer monitors inside each. Blue and grey suited women scurried about with folders in hand and there was a constant hum of conversation. Chris was suddenly acutely aware of her outfit, the shiny black waistcoat and jeans from the last world. That was obviously unsuitable here and she looked around to see a clothes shop, tucked away in the corner to her left. Inside, she found the shop was devoid of people but jammed full of clothes that were virtually all the same, grey or blue jackets and matching trousers with cream or white tops. Only a small rack at the rear with men's clothing.

Chris quickly changed into simple white underwear and then chose a cream top and grey suit. She emerged, more confident now. On her left was a row of three large houses and beyond them, what looked like a restaurant. She strolled towards it.

It was a smart, modern establishment and full of women eating from plastic packets. No counter, just shelving along one wall that was divided into three sections. The first was clearly labelled 'Chicken and Tuna', the second, 'Tuna and Chicken' and both of these were piled high with what appeared to be identical sandwiches in plastic wraps. The third section was labelled 'Sugar, with added Water and Orange Flavour' over a stack of plastic bottles.

The women clustered round gleaming stainless steel tables with a pile of the plastic packets in the centre. They were eating ravenously. No refinement here, they simply shovelled the food down as quickly as possible. At the same time they chattered constantly, bits of food falling from their mouths as they babbled. Occasionally, they gulped down some of the orange coloured liquid.

As Chris watched, two women on opposite sides of the table grabbed the same packet from the heap.

"That's mine," one screamed, a thickset girl with shiny, dyed blonde hair.

"I had it first," responded the other, also chunky but with brown hair.

A tugging match ensued, won eventually by the blonde. The other girl began a loud conversation with those next to her.

"She's a greedy bitch. Those were my sandwiches."

The adjacent women murmured agreement.

"She had mine the other day," said one.

"I always said she was a selfish cow," added another.

The bitching continued while the blonde simultaneously wolfed down the sandwiches, grinned and gabbled to her group of cronies.

Chris looked on with disgust. There was enough food to feed all of them 20 times over and the infantile argument was beyond her patience. The women had completely ignored her and she now had no desire to communicate with them.

She left the restaurant and listened in to a conversation between two women in one of the work cubicles.

"... and he said, 'would you mind taking the printout to Anne'. Those were his exact words," the first confided in a secretive but very audible tone.

"Did he really?"

"Yes, I promise you."

"He didn't say will you mind?"

"No, he said would."

"And you're sure he didn't say carrying, he actually said taking?"

"Yes, taking was the word. To Anne, he said. Can you imagine how I felt?"

"Did you say anything?"

"No. I was too shocked."

"Well, I would have. Just wait until he asks me, then I'll say something. It makes you wonder about him."

"He seems to behave normally but you can't tell what's going on underneath."

"I'd rather not think about underneath. I've heard that some men have perversions, you know."

"My lord, I never thought about that. Taking could mean something different, couldn't it?"

"I'll warn everyone to be very careful. We should never go to him alone."

"That's a great idea. His sort needs to be watched carefully. I'm really stressed out now."

"Why don't you come to my place tonight? Mr Soundcard will be in and three of the other girls are coming."

"He's nice, always slapping my bottom when I walk past him. Would five girls be too many?"

"No, I'm sure he will be able to manage."

Chris was inspired by the banality of this conversation. Inspired to leave the area and return to the stairway. She descended quickly, passing the point where she had arrived and then continued down for some time, eventually reaching a double wooden door at the foot of the stairs.

She was more confident now, dressed in the clothing of a resident and opened it without hesitation. But she wasn't ready for the blue sky, bright sunlight and the scene in front of her. Farmland. An expanse of fields with vegetables growing and perhaps a hundred people busily tending the crops. Their clothing and demeanour were totally different to the office above. They wore 17th century countryside outfits. Long skirts and thick blouses for the women and simple rough cloth garments for the men

Right at the centre was a statue, carved from a thick tree trunk. The figure was of a small, heavy man with a square face. His eyes were made of large, bright green stones, emeralds perhaps. Piles of flowers, some in wreaths lay around the base.

Chris was still absorbing the scene when a loud gong sounded. Everyone stopped their work and immediately began to remove their clothes. She noticed that only about a quarter of them were men. When all were naked, they joined hands to form three circles around the statue and began to revolve slowly with the participants dancing in abandoned fashion while shouting with delight. The women all looked young but the men were a variety of ages, mostly middle. Their random cries developed into a chant and everyone joined in. The words gradually clarified.

"We thank the Green Man, we thank, we thank. Bestower of fertility, we thank, we thank."

The circles moved faster and faster until they were running at full speed. Then another gong and all the people fell to the earth. The sweating, gasping figures were temporarily immobile from exhaustion but didn't stay like that. After a few seconds, a communal orgy began. No one appeared to be selective as to sex, they just mingled together into twos, threes or fours in a writhing mass of flesh. The bodies became caked in grime and mud as they squirmed amongst the carrots and onions and the air was filled with the squeals of women and hoarse shouts of men. It lasted maybe 30 minutes and then a torrential rain began and the people rose to their feet and allowed the heavy shower to cleanse the earth from their bodies. Another few minutes and the sun returned, hotter than before. They were quickly dried and moved to their clothing, dressing as before. Then they returned to their work as if nothing had occurred.

Hot baths existed in prehistoric times, even before the discovery of fire. The bath was, of course, constructed of wood as this was well before the age of aluminium. It was filled with water and the tribal chief sat inside while all his subjects rubbed their bodies vigorously against the sides to increase the water temperature. A later development was the first shower, where the bath was placed in a tree with 20 holes bored in the base. Six of the tribe sat in the tree with fingers over the holes while the water was poured in. The leader stood underneath and adjusted the flow by calling out the number of fingers to be released. After Kings were invented, this became known as a reign shower.

Chris speculated that the ritual had been copied from some rural tradition on earth from hundreds of years ago. She was about to continue her exploration when a voice came from behind her.

"You did not join the ceremony."

The speaker was a tall, Amazonian woman with short cropped black hair. She wasn't dressed in the long skirt outfit. Instead, she wore brief leather armour with a fringe of wide leather straps hanging from her waist to mid thigh.

"I'm a visitor."

The woman's eyes sharpened and she drew a short sword.

"You look and sound like a Tekkie."

"Sorry, I don't understand."

"You will be questioned. Now move."

She jabbed the sword and directed Chris to follow the boundary of the cultivated area. As they walked, Chris could see that the edge was a tall stone wall and, above this, a screen of blue sky. It looked as if this two-storey structure comprised the whole world.

They reached a building and entered a large room with a row of barred cells on the far side. Several women in the leather armour crowded around them.

"Who's that you've got, Glenda?" asked one.

"Says she's a visitor," the amazon replied.

"Bring her here," called a voice from the back. The crowd parted and Chris was prodded towards a heavy, muscular woman with short brown hair who sat at a desk.

"I am Commander Polly of the People's Forces. You will answer my questions truthfully or be summarily executed."

Chris nodded. She felt she could handle this.

"First, your name."

"Chris."

"How did you get here?"

"Through the Gate."

"Gate? What Gate?"

"I came from another world."

The women began laughing until Polly stopped them with a fist to the desk.

"You are being flippant. Cut off her arm, Glenda."

"No, wait. I was sent by the Green Man."

A reverent silence.

"You came from him unannounced?"

"I did."

It felt like the correct response.

"Why have you come?"

"He has given me a task. To find a question mark. It is probably somewhere on the floor, perhaps set in a metal or stone square."

Another silence.

Chris saw the women murmuring negatives.

"We have never seen this," Polly responded but her attitude had changed. Much more conciliatory.

"Does he require us to assist you?"

"Yes, if necessary. There must be no delay."

"I will organise a team."

"No. Just one may accompany me. I choose Glenda."

Chris didn't want to be slowed by a large group and Glenda looked more than capable.

"Very well. You will leave now, Officer Glenda."

The tall woman nodded and then escorted Chris out of the building.

When they were clear of the guard post, Chris paused.

"We need to stop and talk. The Green Man did not give me details of his domain. It is part of my task to discover them. First you must tell me about your civilisation and remember I'm a visitor."

"You know nothing?"

"Nothing."

Glenda glowed with pride.

"We are the Righteous who live in harmony with nature. We number 81 citizens in total, 60 women and 21 men. After the Rift, we formed the People's Army with a force of seven and I am privileged to have been chosen as a member. The central area of fields is called the farm and the buildings on each side are the East and West villages."

"Who owns the houses?"

"They are called cottages. There are owned by all of us, the community. There are 16 cottages, each with five residents."

"That leaves someone without a house."

"One of the People's Army is always on patrol."

"So husbands and wives don't live together?"

Glenda grimaced.

"Absolutely not. A woman's body is a temple that the men must respect and not invade. We are the Righteous, not decadent Tekkie whores."

"Tekkie? What does that mean?"

"The disgusting creatures from the hell above us, who live in eternal debauchery. They are the garbage of existence."

"You are talking of the office people up the stairs?"

"Office? I don't understand. Have you seen these vermin?"

"Yes, I visited them first. That's where I got this outfit."

"Those are Tekkie clothes? Perhaps they deceived you, as I know they normally prance around in flimsy undergarments."

"Have you ever seen them?"

"Of course not. No one has had sight of the hellspawn for 230 years, since the time of the Rift."

"What was this Rift?"

"Naturally, you wouldn't know. One of their lascivious males named Smith, was betrothed to Alice, a sweet virgin of our community. He tricked her into allowing him to enter her temple but immediately afterwards, began an association with one of his Tekkie people, a brazen trollop called Angela. Our leaders met and decided to break off all relations with the corrupt Tekkies. Since then we have had no communication at all and from that time, the women here have dedicated their minds and bodies to our benign lord, the Green Man. We now reside in perfect purity and our bodies are forever chaste."

"But I saw the orgy on the farm."

Glenda looked puzzled.

"It is not an orgy, it's a ritual. Our twice-weekly celebration of thanks to the Green Man and all the bountiful fertility he bestows on our crops. Of course I've participated in hundreds of them but I am proud to be a virgin."

Chris didn't pursue the question.

"Why do you have an army?"

"We know that the Tekkies fervently desire to annihilate us and rule our land with their obscene laws. The People's Army was formed as our defence."

"Are there no men in your forces?"

Glenda looked contemptuous.

"Men are weak. They lack the courage and ability to execute our enemies."

"Well, I am going back to the Tekkie place to find the question mark and also one or maybe two companions who must be there somewhere."

"Then I shall accompany you and with the Green Man's blessing, I will have the chance to kill some of the creatures."

"We're not going to kill anyone, except in self-defence."

"Yes, self-defence of course," Glenda responded but Chris noticed an unwelcome gleam in her eyes. She knew the amazon could be very useful if it came to a fight but would have to be careful to keep her restrained.

"You can come but I am the leader. My instructions must be observed. The first job is to find you suitable clothing."

"I will not wear garments of a courtesan."

Chris looked at the acres of flesh exposed by her brief leather armour.

"No, you will have an outfit just like mine."

She led Glenda to the stairway and they ascended rapidly, the muscular woman easily keeping pace with her. At the top, Chris told her to wait and moved quickly into the central area to reach the clothes shop. She picked out the largest sizes she could find and was just leaving when she heard a rusty voice.

"Routine security check. Provide your name."

She turned to see a woman made of wire. Her body was composed of a mass of different coloured strands and her face made up of two bunches of blue cables for the eyes and a red one around an orifice representing the mouth.

"Routine security. Your name," the wire woman repeated.

"Chris. Chris Darmant."

Chris answered instinctively but then realised that her response could be compared to a population database. She prepared to run as the figure hummed in cogitation. Then, with a faint buzz, it raised a hand.

"Thank you. Have a pleasant day," it said.

Chris returned to Glenda and waited while she changed into a grey suit.

"My legs are covered. That will displease the Green Man," she grumbled.

"He set this task and I'm sure he'll understand," Chris reassured.

As they entered the passageway, Glenda began to stumble on her heels.

"I'm unused to these streetwalker stilts," she complained.

"You need to take shorter strides."

Fortunately the heels were not too high and Glenda managed to achieve an uncomfortable, wobbly walk.

When they reached the edge of the office area, Chris saw her stiffening with anticipation.

"So these are the flaunting sluts. May my sword be granted power today."

168

"You haven't brought your sword?"

"Of course. It is hidden inside the legging of this costume."

Chris sighed. She wanted them to merge into the background, not begin a war. Her plan was to get an idea of the layout and then find Selena and the Gate, plus Franco, if he still lived. The layout proved easy to discover. An exact square and the perimeter was the passageway where she had first entered, that ran around the four sides. Inside this were rows of buildings, also arranged in a square shape and they surrounded the massive office area in the middle. A corridor to the outer passageway ran between the houses on each side of the square. Chris also noticed a large brick built structure in the very centre of the office section.

The buildings comprised three large houses on each side of the square. In the corners were a clothes shop, the eating place, a general store and what appeared to be a guard building. The last was the most interesting. It apparently housed a vast number of the wire women who were constantly entering and leaving on patrol.

"Spawn of the devil," Glenda hissed as she saw them.

"They're a team of robot guards," responded Chris.

"Robot? Is that your word for those inhuman excrescences? These people have descended to unspeakable depths."

Up to now, they hadn't been approached or even received any quizzical looks from the inhabitants. That concerned Chris. Surely someone would have noticed strangers in a small population. There was no point in dwelling on that, she had two places to investigate. The houses and the office area, particularly the building at the centre. Houses first.

She walked to the nearest with Glenda close behind and saw a name above the doorway. Peter Byte. Chris pressed the bell and the door opened to reveal the blonde girl she had seen arguing in the eating-place earlier. But now she was wearing a koala bear costume. Chris heard a grunt from Glenda and blocked the entrance with her body.

"We have come to visit Mr Byte."

"Yes, of course."

The girl smiled prettily as she led them to a lounge.

"Nice outfit," Chris remarked enquiringly.

The blonde responded with a beam of satisfaction.

"It's my best. It's so soft and fluffy and such sweetie colours. I've got lots of spare costumes if you'd like one?"

"No thanks."

"I know, what about the cutie bunny outfit? That would be just you. Absolutely sweet floppy long ears."

"No, I'm fine."

The girl's expression turned cooler.

"As you wish. I'll see if Peter is free."

As the girl left, Chris forcibly restrained Glenda who was already reaching into her trousers for the sword.

"A flaunting tart. She deserves to die," hissed the amazon.

"You're probably right but we're not going to attack anyone."

She pushed the tall woman on to a sofa and sat alongside. It was another two minutes before Peter Byte arrived. He looked to be in his mid-30s with prematurely grey, grizzled hair matched by a weathered, grizzled face. His voice was sombre, like an undertaker.

"Two Greenies from the poor little slum below us. You are Chris but we don't know this big girlie's name."

Glenda began to rise from the seat.

"You will never make me tell you, hell spawn. Torture me if you will but I will not talk."

Byte shrugged.

"I don't really care. You are very simple people and one is much the same as another."

Even his morose voice began to sound grizzled.

"You're saying you know where we're from?" asked Chris.

"Of course. We have watched you on our video cameras since the moment you entered the Complex. You then left and returned with this lumbering creature."

"You are the filth of the universe. Prepare for death," Glenda shouted, her eyes burning death. She reached inside her trousers and pulled out the sword so quickly that she sliced through the material.

"Don't be as stupid as you look," Byte remarked laconically, seemingly unmoved by the threat. He produced a palm sized plastic box and pressed a button.

The sword began to wobble and then drooped dramatically. Glenda swung it towards the man's body but it impacted with all the power of cotton wool. The amazon looked aghast at the limp blade and cast it aside with contempt.

"As a result of your lack of intelligence, you are now intending an assault with your hands in an attempt to throttle me," the man said casually.

That was exactly Glenda's plan and although his words made her hesitate for a second, she tried to carry it out. As she reached for him, he gripped her wrists and pushed with a force that made her stagger backwards into the sofa.

"Please don't try again, it's so tedious."

Chris grabbed Glenda's arm to prevent her continuing the fight and turned to the man.

"You have a gadget that softens metal and have superhuman strength. You must be a god."

He sighed.

"God? Not at all. The gadget, as you call it, is an Electronic Sublinear Molecular Reconstructer, we call it Electronsublinmolecrecon for short. There are different versions that can modify almost any material into another and this one is set for metal. My strength is enhanced by subcutaneous steel fibres that increased my muscular powers. I'm sure you girlies find these words completely incomprehensible."

"But I can't understand why you seem so completely unsurprised by our visit. You have had no contact with the people below for 230 years," Chris observed.

He gave a listless smile.

"We have made regular journeys to your barbaric land right through that time. One or two of us go every week, only the men, of course. You pathetic people are so easily convinced by someone dressed in peasant clothes and naturally, none of you have the intelligence to notice a stranger. I have been myself on many occasions and even participated in the immoral degeneracy of your little Green Man orgy."

Who is the Green Man? The tedious mainstream presumption involves origins in Roman, Pagan, Celtic and other similar concepts. Much more believable is the theory that he is actually the spouse of Gaia, the earth goddess. Every night, he transforms into a tree and thrusts his roots deep into Gaia's fertile, moist, receptive body. This also explains 'earth tremors' and the regular sighting of 'little green men'. It's strange how the most obvious explanations are so frequently dismissed by the scientific establishment.

Glenda strained forward and Chris held her back before speaking again.

"So tell me about this civilisation of yours."

"With your small brains, it will be hard for you to understand. We are the next level of development, a considerable stage up from you simple creatures. We have very advanced technology. That means complicated machines to you girlies. For example, we followed your progress on concealed video cameras and our

Atarons, or mechanical people to you, were also monitoring you. It is a few years since others of your race last visited when two females of your tiny People's Army attempted a suicide attack."

"That's a lie. None of us have come to this abyss of damnation since the Rift," Glenda cried.

"We found out that your stupid community believed that they had been taken by the Green Man as a sacrifice."

"What happened to these two?" asked Chris.

"Oh, we treated them well. They were given to our girls as house pets. We provided a nice wooden box for them to sleep in and placed an eating trough on the ground in front. Of course, after about a year, the girls became bored with them so they were put down."

"You mean killed."

"No, no. We simply injected them and they were at peace within minutes. Naturally, the bodies were cremated."

Chris had one question nagging.

"If you're visiting below so regularly, why is the stairway covered with dust and cobwebs?"

"We constructed another route, a long time ago. Much faster and simpler."

"What's that?"

"No, you are too simple to comprehend it. I was telling you of our advanced culture. The citizens here are supremely happy and content. Each of we nine men possesses a house with up to eight female concubines in residence, the maximum allowed in our statutes. Women who have been unable to fulfil a man's requirements reside in the other three houses. As you would expect, I have the full complement of eight girlies in this house."

Chris was now wishing that Glenda's sword had remained erect and concealed her disgust with difficulty.

"The massive office in the centre? What is it for?"

"It is primarily a means of occupying the women during the day. We men do the important work in the central building and use the females for routine jobs and errands such as filing and entering data. They are also necessary for cooking, cleaning and sexual purposes."

Chris felt the dam burst.

"Do you know you are an obnoxious, self-centred little worm?"

"What big words for a simple little brain like yours. A little fireball, aren't you? My girls will certainly have fun taming your spirit."

Chris regained control and got smart again.

"They would be too powerful for us, even without their increased strength," she said resignedly.

He laughed.

"We don't waste the muscular enhancement on women. As you say, my eight concubines will be more than capable of handling you two little pets."

That was response Chris had been hoping for and half expecting. She gave a meaningful look to Glenda, hoping the big woman would understand.

"We have no choice. You're obviously superior to us and there's no point in resisting, is there Glenda?"

She gave the look again and the amazon seemed to comprehend, grunting in a fashion that could mean acceptance although her eyes were like bullets.

Chris was reasonably confident that the two of them could overcome his so-called concubines, as they didn't appear to be fighting sorts. Byte jabbed a bell push and six women entered, carrying shining silver coloured manacles and chains.

"Fit the restraints and take them away," he instructed.

Chris hadn't expected the fetters. She saw Glenda resisting violently until Byte rose with a deep sigh and held her down. She was stripped to her underwear and manacles were fitted to her wrists and just above each knee. A chain was run through all four and fixed with a padlock near her right leg. Then a wide leather collar was fitted around her neck. They turned to Chris and repeated the procedure. Her wrists and legs were now joined and the only way to move was to crawl on hands and knees. The girls then attached a stout leather cord to their collars.

"They're lovely. We must give them names," a girl squealed.

"The blonde one is cute. We can call her Fluffy," responded another.

"And this big creature looks mean. I know, we'll call her Gruffy. Fluffy and Gruffy."

They burst out laughing and Chris felt a tug at her neck. She crawled after the girls as they pulled her through the door and towards the back of the house. Passing through the kitchen, they went outside to a lawned rear garden.

"Have a little run, Fluffy," the girl called and released her lead. Chris looked across at Glenda who appeared ready to burst with anger.

"You stupid woman. I should never have agreed to your plan," she hissed.

"Quiet now, Gruffy. Don't be a naughty girl. Run and fetch this," called the girl, throwing a red ball down the garden.

Glenda scrambled around and tried to grab the girl's legs but she stepped back and lashed the lead violently across the amazon's rear.

"You are very bad. We'll have to discipline you."

The other girl joined her and began to strike her repeatedly across the rear with the leather leads.

"Come on," Chris called and crawled quickly to the end of the garden. Glenda followed reluctantly, two cheeks crimson with fury, the other two now bright red from the beating.

Chris spoke in a low tone.

"They can't hear us now. Listen, I have an idea."

"Your ideas are crazy. I'm going to kill all of those evil, scummy tarts."

"We don't need to kill, just knock them out. Let's pretend to sleep and they'll get bored. When there's just one or two left, we'll try and take them."

Glenda grunted but rolled on her side and closed her eyes. Chris did the same, ensuring she could see the girls through a narrow gap in her eyelids.

"Look, the little sweeties are tired. When they wake we'll start to teach them tricks. Salome and Debbie can watch them while we attend to the master's requirements," said one of the girls.

The blonde in the koala suit and a dark haired girl in a short pink dress murmured agreement and remained as the others departed into the house. Chris rolled over on her back and began to make little groaning noises.

"Ooh, little Fluffy's having a sexy dream," cooed the blonde.

Chris saw them coming forward and increased the volume and breathiness of the sounds until the koala costume was bending over her. She knew it wouldn't be easy. The chains forced her to move both legs and arms in the same direction. She rammed her feet into the koala's stomach, knocking the girl backwards. Then she kicked forward again, using the momentum to get to her feet. The girl lay below her and she fell forward, fists joined together. The girl's eyes opened wide just before the impact on her jaw. She was out cold.

Chris looked across at Glenda, ready to help. She didn't need any. The pink dress girl was lying still on the ground with the red mark of a chain on her neck.

"I enjoyed that. Let's get the others," the big woman said with relish.

"We need to get out of these chains first. Check the women to see if they have a key."

No key. They crawled quickly to the door and Chris quietly turned the handle and opened it a fraction. Through the crack she could see the back of a woman dressed like a fairy who was arranging vol-au-vents on a plate. Chris was about to turn to her companion when Glenda pushed past and made a massive hop to the girl. She jumped up and stretched the chain between her wrists around the girl's throat, pulling her backwards. Before Chris could reach them, the fairy was as still as a doughnut with wings crushed beneath her. Glenda looked crazed and exultant.

"That's three of the whores. Must get the rest now."

She started for the inner door.

"Wait, you mad woman. See if she's got the key first."

She did have the key, hanging from her rhinestone belt. Within seconds, Chris and Glenda were standing upright again.

"Ha! Now I can kill the other sluts," Glenda cried.

"Listen, no killing and I need one of them conscious to ask about the question mark and my companions."

A look of disappointment crossed Glenda's face. Then she brightened.

"I'll only use sufficient violence to disable them. Just what is necessary."

"Right."

Voices coming closer. Chris motioned to Glenda to hide behind the door and took cover under the table, ready to spring out. Four girls entered, three in dresses and one in a panda costume. Before Chris could move, Glenda was on the girls like a ravenous panther, late for Christmas lunch. She rained clubbing blows at their heads and stomachs, like a demented penguin and they fell to the floor like inebriated parakeets. Then she uttered a wild cackle.

"There must be weapons here," she said, looking round the kitchen.

Chris saw her eyes fix on a carving knife, lying on the table. She grabbed it and fought off Glenda's attempts to wrest it from her.

"Stop. Everyone will hear us."

"These perverts need to be killed. I must have their blood."

"No, you idiot. I wanted to ask questions. Use your brain. We're only dressed in underwear, so the first requirement is clothing. Our best chance is to wear the costumes. You take that panda outfit and I'll get the koala."

A curious pair stood in the kitchen five minutes later. The panda stood awkwardly, as if it had suffered an intimate injury while the koala had a saggy chest since Chris didn't have as much bosom as the previous wearer.

"I feel like a harlot in this thing," Glenda complained, the panda suit stretched to its limits by her muscular frame.

"Careful you don't burst the seams. Remember, I want the next one conscious. Byte said he had eight women and we've disposed of seven so far."

They crept into the hallway and up the stairs. Chris was moving across the upper hall when she heard a slight noise behind one of the doors. Putting a finger to her lips, she opened it slowly. A bedroom but the noise came from the adjoining bathroom. Glenda started forward but Chris pushed her back and edged the door open. A blonde in a bubble bath. She was lying back with eyes closed. Chris tiptoed to the side of the bath and held the knife in front of her face. Then she whispered softly.

"Don't move or I kill you."

The blonde's eyes opened wide and her body jerked in shock, splashing water over the side of the bath.

"You escaped. What you want?" she asked, her face quivering with fear.

"First, have you seen any strangers, a woman and perhaps, a man?"

"No, but strangers are often taken to the Hub."

"What is the Hub?"

"The building in the centre."

"Have you seen the sign of a question mark, probably on the floor somewhere?"

The girl shook her head.

"Not in any area I've been to. But, of course, no women are allowed in the men's rooms at the Hub."

"Right."

Now Chris had the problem of what to do with the girl.

"Find something to tie her with," she said to Glenda.

"That's a waste of time. Just give me the knife. It won't take a second."

"No. Get something now."

Glenda wandered off, muttering and Chris gestured for the girl to get out of the bath. She had just finished drying herself when the big panda returned, smiling. She held strips of cloth, obviously torn from a sheet.

"You can check if it's clear while I bind her," she said.

Chris left the bathroom and then stopped. Why was Glenda smiling? She dashed back in just as the amazon gripped the blonde by the shoulder and dropped the cloth to the floor to reveal a pair of scissors. Chris caught her arm as she slashed towards the girl's neck. Glenda whirled round, aiming a punch but Chris was too quick. Dodging the blow, she brought the edge of her hand down on the neck of the big woman who fell, senseless. The blonde stood naked and trembling with hands over her face. This time Chris didn't hesitate. She banged a fist into her jaw and caught her as she collapsed. Quickly binding the inert body, she used another strip of cloth as a gag. After carrying the woman to the bed, she pulled the covers up around her face.

She made a quick decision to leave Glenda and go to the Hub. The knife could easily be disabled by their boxes and she hid it in a drawer where hopefully, Glenda wouldn't find it. Now clothing was her first requirement. The wardrobe contained a number of the dour suits as well as a selection of costumes. She dressed rapidly in an office outfit, hurried silently down the stairs and out of the house.

17

As soon as Chris emerged, the ground shook violently, causing pieces of stone and brick to fall from the houses. Another tremor and then another. Chris moved away from the buildings and clung to one of the office dividers in the centre area. Cracks had appeared in the flooring and the walls of the houses. She knew that Hades must have arrived here, probably with his band of vicious creatures. Strangely, after stillness had returned, the people continued to work as if nothing had happened.

Chris began her journey to the Hub, finding it was like traversing a maze. The open plan cubicles were massed together with narrow passages between. She noted that many desks remained unoccupied and there were certainly substantially more than the population. It took nearly 15 minutes to follow the tortuous, winding aisles to the centre and she carefully studied the single storey building. There was a clear area around it with just the occasional girl entering or leaving. The walls had been made to look like red bricks but were actually metal. One metal door and Chris saw a keypad lock at the side.

She waited unobtrusively until the next girl approached the building. An elegant, raven haired woman with a sinuous walk and carrying a thick folder under her arm.

"Hello. Are you going to see Mr Byte?" Chris enquired with a smile.

"No, Mr Soundcard."

"Well, I have to see Mr Byte and I'm a little worried."

The girl paused with concern in her eyes.

"I heard about his strange, er… desires. All the girls are talking about it. We haven't met before, have we? I only moved here two weeks ago and don't know everyone yet. My name is Dolores, by the way."

Chris couldn't believe her good fortune. She had used the conversation she had overheard earlier and had no idea that Byte was the man in question. Also, she was lucky that Dolores was too new to recognise a stranger. The god of this world must have recently brought this woman from Earth to replace someone he was bored with.

"I'm Chris. Yes, I'm worried about seeing him alone. I've never been in here before. Can we go in together?"

"Yes, of course. I can come with you as far as reception."

Chris gave her a smile of gratitude then waited as she entered the door code and they entered a small entrance chamber. Steel walls with two doors, one marked 'Offices' and the other 'Research'.

"I always wonder what's behind that one. It's men only of course, so I'll never know," Dolores remarked, pointing at the second door.

Chris nodded but knew she would need to enter it at some point. They went through the Offices door. An elegant reception area staffed by three lingerie models. At least, they looked like that, dressed in black stockings, suspenders, high heels and lacy basques in crimson, black and purple. One sat behind the reception desk with two others standing behind her, eyeing the visitors carefully. They carried a small box on their hips, similar to the one Byte had used on Glenda's sword. Behind the desk was a corridor, presumably the men's offices.

Dolores checked in while Chris scanned the area for a question mark without success. The girl returned, whispering as she passed.

"Good luck. I must go to Mr Soundcard now."

Her heels click-clacked down the corridor.

"Who are you required to see?" asked the purple basqued receptionist.

"Mr Byte."

"There is no record of your summons here."

Chris noticed the other two girls edging forward, fingering the hip boxes.

"I have only just received the instruction."

The woman checked again.

"All requirements pass through this desk."

The two women moved forward and stood each side of Chris, pointing their boxes at her head.

This tranquil scene of capture and imminent execution was rudely interrupted. The door burst open and a grey flash shot across the area. Chris dodged to one side, just in time to see the heads of the two girls being crashed together and they collapsed to the floor. Purple basque had risen behind her desk but probably didn't expect the newcomer to leap across it and plant a foot directly in her face.

"Now I can cut the heads off these obscenities of the gutter," Glenda cried, producing a kitchen knife from the jacket of her grey suit.

"No. We need to get to the men in the research area," Chris shouted, pulling her back through the door and into the entrance chamber.

Glenda was wild eyed and fermenting nicely with savagery.

"Yes, the men. Those who forced these simple virgins into the ways of carnal deviation. Did you see the gaudy, flaunting garments those creatures were wearing, exposing their flesh for all to see?"

"The men are through that door but we need to know the entry code for the keypad lock."

"More devils' machinery that I don't comprehend. I forced one of the whores to open the outer door that had the same device. I will get another to show us the way through this one."

She went back to the reception and returned, pulling the crimson basque by her long brown hair. Then she slapped her face three times.

"Wake, you slut," she shouted.

The girl's eyes blinked open.

"What is happening," she mumbled.

"Open that door. Now," Glenda shouted in her ear, waving the knife.

"I can't. Only the men know the code."

Glenda gave a groan of annoyance and slammed her fist into the girl's jaw. She fell in a fleshy, lacy heap.

Just at that moment, the floor shook violently with a massive tremor that rocked the building. The floor bowed like a wave and as Chris fell forward, she saw the steel walls splitting apart and parts of the ceiling beginning to fall. One jagged block just missed her head and she sheltered near the wall, arms over her head. This time the tremors continued with increasing force and it was several minutes before they subsided.

Chris raised her head to view a scene of devastation. The inner wall had largely collapsed and the reception area was unrecognisable. The corridor to the offices was completely blocked by twisted metal and concrete blocks. Only the outer wall where she sheltered and the entry door were still intact. Chris couldn't see Glenda or the girl she had dragged in and clambered over the wreckage into what remained of the reception area. The desks had disappeared and so had the people. There was no sign of life and she had to assume that everyone had been buried under the mass of debris.

The only good news was that entry to the Research section was no longer a problem. A large gap where the door once stood. What was a problem were the things emerging from the gap. Yellow-brown, shiny bodies with thin, bent limbs. They were like four-legged ants, their serrated jaws oozing a green slime. Chris could see their tiny eyes darting everywhere, and then fix on her. They immediately began a high-pitched squealing noise that jarred her nerves as they moved towards her. She counted seven in total and knew there was no chance of making friends.

This wasn't good. Chris checked the debris at her feet for anything she could use as a weapon. The chunks of concrete and slices of metal were too large. She pulled off her shoes, a woman's last resort. As the first monstrosity approached, she swung the heel against its head. It sank in momentarily but had no effect. Another creature came at her and the two of them pinned her arms and legs against the wall. She tried to resist but their strength was far too great. She couldn't move as the drooling green mucus slobbered onto her clothes and dribbled through to her legs.

She was helpless to defend herself against the other five creatures. But they didn't attack. Three of them went back through the opening and then emerged again, carrying a naked body.

Chris recognised Dolores, the woman who helped her enter.

She appeared to be semiconscious and squirmed constantly, her face contorted in acute pain.

"Leave her alone, you scum," Chris screamed, twisting helplessly in the iron grip of the two creatures.

They ignored her cries and began to maul the body, dripping saliva as they moved. Soon, the face and bare torso were covered with green slime. The only sound was the excited, squealing cries of the monstrous things but the agony in the woman's face was obvious.

"Stop and fight me, you vermin," Chris yelled, tears rolling down her cheeks.

No reaction except the mutations continued their bestial activity with renewed vigour. The naked limbs began to thrash violently and then Chris heard a human cry amid the screeching of the creatures. A scream of finality as the girl shuddered one more time and then was still. The body was carried back through the opening and out of Chris's vision.

She knew that she would be next and a wave of sick revulsion spread through her. Then she noticed something glinting amongst the rubble. One of the small boxes worn by the guards lay less than a metre away.

Her only chance but how to reach it? Chris let herself go limp and allowed her head to slump forward as if she had fainted. She felt the grip on her arms loosen slightly and she made herself fall forward, hoping they would let her drop. They did. As she fell, she twisted to land on top of the box and although her hands were beneath her, her chest, stomach and arms impacted painfully on the stone and metal debris. But her hand was now on the box. She had no idea if it would have any effect on the creatures but there was no other option. She wasn't going to let them use her body as well.

Chris rolled on her side, aimed the box and pressed the button. It certainly had an effect. The thing on her left disintegrated into a ball of putrescence and a disgusting smell radiated from it. She fired again at the one on her right with the same result. Five left.

She rose and moved quickly to one side but her foot slipped on the glob of filth and she fell against the wall. One of the things was nearly on her and she pressed the button as the head touched the box. The beast exploded over her in a foul deluge, the sludge covering her face and body. For a moment she was blinded and fired the box by instinct as she cleared her vision with the other hand.

Globs of slime were still dripping over her eyelids but she could see a panorama of glistening putridity in front of her. Nothing was moving but the overpowering stench made her retch violently. She desperately attempted to wipe the mucus from her body but it clung determinedly. As she pushed a lump of slime from her hair, the box slipped from her grasp and fell into a crack between two massive concrete chunks.

Then the thing appeared from behind the broken wall. One of them still alive. It must have sensed the weapon had been lost and approached rapidly, screeching death. Chris looked down and grabbed a twisted metal strut, about as long as her arm. As it attacked, she rammed it at the join of its head and abdomen. The tiny eyes opened wide for a second and then it liquefied like the others.

She wanted to vomit again but her stomach was empty. Loudly cursing Hades and his malignant servants, she sat against the wall to regain composure. Nothing was going to stop her entering the research area now. She wasn't going to forget the evil scene she had witnessed. Someone would pay for that.

The Blessing ensured that her strength returned quickly. She was still covered with lumps of mucus that clung to her body and clothes like adhesive jelly but thankfully the vile stench had subsided a little. She moved carefully through the mass of twisted metal, concrete and stone to enter the gap where the door to the research area had once stood. Just a small chamber, apparently unaffected by the tremors, and sliding doors in front of her that parted as she approached. An elevator. She went inside and pressed the single button. It descended for a few seconds and then the doors opened.

Byte stood in front of her. Chris jumped at him, attempting to bury her heel into his groin but he grabbed her leg and twisted her to the floor. She was unable to resist his enhanced strength as he gripped her arms and forced her to walk in front of him.

"Girlie, you are filthy," he remarked as he pushed her through a door and slammed it shut.

She was in an enclosed shower cubicle with blue plastic walls and three shower heads that seemed to follow her movements, always centering the spray on her body. Chris stripped off her clothes and this time she didn't care about her nudity. The slime had seeped through the garments and her skin felt contaminated by its touch. It took 15 minutes before she was satisfied that all had been removed from her body and hair. As if in recognition, the shower stopped and now clothes became vitally important again. She squeezed as much water as she could from the bra and pants and pulled them on. The other clothes were still covered with the mucus and it was now starting to solidify.

She was just considering the possibility of creating something from the cleaner parts when the door opened. Byte was there with another man and Chris instinctively moved her hands to the areas covered by the wet underwear.

"Don't be so stupid, little girl. You haven't got a body worth covering," Byte said dismissively.

The other man was fatter and younger, with a chubby face. He gripped her wrists tightly and pulled her into another room, then propelled her violently into a tall box made of transparent plastic. There was just enough space to stand upright and she noticed a number of holes at face level. The man slammed the door of the box and Chris looked around the room.

She was facing a long, crescent shaped table with men sitting behind it. Byte and his companion took their places in the centre. Nine of them, all the Tekkie men together.

Byte tapped the table and began to speak.

"Gentlemen, the first item on the agenda is to decide the future of the two girlies we have in our possession. This little thing is the first."

"Not much of a chest. She looks inadequate for sexual purposes," observed another man.

There was a murmur of agreement.

"Then I propose we utilise her for experimentation in the laboratory."

The heads nodded again. All except the one on the far right, a middle-aged man.

"I want her as a pet. I can teach her some tricks and she can perform for us at our party next week," he said.

"Are you sure, Mainframe?" asked Byte.

"Yes, she looks fit enough and it will be a change from the strippers and lap dancers."

"Very well, you take her. When you find her tedious, we'll use her in the experiments. Bring in the next piece of flesh, Mr Soundcard, if you'd be so kind."

The chubby man who had pushed Chris in the box left the room.

Chris saw Mainframe looking at her with his hand against the side of his head, masking his features from the others. His eyes changed. Golden. She knew who it was, despite his appearance. Franco. He winked and the eyes returned to normal just as Soundcard returned, followed by a woman in a diaphanous dress.

For some reason, Chris felt a surge of relief to see Glenda again but was surprised by her tranquil expression and meaningless smile as well as the dress. Byte beckoned her forward.

"Gentlemen. As you will observe, this creature has received obedience treatment. I think we should congratulate Mr Soundcard here, who undertook the therapy. I can assure you from experience that prior to the treatment, she was violent and intransigent."

"Make her do something," called one of the men.

Soundcard grinned.

"Do your little dance, girl," he instructed.

Glenda began a balletic performance, her face fixed in a stage smile. Soundcard took his seat to watch the display and the end was greeted by a round of applause.

"Well done, girlie," shouted one.

"She's a good size. I'd like her as a concubine," yelled another.

Glenda put a hand on her hip.

"Sorry to disappoint, chaps but there I draw the line."

"What did you say," Byte bellowed angrily.

"I said you are a bunch of self-important, chauvinist gutter swine."

Yells of outrage. The men rose from their seats and started towards her. Glenda calmly produced a box from her dress and pressed the button, sweeping it in an arc from the left. Just as she reached the last one, she saw the man's eyes aglow with gold and swung the beam away.

The other eight had become wobbly, their legs unable to support them. They fell to the floor like the ears of a rabbit with aural erection problems.

"I'm pleased to say you won't recover for a week and by then you'll have a completely different memory," Glenda remarked dispassionately.

She turned to see the ninth man transforming into Franco.

"You were lucky I saw the eyes. Well, Franco, as you now call yourself, I should kill you for what you did to my daughter all that time ago."

"Demeter, I was forced to help them. You know that I changed later," he offered ingratiatingly.

She gave him a disbelieving look.

"I assume this is one of your companions. Better release her," she said, turning to Chris.

Franco obeyed immediately, opening the door of the box. Chris stepped out, please to be able to walk freely again but uncomfortable in her still wet underwear.

"I'm not allowing her to be dressed like that. Go quickly and find clothing, Franco. And towels," the woman demanded.

"Yes, immediately," he replied and scurried out through the door.

Chris smiled at the god.

"Thank you. I'm surprised at this world you created. It's very male dominated."

"I just can't get it as I want. This must be the thousandth world structure I've tried. I only started this one a couple of weeks ago. Every time, I have to implant each of the humans with new memories and characteristics. My previous attempt was only men on this level and all the women downstairs and I let them do what they wanted. After a week, the men had all died from exhaustion and I had to get another batch for this scenario. Now Hades is destroying everything and I don't know if I'll ever be able to start another world."

Franco returned with towels and clothing and Demeter sent him outside again while Chris dressed. Dry underwear but another grey suit.

"Don't bother about these eight men seeing you. They won't remember anything in a few days."

"I really appreciate your help," Chris responded.

"You're a bit precious about your body, aren't you? That's good in a woman. I suppose you just need to find the Gate now. I'm sorry about Hades' creatures killing Dolores."

"How did you know about her?"

"If you press a switch, you can see through some of the walls. I gave these people that knowledge. I was looking on when those monsters entered."

"You should have stopped them attacking Dolores. It was obscene," Chris exclaimed.

"I think I would have probably have saved you if necessary but you seemed to manage very well. Then I surrendered to the men and pretended to be pacified by that disgusting pig, Soundcard."

"You let the girl die. I'm sorry, I can't forgive that."

Demeter laughed.

"I'm pleased you were deceived."

"But I saw her."

"Come with me."

Chris followed her from the room and through a door opposite. Two Dolores but only one had a body. A body covered in hardened globs of slime from the foul creatures. The other was just a head mounted on a metal skeleton.

"I probably made a mistake in giving them the expertise to make androids. I pre-programmed the woman's body construction in their computers before I launched this world. The men here thought they had been working on it for years. The real Dolores is alive and well, back in the office area."

"So where is Selena? Do you know?"

She addressed the question to Franco who had wandered in to join them.

"I arrived through the Gate in one of the laboratory rooms here. A man was just completing an electrical experiment and when he saw me, he must have pressed the wrong switch. Electrocuted himself. So I disposed of his body, changed to his appearance and took his place. I haven't come across Selena here."

"Then you must have seen her, Glenda? Sorry, Demeter?"

"As you know, I've been with you most of the time but I suppose she could be hiding somewhere in the world."

"You don't know Selena. She doesn't hide."

Chris was now becoming increasingly concerned.

"I'm going to search every centimetre of this place until I find her. Before I go, I'd like to see the Gate. I assume that must be here."

Demeter smiled and shrugged but Franco responded.

"I've seen a picture of it on a wall. In the travel room."

"Let's go."

He led her past two doors and entered a small chamber dominated by a large metal cylinder, buried in the floor. It had a large opening and Chris could see a cigar shaped pod inside, obviously designed to house a human body.

"Is this what they use to get to the Green Man area?" she enquired.

"Yes, it's operated by simple hydraulics. It comes out inside a false wall near the farm and you exit by a concealed door. I've seen a few men leaving and coming back. Now, there is the picture."

He pointed at a pine framed painting on the wall. It was just a gold circle around an inverted question mark, also in gold.

"It's the only representation I've seen and it indicates the Gate is about somewhere but there's nothing on the floor. I suppose you could always take it down and stand on it," he offered flippantly.

"That's exactly what I think we need to do."

As Chris reached for the picture, there was a mighty rumble, followed by a huge blast. The room shook violently and they were thrown to the floor. Enormous cracks appeared everywhere and a series of dull but massive explosions continued to rock the complete structure.

"Hades is demolishing this world. We've got to go," screamed Franco, eyes panicky.

"Wait."

Chris scrambled back towards the picture, her body tossed from side to side as the detonations continued. She grabbed it and immediately fell, jarring her elbow. Then she crawled along the undulating floor to reach Franco.

"Take it. I'm going to get Selena. If you find the Gate works, you'll know we're dead," she yelled, over the noise of crashing concrete.

He nodded and began to place the picture on the floor. Chris had started for the door when a bright white light filled the chamber. She turned to see Selena emerging from the brilliance above the picture.

"So we've arrived together this time," she said, looking round.

"Chris, quickly," Franco yelled.

She scrambled back and the three joined hands on the surface of the picture, just as the room began to crumble and collapse around them.

Immersed in the comforting whiteness, Selena looked puzzled.

"What the hell are you doing? We only just got to that place and now we're going. And how did you get that grey suit, Chris?"

"There is no time in the whiteness," observed Franco.

Chris smiled.

"Selena, I'm going to tell you a long story."

And she did.

18

Chris began to feel the white clinging to her like a suffocating blanket. Suddenly, her body was shaken by a violent tremor as if the destruction of the last world had followed her into the Gate. She knew Hades was now demolishing the universe and there was very little time left to reach Jerome Jones before he died. The shaking continued in varying degrees until she was thrown forward, out of the whiteness.

A long, curving passageway, wide enough for two people to stand alongside and about the same height. No sign of her companions and Chris instantly felt very much alone. She forced the negativity to one side and surveyed her surroundings. A wall directly behind her and no exits that she could see. The sides of the passage were solid steel and the floor had the resilience of a running track but was pure white. She looked up and saw herself. The ceiling was mirrored.

No choice, only one way to go. She followed the curve round to her left. After 50 metres she could see someone approaching. It was her reflection in a mirror that filled the passage. She reached forward tentatively and gently touched the surface. As soon as her fingertips made contact, she was sucked in to it.

A gloomy, square chamber. A small, lean man was sitting on a metal chair that had a thick cable attached. An electric chair. Chris looked closer at him. He had a rat-like, greasy face with narrow eyes and thin lips and just a few strands of dirty hair across his head.

Suddenly, the chamber was filled with a woman's voice.

"This man is a thief. The only way to get back what he has stolen is to execute him."

"Killing is not a punishment for that," Chris responded.

"He has stolen from you."

Chris thought quickly. Did the woman mean stolen here or on earth?

"What has he taken?"

"Memories. All your memories of your parents."

Chris felt a sinking feeling. She had lost her parents in a car accident, just before she turned 17. She tried to think of them. Nothing. The memories had gone. She still felt close to them but now couldn't even recall their appearance. A complete void. Chris tried to gather her composure but felt perspiration running down her forehead.

"He should be punished but his life should be spared. In restitution, he should restore my memories."

The man's lips curled in a leering smile.

"No chance. I'll never give them back while I'm alive."

Chris felt her eyes moistening and a chill emptiness inside. One of the main foundation stones of her life had been destroyed. The vile face in front of her reverted to a smug expression of victory as the woman's voice came again.

"You only have to say the word and he will die. Then you will again know your parents."

"I need time to think," she responded but her voice seemed weak and unsteady.

She sat cross-legged on the floor and closed her eyes. Losing her parents had been bad but they would have inevitably passed away at some time. To take their memory from her, one of her most valuable possessions, was unthinkable. She only had to say the word. The man was unknown to her. Who would miss a creature like that?

"You've had time. Your decision is required," said the voice.

Chris rose to her feet and blinked back the tears.

"No execution. He lives but should be incarcerated for the rest of his life."

"Are you sure? Your memories were beautiful and happy."

"I'm sure."

The scene disappeared and she was back in the passageway. It was now like a maze with turnings everywhere. She vaguely recalled someone mentioning that you should always keep a wall on your right to get through a maze. It could be a circuitous route but should lead somewhere. No other ideas, so she took the first right turning, then another and another. The passage ended in another mirror and this time she entered without hesitation.

A corner shop, one she knew well as a child. Mr Tarvery was behind the counter, his wide red face full of smiles as usual. He was chatting to that old lady who lived just four doors away. Then she saw Jackie, her best friend. She was stealing, pushing packets of sweets and chocolate into her coat. Chris recalled the scene. She had been ten years old.

"Old Tarvery won't miss it," Jackie had said as they shared the confectionery outside the shop. Everyone knew he was rich with a big house, two cars and a spoilt, petulant daughter who was in their class at school.

"It's stealing," Chris had responded.

"It's not stealing, just being fair. It just means that horrid girl will have less money to flash around."

Chris hadn't been able to disagree. It did seem fair and just.

Now, 16 years later, she was there again. She had often thought back to that time, wondering if her decision had been right. Theft or justice? She knew if she had said anything, it would have made her very unpopular with her best friend and all the girls she knew in her class. A decision of morality, of principle. Would she do anything different now?

She followed Jackie out of the shop, just as before.

"Want chocolate?" her friend said with a grin.

"Someone stole from me and it wasn't nice."

"I told you we're not thieving. Old Tarvery's got plenty and it's our best way to get back at that cow."

The daughter walked past, sneering at them as usual.

"Anyway, who stole from you?" Jackie asked.

"An ugly man. He took my parents."

"What?"

"Doesn't matter. Everything we steal is a little bit of someone's life. If we keep taking, they die."

"That's stupid."

"Give me the stuff, I'm taking it back."

"No."

They grappled but Chris was stronger. Jackie's face contorted with anger and tears.

"I hate you. Never going to speak to you again."

After she had run away, Chris returned the items to the shelves in the shop. Tarvery was talking to his daughter but looked across at Chris as she moved to the door.

"I hear you're the stupid one in your class," he called.

Chris turned to face him and smiled.

"Yes, I'm stupid," she said quietly and then left.

The scene disappeared. Chris couldn't recall what had happened since entering the mirror. Something in her childhood? But she didn't recollect much about that time. No friends at school and her home life was a complete blank. She was back in the corridor and continued to follow the right side wall. A hollow feeling was growing inside her, gnawing at her concentration.

Another mirror and she entered it without thinking. A familiar bedroom. The bedroom in the house of her lover, Jerome Jones. He was in bed with a beautiful girl resting her head on his chest.

"It's not real," Chris cried out but the certainty had left her.

She heard the girl speaking.

"You said you'd never sleep with me."

"Times change," replied Jerome Two.

"But you had that other woman, Chris?"

"She never had time to love anyone. Always too busy. I kept asking her to stay with me for a couple of days, just to be together."

"Two days in bed, you mean."

"Not just that. Two days alone to talk and touch, just be intimate together. She either never felt like it or was doing something more important."

"Sounds very selfish."

Chris felt the tears running down her face. Shafts of pain and guilt went through her like ice. Jerome Two had asked her to stay several times but it was always so difficult. She remembered that she hadn't slept with him for over a month.

"Not true," she shouted, but didn't believe herself.

The tears began anew and she knelt down, sobbing quietly.

"She's still away then?" She heard the girl ask.

"Yes but it won't change when she returns. I suppose she'll call me sometime when she needs help."

"Not true, not true," Chris mumbled through the tears. Then she lifted her chin and rose to her feet.

"I love you," she shouted as loudly as possible.

There was no indication he heard her and the scene vanished.

No corridor this time. A lush, green garden. Somewhere warm. She was looking over a pruned hedge at a deserted beach with the bright blue sea beyond, lapping gently on the sands. A squeal behind her and she turned.

Two young children were playing ball on the grass and a woman sat behind them. Chris was looking at herself, propped up reading a book on a sun lounger. A man came from the house, carrying a tray of drinks. Jerome Two.

"Orange juice, kids," he called and her two children rushed towards him to take their drinks. He moved next to the woman and kissed her tenderly on the cheek.

She smiled and softly returned the kiss. He handed her a drink and wandered off to the children.

The woman turned and looked directly at Chris, with a gentle smile.

"I have wonderful memories of my parents, lots of friends at school and I know how to look after a man," she said, in a mellow tone.

"Then you killed the one in the electric chair and participated in theft," Chris responded.

"You're using words like weapons to make yourself feel better. Everything I did was just and fair. My life now proves that I have been rewarded in my judgments."

"But how do you feel inside? Your conscience?"

"I feel fine. No regrets. A wonderful house, husband and children."

"I still wouldn't kill the man, wouldn't allow the theft. I believe that Jerome Two knows that love has many patterns like a cut diamond but sometimes the facets are sharp. The diamond is still beautiful and everlasting."

"Then I'm sorry for you," the woman replied without bitterness.

Again the scene began to dissolve but Chris thought she saw Jerome glance at her with something hard in his eyes, something she didn't recognise. Probably her wishful thinking. She couldn't, wouldn't change and go back now.

A park, maybe in October. Leaves were scattered across the paths, scuttering like flakes of gold in the bitter, gusty wind. Chris was tired and hungry. She pulled a thin coat around her throat and saw her hand. It was bony, dirty and weathered. She quickly felt her face. Leathery cheeks with deep etched lines. Her eyes felt sore and her hair was matted with filth. A shabby bag lay at her feet. It was all she had now.

Couples walked past chatting in familiar togetherness. Two women meandered along, wheeling prams and perpetually peering at their offspring while maintaining a constant, meaningless conversation. Lone men strode quickly, talking on mobile phones. They all deliberately avoided looking at her, a filthy old woman seated uncomfortably on a wooden bench.

Why go on? She had nothing. No home, no family, no friends and no lover. She was old and all used up. Nothing to look forward to. Just more days and nights of pointless misery. Too late now, she realised that. Much too late. Was there any reason to live for tomorrow? No one spoke to her, no pleasure, no laughter, no hope.

A woman stopped and put a couple of coins on the seat beside her. Chris tried to say thank you but it emerged as a hoarse grunt and she saw the disgust scurry across the woman's kindly face. Unless something changed, Chris contemplated willing herself to die tomorrow. And nothing would change. She considered whether to stop eating today and with luck, death would take her in the night. Then they would cremate her and scatter her ashes in the wind. Just another passing cloud of dust that no one would notice.

She just had one choice left to make in life. To die or to live. While everyone else was picking from so many options of friends, relationships, entertainment, shopping, holidays and the rest.

"You'll have to decide. Beef or pork tonight?"

Chris looked up to see a chubby woman with a bespectacled man. Both were impeccably dressed in top brand, padded anoraks.

"I don't mind," the man replied.

"You know you like beef best."

"Okay, beef will do."

"Are you sure? Don't forget we have the Carters coming over tomorrow and they like beef. So it'll be the same meal again."

"Then let's have pork."

"But you prefer beef."

"Well, what would you like? You choose this time for a change," he said mildly.

Her lips tightened.

"You're so difficult sometimes. You said you wanted beef, so we'll have that."

They moved off and Chris heard a rasping noise. It took a second before she realised she was laughing. A strained, hoarse chuckle that sounded like the breath of the Reaper. It was the first gasp of life.

She was hungry and cold on the bench. Get food first and then walk around the town. Tomorrow, she'd stand by the cafe. They often gave her a free tea.

The picture fragmented and disappeared. She was back in the passageway. No, not the passageway. A square cubicle with mirrors on each wall. Chris looked at her reflection and saw a pale, tired figure. They had taken her memories, her friends, her man and showed her the unwelcome future. Her life was an undermined building about to collapse and a bleak, empty existence was waiting. A wingless bird on the stony seashore. She had to find something positive.

Chris didn't want to enter any more mirrors to find another part of her crumbling away. Then from inside, she sensed a particle still glowing dimly. Maybe all that was left of her soul. The light was slowly expiring and uttered the words with difficulty.

'Make me shine again.'

Precious. Like a baby inside her. She lifted a tearstained face and pushed into the mirror she was facing. A half-lit room and in the centre, on a stone block, lay a corpse. Even before she reached it, she knew it was Selena. The body was covered with deep cuts with dried blood congealed around them and the face was twisted in an expression of agony. Words had been carved with a knife across the stomach.

'Die In Pain'.

Selena was not a friend but she was the only person Chris now knew. The only one she was close to. And she was dead. Nobody left now.

But the spark inside was glowing brighter and the words came to her.

"No. I will go through."

The fortitude and calmness of her voice surprised Chris. She walked past the corpse to the wall. She knew the door was there although nothing was visible. Pressing both hands against the rough surface, she pushed with all the strength she had. It gave way just a little. Straining every muscle, she edged it slowly open until the crack was wide enough to squeeze through.

Another gloomy room but she could see a desk and behind it, a man writing furiously. He looked up as she approached.

"Name?" he asked coldly.

"Why should I tell you?"

He sighed loudly.

"I require your name. We cannot proceed without it."

"We will not proceed anywhere. I decide what I will do."

"Then I must ask the birds to encourage your response."

Chris felt the shudder of fear running through her. Birds were her only phobia. She didn't know why, all her childhood memories had gone.

The slapping of feathered wings against the air and a spear of horror twisted in her body. Then they were on her, feathers beating against her face, her eyes. Sharp claws frenziedly tore at her hair. Her heart was beating like an express and in desperation, she flailed her arms at the creatures.

"Just say your name," the man's voice pierced the screeching morass.

"I will not," Chris shouted as she fell to the floor, covering her head with her arms. The talons ripped at her hands and body and she felt warm blood oozing from the wounds.

"I will not," she screamed again as the venomous assault continued. She repeated the words, time after time. But the birds didn't stop. She could feel more and more of them joining the rape of her mind and body. More wings were beating, throbbing against her skin. Beaks thrust into her flesh, spiking with pain while the claws continued to rake and scar. She barely heard his voice this time.

"Just tell me your name, you stubborn bitch."

Chris pulled her arms away and instantly felt the beaks and claws tearing at her cheeks. She ignored them and rose to her feet amid a maelstrom of feathers and hammering, feathered wings.

"I will never tell you."

She felt a sharp talon rip across her forehead and blood began to drip into her eyes. She reached to wipe them with the back of her hand.

Then they were gone. No birds but still a man at the desk. A different man. This one had grey hair and a round, friendly face.

"Hello, you must be Chris."

She wasn't going to respond and he seemed to understand that.

"You have taken something. You will be punished but your life will be spared. In restitution you should give back what you have taken."

"I've not taken anything. You'll get nothing from me as long as I live."

"Then we can kill you now."

"You can try."

Chris started forward but her wrists were gripped by metal straps. The metal chair was hard and uncomfortable. The electric chair. The old man smiled benignly.

"There is a button on this desk. If I press it, you'll fry nicely. Just give back what you have stolen."

Chris glimpsed her reflection in the shiny wrist strap. It showed a rat-faced man with thin lips and a few dirty strands of hair.

The old man spoke again.

"Look, you have nothing to live for now but if you sacrifice yourself, then you'll give someone their life back."

"As I haven't stolen, I have nothing to give back. My death would serve no purpose."

"So your final answer is no," he said, reaching for the button.

"Explain what I have taken."

"If we knew that, there wouldn't be a problem."

"You don't know what I'm supposed to have stolen?"

"No. If you tell us then all will be well."

Chris paused, studying her repulsive reflection.

"In my whole life, I have only taken three things that have all been given to me. Existence, time and something else."

"What else?"

"Love."

Suddenly she was back in the corridor, directly in front of a golden door. It opened as she approached and a man beckoned her inside. A tall young man with tousled brown hair.

"Hello Chris. I am Poseidon," he said casually.

She touched her face. The cuts had disappeared and the tears had dried but she still felt unclean. Inside, it was very different. The spark had grown to fill her and now shone like a star. Her parents, her friends and most importantly, Jerome Two were in her memories again. Exhilaration coursed through her.

"I must look terrible," she said ruefully.

"But you feel like a newborn butterfly in the morning sun."

"Yes, that's exactly how I feel."

"I'm sorry about Selena."

Chris hesitated and then smiled.

"You should be. The duplicate was not perfect. You missed a tiny birthmark in a place you wouldn't know about."

He laughed.

"Come in and take a shower."

She walked through into a deep carpeted hallway. Crystal chandeliers hung from the gold ceiling and the golden walls displayed lifelike portraits of each major Greek god. Poseidon pointed at the first door.

"In there."

Chris wallowed in the warm shower, emerging refreshed and renewed. She noticed a neat pile of clothes near the door. A short mauve dress and medium heel shoes.

Poseidon was waiting outside.

"Better now?"

"Thank you but I'm puzzled. You should have a water world, not an ordeal like this."

"Water is my job but this is my leisure. I never want to see the stuff when I come here."

"I learnt that the happiest lives on earth result from selfishness and deceit."

"Yes, that is absolutely true."

Chris stared at his friendly, handsome face for a few seconds.

"How did I perform?"

"There was no performance. You changed your past and found something that you didn't know you'd lost. You're smart and courageous, characteristics I admire in a woman."

"That's the first time I've had a compliment from a god."

He laughed. Attractively.

"Now you're going to ask me about Selena and Franco."

She grinned and nodded.

"Selena told me you met her on earth."

"Yes. Maybe she also said that I failed to seduce her there."

"Sort of," Chris said uncomfortably.

"Come with me."

He led her to the end door on the right, opened it and stood back.

A bedroom as luxurious as the hall with a figure in a white negligee lying on a four poster bed. Selena.

"Hello, Chris. It's been a long wait," she said without surprise.

"Have you just been lounging in bed while I went to hell and back?"

"Yes and no. I told Poseidon you would get through. I knew you'd be here."

"Small consolation. I hope you enjoyed yourself?" Chris remarked with a little ice.

"It's been an experience I wouldn't have missed for anything."

She rose from the bed and hugged Chris tightly.

"Now we'll try to save Jerome. Time is very short."

Chris smiled.

"You're impossible, Selena. We need Franco and the Gate."

"Franco is here and Poseidon has shown me the Gate. Would you leave us for a minute so I can say goodbye and get dressed?"

Poseidon walked past Chris and she moved to the hallway, closing the door behind her.

Four minutes before it opened. She saw Selena reach up and kiss the god, very soft and long. She recognised a special kiss when she saw one.

"I hope I'll come here again," Selena said as she detached.

"That would be nice. I wish you good fortune on your mission," replied Poseidon.

They left him standing in the hallway and passed through the golden door. The outside was different now. Not a passageway but a room and in it, Chris could see Franco, lounging on a sofa with two stunning women, each wearing a tiny black stretch dress. He smiled briefly.

"Off you go, girls. I have to leave now," he said in the new, commanding voice.

They murmured protests and departed reluctantly, glancing back at him as they left. He waited until the door was closed, then pulled the sofa to one side to reveal an ornate golden design on the floor. In the centre was a question mark.

"I thought Hades had killed you as we left the last world," Chris observed with a smile.

"So did I, until I found myself here," he replied.

 Selena grasped his arm and then Chris's hand.

"We have under four hours left to reach Jerome. If he's on the next world, don't waste time exploring or finding each other. Just get to him quickly," she said tersely.

"Only you and Chris can release him," observed Franco.

"Yes but if you find his location, you must find a way to contact us."

Chris took Franco's hand and they stepped onto the gate.

19

The whiteness wasn't pure this time. Bright red sparks hovered and flashed with a crackling sound, as if near an open fireplace. Chris was full of unanswered questions. She felt lacking in information after the visit to Poseidon's world. There hadn't been time to find out more from Selena and she knew that reaching Jerome was the first priority. She also remembered the kiss Selena had given the god, a true lover's kiss. Adding the soft look in her eyes gave an unmistakable recipe. That pleased Chris. She knew a brick had been missing from Selena's life and wanted her to achieve happiness.

The crackling white cleared but she wasn't ready for the sign. A massive, roadside advertising sign that displayed just three words in red on a white background.

'Jerome Jones Is Here'.

She was on a road, a country road. It wandered away to her left through green meadows and in the distance, she could see a small village. She took off her heels and ran towards the group of houses. As she approached, she saw an old man leaning against a fence. He was dressed in thick dark trousers, scruffy white shirt and leather jerkin.

"You're in a hurry, lady," he called.

"Where is Jerome?" she responded abruptly.

"He's here, there and everywhere."

"I haven't got time for riddles. Where is he?"

"Wind down a bit. Speed and knowledge are distant strangers."

Chris stopped and walked towards him.

"I am a very patient woman. Can you give me some indication of what you are talking about?"

"All the other men in our village are called Jerome and those that aren't are called something else."

"If they are all called Jerome there can't be anyone else."

"Yes, that's true but if there were, they be called something else."

"So you are a Jerome?"

"No. My name is Else. Something Else."

Chris retained a shred of patience.

"What are the women's names?"

"All except three are called either Chris or Selena."

"And the three are called Something Else?"

"No. Tracy, Jackie and Amanda."

"I'm looking for Jerome Jones. Can you help or not?"

"I wouldn't ask Jerome Knot, he's always tied up with something. I can help you."

"I will ask again a very simple question. Where is Jerome Jones?"

"You mean the visitor? The one who is going to die unless you reach him?"

"Yes."

"Never seen him."

"I didn't ask that. One final chance before I hit you. Can you tell me his location on this world?"

"Theoretically, yes but we are sworn to secrecy."

Chris walked away towards the village and waved a hand.

"Goodbye," she called.

"Good luck and watch out for the big man."

She looked back quickly but he had gone. Hopefully, he wasn't typical of the whole population.

The word typical is a perfect anagram of 'Tic Play', more correctly spelt Tick Play. The Tick is a tiny arachnid, no more than three millimetres or an eighth of an inch long but has been found to possess superb acting skills, far beyond the capabilities of fleas. A group now present the world's greatest plays in their own theatre situated in central England. The performance is accomplished at lightning pace by the rapid eight legged creatures, with four hour plays being completed in under five minutes. As they are unable to speak, they use high-speed mime with subtle movements of their legs giving depth and meaning to the words. Unfortunately, those without highly magnified vision cannot see any of this, sadly missing out on the torrid love scenes and subtle nuances in characterisation.

The village buildings were modern. No old stone cottages here. Brick built, double glazed, tiled roofing. Just like a new housing development in rural England, except for the lack of garages. No cars but plenty of road signs and every one was the same. 'Jerome Jones Is Here'.

Two women walked towards her. Hair sensibly cut but finely groomed, just enough cosmetics not to be apparent and the required dark trousers and jacket outfit. Self-centred introversion personified. The couple were talking intently.

"I had a terrible shock when I got home yesterday. Tom had gone out for a walk, so I dashed upstairs to check his wardrobe. He'd forgotten to change into his walking shoes!"

"What? Really?"

"Yes, I was totally shaken. Anyway, when he got back, I made sure we checked his feet thoroughly for a couple of hours. You'll never guess what we found."

"Go on."

"He had a patch of hard skin on the sole of his foot, just below his little toe. Of course, he couldn't see it properly so I took photographs. I'll show them to you next time you come round."

"I'll be there tomorrow. I can't wait to see them. I really don't know how you handle all this, Selena. I'm sure I'd just collapse if anything like that ever happened to me."

"Well, neither of us got much sleep last night with all the talk and worry about his foot. I wanted him to go to the surgery immediately but Tom is such a baby. He was too scared."

"You must have bandaged it?"

"Yes, immediately. Obviously he's had to stay at home today, looking…"

"Excuse me."

Chris interrupted their conversation at a critical point. Two frigid looks.

"Yes?" said the one with the critically injured man.

"I'm looking for Jerome Jones."

She could see them studying her carefully and knew she would be the subject of conversations for months to come.

"What you want with him?"

"I'm a friend. Do you know where he is?"

Chris tried to keep her voice calm but saw the women grip each other's arms for protection.

"We don't want trouble here."

"There's no trouble. I'm just looking for my friend."

"Well, we don't know anything."

The women dashed off, looking back at her as they ran.

Chris decided to abandon conversations and conduct a search herself. It didn't take long. The settlement comprised only about 20 houses, all exactly the same design. Jerome was either hidden inside one of them or he was somewhere else in the world. Her instincts told her he wasn't here.

She was following the road out of the village when it began. A mighty explosion shook the earth and sky. The ground trembled and split and she saw trees falling on the roadside. A deeper rumble and her feet were pulled from under her. As she lay prone, her body was pummelled by the ground beneath and her eardrums almost shattered by a loud explosion. She was thrown a metre in the air and thudded back to the hard, gravelled road surface. Suddenly, it stopped.

Chris waited for a minute before rising. She stood up to see a changed landscape. The village had disappeared. All that remained was a large depression in the ground filled with a variety of bricks, tiles and slabs. The grassy hills around her were now scarred with wide cracks and she could also see the black lines of fissures in the blues skies. Remarkably, the road ahead was completely unchanged, curving upwards to the brow of a large hill in front of her.

A movement caught her eye. Something was emerging from the wide crack in the land to her right. At first she thought it was a white dog, maybe an Alsatian. Then she saw its body was smooth and gleaming and its head looked more insect than canine. Other, similar creatures scrabbled out until they formed a group of about twenty.

Then she saw the first turn towards her. Its eyes were round, bulbous and a startling ice blue colour. The others joined in the stare and she felt forty blue eyes burning into her like ice picks. Then the leader gave a loud grunt and began to lope forward.

Chris ran, sprinting up the road towards the brow of the hill. The air was now filled with the malignant cries of the creatures. She briefly glanced behind. They were already on the road and pursuing with long, bounding strides. Chris was fast, nearly Olympic standard but she sensed they were gradually closing. She was thankful she still wore the short skirt for freedom of movement and had already discarded her footwear. Running shoes would have been preferable on the hard surface but she had no choice.

As she approached the top of the hill, she knew there would be no time for delay. Whatever was over there, she would have to decide instantly where to go. The creatures were much closer now, maybe just ten metres away and the malevolent noises had become louder and more insistent.

Just before she reached the top, she came to a crack, about a metre wide and directly across the road. Measuring her stride, she leapt across but something caught her trailing foot and she sprawled to the ground on the other side. She saw immediately what had tripped her. An arm. A dark, hairy arm coming out of the crack. Another arm followed together with an equally hairy body. It paused, directly at her feet. The arms were longer than a human, twice the length of its globular torso. Two hostile red eyes glared balefully and it opened a large crimson mouth full of shiny, steel-like fangs. The ice hounds had stopped the other side of the fissure and waited expectantly.

Not the time to contemplate. Chris jumped to her feet and ran again. She heard a loud shriek behind her like the magnified cry of a seabird, followed by a wild cacophony of grunts. They were coming and their purpose was slaughter.

Chris reached the summit. A tiny valley with higher hills beyond. The road led down to what appeared to be a monastery or temple. A round, single storey building with a tower in the centre. She continued downhill without hesitation. Then, suddenly, she heard a 'throp' sound and a little pool of flaming lava appeared on the road to her left. Another 'throp' and she felt a sharp stinging pain on the back of her right thigh. Glancing behind her, she saw the source. The hairy creature was using its two arms as legs and running like a biped panther. It spat at her again and she saw the glowing spittle arc past her shoulder. The pack of ice hounds followed close behind the shaggy creature.

Chris maintained her speed, feeling the Blessing working to heal her leg. The pain had almost gone and she knew the wound would disappear in just a couple of minutes. Her main objective now was to get inside the building without any delay at the entrance. The circular, outer wall seemed to be windowless and the road led directly to the only apparent entrance, a large, wooden door. It was less than 80 metres away now.

"Open the door," she screamed, hoping someone inside would hear. Nothing.

Another glob of lava hit her skirt and she could smell the burning as it ate into the cloth.

50 metres and she yelled at the door again but it remained firmly closed.

20 metres.

"Let me in," she shouted for the last time and quickly decided to lead her pursuers around the building. She began to veer left but then the door opened. Swerving back, she jumped inside and heard it slam behind her. A ball of flaming lava entered before it closed and burnt merrily on the stone floor.

The cries and grunts continued outside as the creatures began to hammer at the door. It started to bend inwards.

"Naughty little rascals," said a voice.

She expected a tall figure in a hooded monk's habit but was wrong. It was a short figure in a hooded monk's habit. The habit was blue and it was a woman's voice.

"Did you see the things that were chasing me?" asked Chris.

"Yes, I'm not surprised you were running."

"Is the door strong enough to hold them?"

"No. They'll break through eventually. We'd better go before that happens."

Chris looked around. A stone chamber with an arched portal. It was poorly lit by the flames of a couple of flickering torches on the walls. She followed the woman through the arch.

"I'm Chris. Sorry, I don't know your name."

"Call me Peregrine."

"Well, thank you Peregrine."

They continued down a near dark passageway and the woman opened the door at the end. Chris was dazzled by the bright sunlight and it took a few seconds to adjust her eyes. A massive, circular room in the middle of the building with a large dark hole in the centre, surrounded by a tall, silver fence. All around were hooded figures with the same robes as Peregrine but in a variety of colours. Unusually, they were all playing sports. Running, jumping, boxing, wrestling and various ball games. Some of their hoods had fallen back, revealing an equal mixture of young male and female faces.

"I thought you were a sort of sect?" enquired Chris.

"We are worshippers of Mathfellas, the ruler of this world. He resides in the perfect lands far below us."

"Then what is everyone doing?"

"All his worshippers are undergoing the monthly trials. At their completion, the lowest three are sent to Mathfellas for restitution."

"How do they get to him?"

"We send them through the great portal," Peregrine responded, pointing at the central hole.

Chris appreciated that must give them an excellent, if extreme incentive to excel at physical pursuits but she was more concerned about her own problems.

"Those creatures must have come from Mathfellas. They appeared through the cracks caused by the earthquake."

"Earthquake? We had no earthquake here. Perhaps you have angered him."

She beckoned towards a group who were attempting to wrestle despite being hampered by their robes. They ceased immediately and surrounded Chris.

"I haven't angered anyone. I was just walking down the road when they appeared."

"It is punishment for a sin," Peregrine responded, apparently not listening to her explanation.

"No, I just explained what happened."

"Confess all to me now and forgiveness is yours."

Chris was running thin on patience.

"I think I'll go now. Is there another way out?"

"There is no way to escape your transgressions. In addition, we find your garments totally unacceptable. Your limbs are displayed for all to see, a sure sign of lasciviousness."

"Okay, I confess. I've been naughty. Am I forgiven now?"

Peregrine pulled back her hood. Long, blonde curly hair and an attractive, round face with twinkling eyes. She looked about 35.

"That's much better. A confession. Of course you are forgiven, child. You only have to complete your penance and all is forgotten."

"What's the penance?"

"To descend in contrition to the land of Mathfellas."

"You mean jump down that hole? How can that be a penance? It's certain death."

"Then afterwards, all your evil deeds will be purged from you and you can be amongst us in joyfulness."

"But there is no afterwards if I'm dead."

"Of course there is."

"How many have served this penance?"

"Oh, nearly 200. Poor, tarnished souls."

"And how many have returned?"

"Up to this moment, none. But they will come back to a celebration. We will all greet them with warmth and love."

Chris had been constructing a plan while she spoke.

"That is excellent, Peregrine. You have passed the test set by Mathfellas."

"I don't understand."

"Our ruler has dispatched me to verify your worthiness. My words and my attire were a part of the test as were his servants who accompanied me and pretended pursuit."

Chris reached out and laid a hand on the top of the woman's head.

"You have done well and Mathfellas will reward you for your obedience."

She saw the hooded figures around her nodding with approbation but Peregrine didn't appear over impressed.

"I am most grateful. Is your work now completed?"

"It is and I will leave you with joy in my heart."

The woman smiled sweetly.

"Then of course you will return through the entrance to his world. Come, we will escort you."

She waved to the crowd which had now grown as others joined and they began to usher Chris forward. Some of them rushed ahead and opened a gate in the silver fence. By the time Chris reached it, the whole population had gathered around her.

She turned at the gateway and held her hands high.

"Open all the doors to allow my companions to join me."

Before Peregrine could speak, a crowd opened the door to the room and she saw them disappear towards the outer portal. Meanwhile, the gathering in front of her parted to allow a clear way through. Then she heard the sound of communal screaming. They must have let the creatures in. The hairy thing appeared at the doorway, streams of blood marking its fur. It looked around and then fixed its gaze on Chris. Behind it, the pack of white hounds was grunting enthusiastically.

Then the creature uttered its strange cry and charged towards her. The pack followed, ripping off the arms and legs of the front row of onlookers as an aperitif. Chris waited until they were less than three metres away and then jumped for the gate, taking a firm grip and quickly hauling herself to the top. The hairy thing and most of the hounds were unable to stop, falling into the dark pit with anguished cries of frustration.

Just the rear four of the ice hounds were left. They stalked around the gate and tried to climb and jump but she was well out of reach. After continuing unsuccessfully for a short time, the blue-eyed creatures began to eye the remaining congregation of hooded figures who stood frozen with horror. In a flash of white, they attacked. Robes were shredded, limbs and heads torn off in a feverish lust to massacre. The air shuddered with screams and Chris saw Peregrine running for the door, her face appearing more angry than terrified.

The four creatures appeared insatiable in the bloodlust, unceasingly ripping and shredding with their forelegs and pincer-like mouths. Chris had to move now. They would soon turn back to her and she had no weapons to defend herself. Waiting until the creatures were clear of the fence, she descended rapidly and immediately sprinted for the door. She heard the grunts and sensed them coming behind her. Suddenly, she felt a tug on her skirt and was pulled backwards. One of the things had caught the garment between its jaws and was clinging tight.

Rolling to one side, she kicked back with her foot, striking the creature directly in its ice blue eye. She kicked again and pulled away. The skirt ripped off and she ran for the opening in front of her, just as the other three hounds were nearly upon her. No time to close the door, they were too close. She sprinted along the passage, and then saw an opening on her left that hadn't been there when she entered.

A long corridor lined with flaming torches. Her chances outside were almost zero so she turned through the new doorway with the grunting pack close behind. As she ran, Chris saw small chambers on each side. Most were empty but halfway down, she saw one that had walls gleaming with metal objects. Swords, knives and shields. Turning in quickly, she grabbed the first sword and swung it blindly behind her. It hit something. Turning, she saw the something was a neck. She had neatly sliced the head off the leading creature. The other three paused uncertainly at the doorway.

Chris charged towards them, swinging the sword in front of her. She struck one on the head and the blade bounced off. The creatures had an exoskeleton like an ant. Aim for the joints. Target the neck and top of the legs. They grunted and snapped at her but she knew they feared her weapon. She cut off another head and then hacked one leg from the third, followed by its decapitation. One left. It crouched for a second and then leapt at her. Chris fell backwards to the floor and jabbed the sword up as she went down. It found soft flesh and she pushed it in to the hilt. The creatures had soft underbellies. She heard it give a final grunt and thud to the floor behind her.

She rose to her feet. No injuries but she was concerned that her short skirt had been torn from her, leaving just the black lace pants. Taking another sword from the wall, she clambered over the white corpses and returned to the corridor and continued to follow it. There was a chance Jerome could be here. More side chambers, the first four empty but she sighed with relief when she saw the fifth. Nothing inside but the walls had long, orange drapes. She sliced one in half and wrapped it around her waist. A skirt of sorts. Just above the knee and not the colour she would have chosen, but still a skirt.

At the end of the corridor was a door. Chris readied her sword before entering, aware that Peregrine had probably come this way. Then she opened it.

"Good day. May I convey you?" a voice asked robotically.

The shiny steel buggy was out of place in the old stone building. So were the modern, marble tiled walls and fluorescent lighting. The buggy was a clear plastic sphere with two seats inside. Behind it, Chris could see the entrance to a tunnel.

"May I convey you?" it repeated and a panel in the front opened. Chris entered and sat. The door closed and the buggy shot down the dimly lit tunnel.

"Where are we going?" she asked, not expecting a reply.

"To Jerome Jones, of course. That's my only destination."

The answer was a surprise, but a nice one. The buggy stopped and the door opened. An identical chamber to the one she had left. However, this one had a large sign on the wall.

'Jerome has 22 minutes 14 seconds to live'.

Even as she watched, the seconds were counting down.

She jumped from the buggy and left the room. Outside. A flat desert, stretching all around her with a scorching sun burning her skin. A trick. Jerome wasn't here. She went back into the chamber. Except it wasn't the chamber. It was a brothel with five near naked girls posing, writhing and teasing. Every one looked like Selena.

Chris hesitated and immediately the girls surrounded her, wrapping their arms and bodies around her and pulling at her clothes. She tried to fight them off but they were powerful, stronger than the real Selena. The sword was twisted from her grasp and fell to the floor. Then she felt her makeshift orange skirt being pulled from her and began to fight seriously. She kicked and punched, constantly moving and twisting her body. The Selenas began to give way. One fell from a kick to the stomach, another from a punch to the head. Chris finally squirmed free and rushed out into the desert again but as she moved, one girl ripped the shirt from her. The situation was now grave. She had just her underwear left and someone was going to suffer for that.

She waited just a few moments in the blinding sun before entering, this time with grim determination in her expression. Now she was in a palatial room, much larger than the previous two chambers. Two thrones of blue marble stood on a raised stone platform at the far end. Peregrine sat on one and was now clad in a long dress with her blonde hair cascading around her shoulders. On the other was the big man, his right arm outstretched holding the hilt of a sword with the point balanced on the floor in front of him. Before them stood a mass of creatures. All the ones she had seen before and many more horrendous and disgusting shapes that were completely new.

"You are here to die."

The powerful voice of Hades filled the chamber. Peregrine turned to him, smiling as he spoke.

"I have come for Jerome Jones and you're not stopping me," Chris announced firmly.

A burst of noise came from the creatures, their expressions turning even more malevolent.

"Silence."

His command was obeyed immediately and nothing moved. Chris cursed her lack of clothing but kept her gaze on him.

"Jerome Jones is in there," he declared, gesturing towards a door to the right of his throne.

"Will you try to stop me entering?"

"You have just eight minutes left. To enter the room, you simply have to defeat me."

"Stop talking and let's do it."

He rose and walked slowly through the ranks of indescribable horrors. They parted subserviently in front of him.

"Form a circle," he commanded and the creatures moved, creating an area some ten metres in diameter. Hades placed his sword on the floor in the centre and walked to the far edge. Chris stepped back until she felt the foul breath of the things on her naked shoulders.

"I will shout begin," announced Peregrine, who had remained seated on her throne.

Then silence. Chris assessed the distance to the sword and tried to predict the movements of the big man.

"Begin."

Hades rushed for the sword but Chris sprinted up the side of the circle. As he reached down for the huge weapon, she launched herself at him from the side, feet first. Her heels rammed into the side of his head with all her weight and velocity behind them. She felt something crack, then landed on her side and sprang up quickly. Hades had staggered to one side and she could see his jaw was broken. The sword lay in front of her and Chris reached to pick it up. She grasped his huge weapon with both hands, expecting a substantial weight but as soon as she touched the hilt, it shrank to the perfect size for her to handle.

"I do not like my clothes being removed. That makes me quite ready to kill a god or two, if necessary. I will go through that door and then you can continue to destroy this universe as you please."

She swung the sword and Hades lifted his arms to deflect the blow from his head and heart. That wasn't her target. The tip of the blade cut down just around his waist, leaving a bloody gash that ended on his thigh. It also neatly sliced through the leather skirt he was wearing and garment fell to the floor, leaving him fully exposed.

"How do you like it?" Chris remarked with feeling.

She also noticed that the critical part now revealed were totally out of proportion to the rest of his body. A very much smaller proportion. She wasn't going to dwell on the subject and made no further comment.

She walked directly to the door, the creatures standing back from her path with eyes lowered. After entering, the door slammed shut behind her. A smaller room than expected but her eyes were fixed on the back of a head that rose above a leather chair facing away from her. Around it, the spikes of the halo now were buried in the hair. Chris rushed forward and pulled the ring upwards and clear of him. Then she threw it in a corner.

"Jerome," she cried and moved round in front of the chair. She had been just in time. Trickles of blood were running down from a series of marks across the forehead and cheeks. A broad grin appeared on the man's face. She had been just in time.

"Thank you, Chris."

She had been just in time to save the body. They hadn't bothered with the legs or anything below waist level. That part wouldn't appear on camera. It was just a torso, arms and head. A dummy, robot, cyber thing or whatever. Just a machine. A perfect replica of the upper half of a man.

"I expect you're wondering what happened to my lower half?" it said cheerily.

"No. Where is Jerome Jones?"

"Try that door in front of me."

She looked at the far wall.

"There is no door."

"There is but it's concealed. You just have to find how to open it."

"Listen, thing. I spent a long and hard time getting here and now I've been tricked. Tell me where the door is or I'll chop you in small pieces and do the same to every god I can find."

"Well, if you put it like that, I'll definitely not help you."

Chris swung the sword downwards, aiming to cut its arm off at the shoulder. It hit something like hard rubber and bounced off. She swung again and again at every part of the thing but with the same result.

"I'd try the door if I were you," it said.

She glared, and then walked to the back wall. Just solid stone except for an unusual design across the lower part. It was an embossed row of swords, point downwards. They were so tight together, the blades almost touched and the hilts overlapped.

"All you need to do is place one finger on the hilt of Hades' sword. Make a mistake and it will be much harder."

Chris thought back to when she had entered the previous chamber. Hades had been sitting on his throne holding the sword with its point resting on the floor. She just had to transpose that view to this wall and decide the exact horizontal position. He had not been right in the middle. There were two thrones each side of the centre line and his had been on her right. Chris quickly measured across the wall using her sword. Just over 14 sword lengths. She marked the centre, a tad over seven lengths in. But how far from the centre? She proportioned the distance and settled on an area covered by three swords. The obvious choice was the one in the middle. She lightly touched its hilt.

No door opened. Instead, the blade swung up and began slashing feverishly, as if held by a hand embedded in the wall. More difficult now. She held her sword in her right hand, parrying the blows and quickly touched the hilt of the depiction on the left of the three. Same result. Two swords now sliced wildly like twin propellers. They seem to sense her position and adjusted accordingly. Impossible to reach the third choice.

She walked back to the chair and picked up the robotic torso.

"Are we going somewhere?" the thing asked.

She held it in front of her and walked to the left of the slashing blades. They began to hack unmercifully against his rubber skin, without effect. She waited for two seconds then threw the torso at the swords, jumped to the right and touched the hilt of the third embossed sword.

The two blades swung back to inanimation and a part of the wall slid back smoothly.

Franco, dressed in a long robe. As usual, he was sitting on a couch with five naked girls around him. One stood behind, stroking his hair. Others sat each side of him, caressing his chest with another two on the floor, running their hands over his legs and thighs. He smiled at her but Chris wasn't in the mood.

"So you've been accepted back by the other gods. That's good for you. Now I want to know where Jerome Jones is."

He shrugged.

"Search me."

"I do not want flip answers. I'm in a bad mood. One last chance. Where is he?"

He shook his head.

"You've been told."

She paused to recall the series of worlds. The gods, the people, the fighting and the conversations.

"No one has told me."

"You don't approve of me?"

"I cannot see the need for a god of sexual desire. It seems you're just used by the other deities when they want to bed a human."

"Isn't that good?"

"I don't think that you're necessary. If a girl likes someone enough, then she will decide. There shouldn't be this sort of coercing. Your powers failed to help Poseidon seduce Selena on earth but I think she may have chosen for herself."

"That's a good point."

"Now I'm tired of lies and trickery."

With lips tight, she moved towards him, sword raised.

"You have one fault. You just won't listen sometimes. There's a fire burning inside you and it drives you forward wilfully. You know my answer," said Franco.

She stopped and then grinned.

"Yes, you're right. I don't listen sometimes. Stand up while I search you."

He returned her smile and rose to his feet. His robe had a pocket, cut kangaroo style in the front. She reached in quickly to avoid any contact with his body. A Squark. She pulled out the metallic square.

It came to life immediately she looked. A video screen displaying a beach, maybe in the Caribbean. In the middle distance, she could just see a man sitting there alone, his face mostly hidden under a large sun cap. Beside him was a pile of books. Suddenly, he seemed to sense his image was being transmitted. He picked up one of the volumes and threw it towards her viewpoint. The screen zoomed in on the cover and she read the title. 'Wish I Was There'.

Chris felt a sinking sensation.

"So he was never here."

"Oh yes, he came but the moment you arrived, he was sent back."

"It looked like Barbados."

"A little island not far from there."

"You've obviously wormed your way in sufficiently to know all this."

"You'll see me in my rightful position before you leave. If you're not killed first, of course."

"Well, you will need to hope you survive as well. Hades is destroying this universe and killing all the gods. I don't think he's too fond of me either, after our fight. Is he keeping you prisoner here?"

She saw an uncertainty spread through his expression.

"No. Why?"

"He's in the next room with a mob of his creatures."

"What?"

Franco dashed to the door and opened it. Chris ran to join him when she saw the scene. A large, marble room with a circular pool where an abundance of naked women were bathing peacefully.

"I don't see him," said Franco with relief in his voice.

"It was a different room. I think he's messing with the structure of these little worlds."

He looked at her intently.

"I don't think you'd lie. If you help me, I'll try to reciprocate. You're right that some of the gods have accepted me and I have partially regained my powers. But at the moment, I'm not allowed to return to the gods' domain. They will only permit me to stay here in human form until they hold a meeting. Then they will vote."

"So you are still mortal and Hades could kill you?"

"Yes, I'm afraid so. You said you'd fought him?"

"I won a contest and then cut off his skirt."

"He was ... exposed?"

"Completely."

"That is bad, very bad for you. Of all the gods, he is the most proud of his masculinity."

Chris briefly recalled the unpleasant but insignificant content of the exposure but decided against mentioning it.

"Okay, I'll help you. Let's go now."

Franco scanned her body.

"I would suggest that you're not ideally dressed for the journey."

Chris was annoyed she had forgotten. She was still wearing just black lace underwear.

"I want clothes now."

One of the naked girls opened a cupboard in a corner and returned with a lavender dress. Chris slipped it on and found it fitted perfectly.

"First we must find Selena," she said.

"I haven't seen her but did hear some talk she was planning to stay. I don't think we should wait for her."

"No. If she tells me herself she is not leaving, then I will go. Otherwise we go together."

"You could both be killed. Let's go back to earth now. Please?"

"No chance. I'm going to find her now. You can come or stay here."

She marched off into the pool room and sensed Franco following.

A choice of two doors next to each other on the far wall and she was now well aware that anything could lie on the other side of them. Hopefully she wouldn't have to face Hades again. Ignoring the disporting mounds of naked flesh around the pool, she walked directly to the left-hand door. Then she paused.

"Is it worth asking if your new powers can help see what's through these doors?"

Franco came alongside her.

"Yes and no," he responded.

"You're testing my patience again."

He sighed.

"Yes, it's worth asking and no I can't. You weren't listening again."

"Okay. You choose the door then."

"Why not ask the Squark, as you call it?"

"That's the only good idea I've ever heard from you."

She lifted the metal square and it came to life immediately.

"Which of the doors in this room lead to Selena?" she asked.

"The second," it replied immediately.

"The second from the right or left?"

"It depends where you start from."

"Listen. I'm standing in front of a door now. Is it the right one?"

"No, it's on your left."

"I will ask once more before I drop you on the floor and jump on you. Does the door I'm standing in front of lead to Selena?"

"No. Just to a mob of crazy men with axes who enjoy the sight of blood."

"So it's the other. What's behind it?"

"A mob of crazy women with cleavers and knives who enjoy the sight of blood."

"And I need to get through them to reach Selena?"

"No. I doubt if you get past them anyway without losing an arm or head. Even if you did, you'd just reach the room with the axe men."

"So you lied about Selena."

"She doesn't listen, does she zzzzz?"

The Squark actually used the god name of Franco, represented here by zzzzz for the sake of decency, even in today's broadminded world.

Chris screwed up her face.

"That's totally disgusting. Call him Franco and I assure you, I listen very well."

"Then you don't think."

"I won't be abused by a little bit of metal."

"Tough," replied the Squark and switched off. She had no pockets, so slid it under her bra strap for safe keeping.

"You make friends easily," Franco observed.

"Don't you start."

Chris was more annoyed with herself for getting annoyed. An annoying annoyance she would need to curtail. Then she understood. She turned and saw the door to the room they had left was now closed again.

"Come on," she called and led Franco back past the pool.

"You think my room has changed?" he asked with concern.

"Yes. The Squark must know. This is the way to Selena."

Chris opened the door and was in the snow. She didn't step forward but was drawn inside and engulfed. Engulfed in a warm snowstorm. Not at all cold but it wasn't simulated like in a toy store at Christmas, it behaved just like the real thing, melting quickly on contact with the skin.

It was so thick, Chris couldn't see anything. She didn't even know if Franco was still with her. Bending forward, she trudged into the force of the storm. She could feel her new dress becoming saturated but the warm atmosphere made it similar to swimming in a heated pool. On and on she pushed her body forward. The storm seemed unceasing and, after thirty minutes, she wondered if the trek would ever end. Four minutes later, it did.

As if she had walked through a wall, the snow finished. She stood at the top of a steep, snow-covered hill. Below her, in a valley, stood a log cabin. Suddenly, her feet slipped from under her and she was sliding down on her back, following a curving icy channel in the snow. Below her feet she could see she was approaching the cabin at neck breaking speed. 50 metres, 20 metres, 10 metres.

She would impact directly on the solid, wooden door of the building. One metre and she stopped. No buckling forward, no impact. She simply came to a halt.

Chris rose to her feet. Her shoes had been lost somewhere on the journey and her dress and underwear were clinging tightly, sodden with water. A cry came from behind her. Franco was careering down the slide, screaming as he went. She waited until he pulled up beside her.

"Enjoy the trip?" she asked.

He scrambled to his feet, his wet robe plastered to his body. It hid nothing now and Chris kept her eyes on his face.

"I could have been killed," he complained.

"Don't be childish."

She moved to the wooden door, made with tightly bound, vertical logs. It opened easily at her touch. The room was empty but a crackling fire burnt solidly in the fireplace. In front of it, a pile of folded towels and, beside them, were two bags of clothes. In the first, she could see jeans, cream top and jacket for her and the other revealed a grey suit for Franco.

She grabbed two towels and threw them to him, followed by his bag of garments.

"You stand in the corner to dry and dress yourself. Do not turn round. Is that clear?"

"Perfectly."

She took her bag with two more towels and moved to the opposite corner. Turning her back, she stripped completely and dried every centimetre of her body and hair. She found comfortable white underwear amongst the clothing and dressed quickly. In the bottom of the bag was a pair of trainers that fitted perfectly. It was exactly the outfit she would have chosen and she felt much more comfortable now.

"You can look now, Franco," she called and then turned.

She wasn't expecting Hades to be standing in the middle of the room. He was now wearing a brown leather jacket and jeans, his muscular body bulging with awesome power. Beyond him she could see Franco, cringing in the corner.

"I have not forgotten our last meeting. Instant death or should I have you first?" the big man growled.

"There's no way you get the second choice, so you'll have to try to kill me."

He grunted and pulled out a long, slim knife. The cabin rocked and shuddered. Wide cracks appeared across the ceiling and walls. The building was still trembling as he gestured to Franco.

"Come here, you sickening worm."

Franco obeyed, but kept his head bowed.

"Make this girl want me," Hades instructed.

Chris glared with vitriolic eyes.

"Don't bother asking him. I wouldn't have you if you were the last man on earth."

"We are not on earth. Well, worm?"

Chris could see Franco squirming with uncertainty. Finally he appeared to reach a decision.

"We will need someone to hold her while I perform my work," he said quietly.

Hades smiled sourly, and then clapped his hands mightily together. The outer door opened and a woman entered. The blonde who had been on the throne next to him.

"Persephone. You will restrain the girl while this slimy creature implants her with desire for me."

She smiled sweetly and then moved like lightning. Chris had been ready but found her arms gripped behind her back before she could begin to move. She felt the large bosom of the blonde pressed into her back and a voice whispering in her ear.

"Now just relax, darling. You'll enjoy it."

Chris struggled violently but couldn't break free of the iron grip. She saw Franco approach. He lifted a hand and then began to slowly move his fingers towards to her cheek. She tried to twist her head and bent forward. Then she saw his left hand was moving round her side. He never touched her cheek but she saw the forefinger of his other hand lightly make contact with Persephone's arm. Chris felt her grip relax.

"Hades," the woman screamed and was on him before he could react. She leapt up and carried him back to the floor. Sitting astride his body, she began to tear at his clothes.

"I want you now," she squealed.

"Stop this," Hades shouted but the words were muffled by her large bosom pressed into his face. The wrestling match continued, the might of Hades more than offset by the desperate passion of Persephone's assault.

Franco stood over them for a moment, his eyes now pure gold and a smile playing across his lips.

"Don't ever call me a worm," he cried exultantly.

Chris wasn't going to miss this opportunity to escape. She grabbed his arm and pulled him through the outer door.

No snow now. No land. Not even a planet. They stood on a metal disc about 100 metres across that was floating in space. Black void, with the shimmer of a thousand stars above and below them. The disc had a big hole in the centre and floating in the middle was a much smaller disc, no more than 5 metres diameter. Even from a distance, she could see it had a bright red question mark in its centre.

"We need to get to the inner disc," she called to Franco and began to advance cautiously towards the centre. As she walked, she could feel a smooth, growing movement underfoot. The disc was spinning and the closer she moved to the centre, the more rapid the rotation until it reached the point where she could barely keep her balance. She retreated and the spinning decreased.

"It's a little physical test. We need to get as close as possible to the centre, then jump onto the small disc."

Franco looked unenthusiastic.

"I can't do it. We'll spin off into space," he muttered.

"You have no choice. The door we came through has disappeared. Hold my hand and copy me."

She began to run in the opposite direction to the spin. At this outer point, they moved forward rapidly. After a few seconds to build up pace, she swerved quickly towards the centre. Their speed slowed dramatically as the rotation began but they still had sufficient momentum to be just holding their place within a metre from the edge.

"Jump," she shouted and pulled him with her as she leapt for the centre disc.

Chris landed on her knees but Franco fell short. She felt his weight on her arm dragging her over the edge. Gravity clearly worked as normal here and she was going to follow him into space. She reached round with her free hand and felt the top curve of the question mark. It was heavily embossed, rising several centimetres above the surface of the disc. She gripped it firmly and dug the rubber heels of her trainers against the surface. Then she pulled, using the power of her legs to push backwards. Her arm and shoulder were giving way under his weight and she felt Franco's grip loosening.

"Get up here," she screamed, mostly for adrenaline purposes.

Chris tightened her grip on his arm and pulled hard, arching her back as her legs took the strain. Suddenly, he was grabbing her foot and hauling himself up beside her. She fell back, panting with exertion. They lay together for 30 seconds and then Franco raised himself on his elbow and looked down at her. His eyes were pure gold but there was something else in them now. Something magical.

"I will not forget that," he said quietly.

She rose to her feet and took his hand again. For a second she wondered if the Gate would work, as Selena was not with them. But then came the whiteness.

20

The white was pure again, just as when they first arrived. It cleared slowly and Chris found herself facing a beautiful woman. A woman clothed in a flowing, pure white dress and on her head was a tiara of exquisitely cut diamonds.

Chris smiled broadly.

"Selena, you look wonderful."

"You're heavy competition."

"Don't be silly."

Serena gestured to a large wall mirror and Chris walked in front of it. The reflection was her but not a her she had ever seen before. She was wearing a similar silk dress to Selena, this one in the palest blue. Her curly mop of hair was now styled like a queen and she also had a gold tiara, encrusted with rubies and emeralds. Around her neck was a massive diamond on a gold necklace. Chris had never considered herself attractive but this was as close as she'd ever come.

"Wow, they did a good job," she murmured.

"Well, that's the gods for you."

"You know about Jerome?"

"Yes and surprisingly, I wasn't angry."

"I heard that you'd decided not to return to earth."

She saw Selena walking towards her and felt the light kiss on her cheek.

"I'm going back. I have a duty to perform in 2019. Also, I'd miss you and Jerome too much."

Chris didn't hide her relief and pleasure. She hugged her companion tightly.

"You'll be leaving Poseidon and Athena."

"Yes but this is their world and I belong somewhere else."

"You'll have to tell me all about these gods when we get back."

"Actually, I don't know that much about them. They aren't big talkers in bed."

"Right. Where do we go?"

"Poseidon brought me here and asked me to wait. Then you arrived. I've no idea how to find the way back to Earth."

"I was with Franco. Then we went through a Gate and here I am."

"Franco? I would have thought the other gods would have killed him by now."

"He's very much alive. There's a chance he could be accepted back but they need to vote on it. I've also crossed paths with Hades a couple of times. You know he's nearly demolished this universe?"

"Yes, I gather he didn't join in when they created it. Now he's like a jealous little kid."

"The main reason for the destruction is because it was the route for Franco to return. They just met and it's obvious they hate each other. I'm sure Hades will try to kill him next time they meet."

Selena shrugged.

"There's nothing we can do. It's a matter for the gods to resolve."

"I still don't want him killed and I'll try to stop it if I can."

"I don't particularly like the little man but maybe we can ask for leniency if we get the chance."

The floor started to shake. Another series of tremors and cracks began to appear. A large fissure opened in the wall like the maw of a giant wall creature. Then the shuddering gradually subsided and a woman emerged through the crack. A blonde woman.

"Careful, Selena. It's Persephone," Chris shouted and began to look around for weapons.

"No need. It's over now," said the blonde with a smile.

"You and Hades have destroyed it all?" Chris asked, still searching for a form of defence.

Persephone's eyes sparkled and her round cheeks were pink with excitement.

"Hades, I want you now," she screamed. A replay of the earlier scene in exactly the same tone.

He entered, his massive figure barely squeezing through the opening in the wall. Then he stood beside Persephone and their gaze became frigid.

Selena took place forward.

"We're going back to earth. I don't really care if you've completed your demolition."

Chris moved to her side.

"You've tried to kill me and seduce me. You can try it with someone else now because I'm going back to someone I love."

Hades moved his hand and she froze. Not by choice. Her body was completely paralysed. He moved towards her and ran a finger gently across her cheek.

"Do you believe she would suit me?" he murmured.

"I don't think she could handle you, big man," responded Persephone.

Then they laughed. The laughter of gods. It reverberated around the room with unquenchable elation. Chris suddenly found her muscles obeying again and then she was laughing with them, irresistibly. So was Selena. The laughter gave a joyous release, a tonic for the soul.

"A good game. The best ever," Hades shouted as he laughed.

"You're not destroying anything, are you?" Chris asked.

"Of course not. I just had to play the evil one this time. It's a pity you never reached my world. We'll enjoy your adventures for ages to come."

He gestured and the far wall transformed into a large video screen. It was displaying the end of her fight with Hades. Chris saw herself grabbing his sword from the centre of the assembled creatures and then cutting off his leather skirt. The big man roared again with laughter and was joined by Persephone.

"Wasn't that a brilliant touch," he cried. The picture had frozen at the point where he was fully exposed. Chris looked away.

"If the poor girl had seen the real thing, she'd probably have fainted," Persephone squealed and the laughter continued.

Selena was studying the screen intently.

"I wish I'd been there. Chris did well and it serves you right."

"So the whole thing was an act. But you killed lots of people," Chris remarked.

"No. It's too much trouble to replace them. You just thought you saw the heads rolling and the blood flowing."

"But you can't use supernatural abilities in these worlds. The referee told us that."

"Yes, so he did."

The large figure shrank and changed as she watched. She was looking at Sophos, the referee.

"Sorry I may have misled you a little. In the big games, we always allow at least one of the gods to use his powers. This was certainly a big game," he said.

"I've never enjoyed one more," added Persephone.

Hades reverted to his normal, massive appearance and the smile disappeared.

"Come now. It is time for the vote on that little piece of slime, Franco."

He moved his hand again and the room changed.

Chris was in front of an assembly of the gods. Certainly not the grand, opulent hall she was expecting. It was a simple, large chamber built of exposed concrete blocks with other blocks scattered around the floor to provide seating for the gods. Their attire was also not as she anticipated. Jeans, plain or check shirts and casual jackets appeared to be the popular choice. Not a single white robe in sight.

There seemed to be no hierarchy. Hades and Persephone walked to the nearest vacant chunk of concrete and sat down. Chris noticed Poseidon and Athena on different sides of the room, talking to those nearest to them. The buzz of conversation filled the air. Then she saw a tall man with bright, long golden hair, seated at the end, slightly apart from the others. His clear blue eyes glowed with power and he wasn't talking to anyone.

She nudged Selena.

"I think it's Zeus," she said quietly.

Selena nodded.

"Perhaps he'll give you a chance to plead for Franco."

Chris sensed a movement behind her. Franco walked past, his head lowered and arms by his side. He was naked. With short, slow strides he reached the centre of the chamber and then knelt down, his eyes still fixed on the rough, concrete floor.

Hades immediately rose from his seat and Chris saw him glance towards the golden haired man who made a slight movement with his hand.

"Today we vote on the possibility of this devious worm returning to our pantheon. I will state my views and any of you may then present your own opinions. We will continue until all who wish to have spoken and then we will vote."

Then he continued for 10 minutes, describing the occasions where he had requested Franco's help but was refused.

"Finally, I have to report one last deceit. I told him to use his powers on this blonde girl. He did not comply and as a typical final insult, he filled Persephone with lust and she assaulted me."

No laughter, just the nodding of several heads.

Next was Athena, who stood up and walked in front of the kneeling man.

"My view is that this obscene creature is not required. We have existed in harmony during his banishment. His so-called powers are simply a vehicle for base lechery and salaciousness, a craving for sexual activity that I find abhorrent. I know his services have been utilised by some of my gender but it is mostly employed to assist the unceasing, licentious urges of the males in this assembly. How many pure virgins have been encouraged to offer their bodies by this repugnant putrescence? I cannot condone his return and I urge each of you to vote again for banishment or, alternatively, send him for execution."

She was followed by many others, including Poseidon, who gave short speeches. All were against him, except one, Hera. She gave Franco limited support but tailed off somewhat when she caught the eye of Hades, who rose again.

"Is that the final offering before Zeus declares his wishes?" he called out.

Chris quickly moved forward.

"May I speak?" she asked.

Hades looked towards the golden haired man who paused for a few seconds before giving a small nod. She moved next to Franco before speaking.

"Then let me say this. All who have met me know that I share Athena's dislike of the nature of his abilities. I wouldn't want to be stimulated by someone to sleep with any man. However, he has helped both Selena and I in our quest here. He never really deceived us, although I'm not sure about his bravery. I don't think there's any great harm in him and Selena proved that a woman can resist his powers if she tries hard enough. It would have been easy for him to help Hades to seduce me but he took the harder option, knowing how much I didn't want it. Some of you gods favour violence and killing and that's something I consider much worse than a walking aphrodisiac. He belongs here, not isolated on earth and I appeal to all of you to take him back."

A long silence and everyone looked at the golden haired giant. Chris knew no one would dare to oppose Zeus and his words would be decisive. Franco seemed aware of this and his head was now nearly touching the floor.

She watched as Zeus rose from his seat. He was even taller than she had estimated, not even Hades could match his height. She looked in vain for any sign of compassion in his eyes. He strode forward, towering over the naked figure that was now shaking with fear.

Then Chris saw Zeus walk across to Hades and sit beside him. And she heard the laughter. Not fear but laughter. Franco rolled onto his back, rocking with uncontrollable guffaws that hammered against the walls and deafened the eardrums. Everyone in the chamber was laughing.

Hades jumped from his seat and grabbed the naked body and they rolled together across the floor. Poseidon quickly joined them.

Chris couldn't speak but heard Selena's voice amongst the raucous mirth.

"Oh shit," she said.

The three men continued to tumble around and Chris saw that Franco was growing, expanding, changing.

"Stop," he shouted and extricated himself from his brothers. Then he approached her.

A most beautiful man. Tall, with a flow of dark hair running down to his broad shoulders and eyes of the purest deep brown. He lifted a hand and lightly touched her chin. Then he kissed her. A kiss of ultimate paradise. An indescribable experience she could never forget. Not passion but love. Universal love that had no meaning for her until that moment. She shared the pure joy with him, travelling a million miles and immersing in the warm glow of a million true souls. Every fibre of her body tingled exultantly.

Her eyes were still closed when he spoke with the softness of majesty.

"I said I wouldn't forget. You are now special to me."

Chris opened her eyes and nearly fainted at his beauty.

"You are Zeus. I never guessed."

She realised her voice sounded like a schoolgirl in heaven.

"Do I get kissed as well?" Selena asked.

He laughed again.

"I'm not kissing a girl that walks in on me while I'm showering."

"I remember Iceland. You're rather more impressive now."

"I believe my brother finds you very interesting."

Selena's brow furrowed.

"Was that part of the game?" she asked with a plea in her voice.

Poseidon shook his head.

"It was not and it is not. My only deceit was omitting to tell you everything. That would have ruined the game. Despite what you said a little earlier, gods do usually talk in bed."

Chris saw the delighted smile spread across Selena's face and turned back to Zeus.

"I assume the game is over now," she said.

"The best ever, as Hades described it."

"If you men have quite finished, I will guide the women back to earth."

Athena had joined the brothers. She was smiling but not as brightly as the rest of the gathering.

"Yes, it's time," Zeus agreed.

Chris looked around.

"I'm not one for long goodbyes but …"

228

"And we've only just arrived," said Selena.

Chris was in a one piece swimsuit, standing on the same Caribbean beach she had seen earlier with Selena in a bikini beside her. About 100 metres away was the shaggy haired man with his large sun hat pulled low over the eyes.

She caught a sparkle below Selena's throat. A beautiful but curious pendant. It was metallic but shimmered blue, like water.

"A gift from Poseidon?" she asked.

Her companion nodded, eyes moist. Then Chris realised she also had something new. A plain bracelet that glowed rich purple and felt soft, like velvet. She grinned.

"Selena, there are two things I'm not clear on. First, how could Franco be Zeus when he'd been at the University for two years?"

"That's simple. I suppose I should have suspected something. Zeus impersonated Franco. He probably hid the real one in one of the rooms at the University. What's the other question?"

"In Beddgelert, that strange room with the picture of the snake holding the man. You said it was a representation of something you'd seen."

Selena's expression changed, as if a chill wind had struck her.

"I'd rather not talk about it," she responded and Chris followed her across to the man in the sun hat.

"We've just wasted a month on a journey to save your life while you've just been sitting here," she said mildly.

"Saving my life was a waste?" asked Jerome Jones.

"It was just a game. I only saved a dummy."

He removed his hat. All around his head were scars, not yet healed.

"As above, so below," he murmured with a grateful smile.